*For Uncle Virgil
with love – Julia Nunnally Duncan
Oct. 2009*

When Day Is Done

a novel

Julia Nunnally Duncan

Copyright © 2009
Julia Nunnally Duncan
March Street Press
3413 Wilshire
Greensboro NC
marchstreetpress.com
rbixby@earthlink.net
isbn 1-59661-114-6

When Day Is Done is a work of fiction. No character is meant to represent or suggest an actual person, living or dead.

1

Esther passed Oak Grove Cemetery every weekday as she drove to work and passed it again on the drive home. Her brother's grave couldn't be seen from the highway, though she always strained to see it, as now while she was heading to the technical college to teach her five p.m. literature class. Stopped in traffic, this Wednesday evening, she stretched her neck to get a glimpse of the square marble stone. Though she could not see it, she knew the stone well: its rippled top and glass-like surface, still shiny today in 1990—twenty years after the burial—still cool to the touch, even on warm June days, as today.

But at the moment she didn't have time to pull off the highway to rest against the stone. Often though she would drive up the winding cemetery road that snaked by wrought-iron enclosed family plots and oak-shaded Confederate graves and led farther still to poorer graves marked only by creek rocks. Beyond the poor section, close to the railroad tracks were the newer generations of Milton dead. Here her brother Sandy lay.

Miniature American flags dotted the hills, probably from Flag Day. The local Veterans of Foreign Wars group was conscientious about keeping Milton's veterans' graves properly adorned. Not Sandy's grave, she thought, for he had been too young—seventeen—when he died to have served in Vietnam. Which would have been worse? She knew this was pointless speculation. Death in the long run is death, after all. Degrees of suffering alone distinguished one kind from the other. At least being killed instantly carried the smile of mercy. Or so the preacher had said at the funeral.

One maintenance worker, a yellow-haired man who wore a bandana around his head, sat on a riding lawnmower, and the other worker, whose hair was dark, held a weed eater. The dark-haired man jerked the string of his trimmer and swept his brow with his tanned forearm. His red tee shirt was patched with sweat.

When this second man looked at her and raised his eyebrows as if just noticing her, she looked away from him to the road in front of her and gripped the steering wheel. Finally the cars ahead of her moved and let her lift her foot from the brake. She moved forward and checked her rearview mirror to see him lowering the weed eater to the grassy bank above the highway.

Take care of their graves, she thought, and lost his image.

But later that evening she looked for him when she passed by again at eight o'clock. Dusk had fallen, and of course he wouldn't be working so late, but she crept in the 35 m.p.h. zone and then headed home.

"Wonder who the maintenance workers are out at Oak Grove?" she asked her mother the next morning while they sat at the kitchen table. Though Esther was thirty-four and had been married and divorced, she lived at home with her parents. Her mother Lyla cooked their meals.

"Maintenance workers?" Lyla said and pushed a jar of apple butter toward her. "Put some of this in a biscuit. I buttered you one."

Esther took a soggy biscuit, saturated with Shedd Spread, opened it, dabbed a tablespoon of apple butter into it. She took a bite and waited for an answer. "Wonder who they are?" she asked again.

"It ain't a job many would want," Lyla said. "You know how it gets hot out there of a day, and they've cut down some of the pines that added shade. Why you reckon they cut them down?"

"Keep criminals out, I guess," she said, referring to an incident of several years back when a Tennessee prison escapee fled to Milton and was spotted at Oak Grove. He hid in the pines and was later shot to death in a cotton mill house nearby.

"Why is it hoodlums come to cemeteries?" Lyla asked, her

blue eyes set in a baby doll stare. "Why can't they leave the dead in peace?"

Esther looked at her mother's lined face, the prettiness of her features twisted in the question.

"That's why they need a caretaker," she said and waited for the shadow of her mother's mood to pass.

"What would draw a man to work at the cemetery?" Lyla said finally. "You know it don't pay much."

"Neither does the cotton mill," she said. "Of course the mill benefits are better—if you don't count brown lung."

"Don't let Arthur hear you say that," Lyla said and glanced across the room toward the kitchen's arched entrance. Down the hallway was her parents' bedroom, not really within earshot of the kitchen, yet Esther knew her mother feared their conversation might be heard by her daddy. No need to worry, though, as her daddy hadn't risen from bed yet. He usually slept till ten o'clock or later since his retirement.

"You know it's true," she said.

"He does too," Lyla said, "but there's no use in bringing it up. This house was paid for by cotton mill sweat. There's pride in that."

"He earned every cent," Esther said. She didn't know why she brought up the brown lung issue. Her daddy had a cough and his hearing wasn't perfect, though she suspected he just didn't want to hear at times, but he had escaped the fate of his brother Dave who died of emphysema before he retired. Her daddy defended the mill and said lung problems ran in the family even before the 1920's when his mother's brothers died of T.B.

Still, she knew his work in the mill had scarred him and retirement had made a fresh wound. Fixing machines was his skill, acquired and perfected over forty years, and without the mill, he seemed lost.

So she dropped the subject of brown lung.

Lyla pulled the plates from the table and wiped the vinyl tablecloth with a wet dishrag.

"Let me help, Mother," Esther said, but Lyla didn't stop her movements or look at her, and when she started to put the jar of apple butter in the refrigerator, her mother said, "Leave that out for Arthur," though they both knew he wouldn't eat a bite until suppertime.

"You can cover the biscuits with tin foil," Lyla said and she obeyed, also knowing the birds wouldn't care whether they were soft or hard.

She left at ten-thirty for her eleven o'clock class. Her mother was hoeing her garden in the back yard; her daddy had turned on the T.V. in the front room and sat on the couch watching it.

"I'll see you after while, Daddy," she said and her daddy nodded though he kept his eyes on the screen. He would be sitting there when she returned.

As she drove through town she passed the Episcopal church where she and Richard had married in 1980; also here on Main Street was Porter's Law Office where the divorce papers were finalized three years later. She wondered if Richard still served on the vestry at St. James and wondered if he played tennis every Friday evening as he had during the brief span of their marriage. Did he still work for his father's insurance agency? Of course he would be employed there. By now he was bound to be a full partner.

She had heard that Richard had remarried and had a daughter. This is what he wanted all along.

She could see his long dark-blond hair as it was when they started dating in the mid-70's. He wore wire-rimmed eyeglasses that gave him a scholarly look and was one of the first young men she had ever seen wearing an earring. At Appalachian State University, where they both attended college and where they began dating, he joined a fraternity that his father didn't approve of and devoured Chinese philosophy. He turned to her for approval, and she listened to him, though she still secretly preferred the philosophy of Rod McKuen.

Her mother never completely accepted Richard.

"Baptists should marry Baptists," Lyla said after the Episcopal wedding. "There ain't any spirit in this church. You don't get the spirit by reading everything out of a book." She meant the *Book of Common Prayer* that the Episcopalians used in their service.

Later Esther felt the same lack of spirit in Richard. Maybe her mother was right. Though she herself hadn't attended a Baptist church service in years, she recalled the revival services of her childhood, the preacher's face filled with blood, the vein in his temple bulging.

She couldn't imagine Richard's family approving such religious fervor. And though Richard might have rebelled against his parents in college, he came back to the fold soon enough. When she and he finished graduate school and married, he cut his hair, discarded his earring, and left his unorthodox views in Boone. His father welcomed him back and she released him. A child was the goal of his desire, and when that wasn't achieved, his desire died. So she was glad he had a daughter now.

It's funny how she'd lived in the same town as Richard for seven years since the divorce and hadn't seen him once.

She hadn't seen Martin, the boy she considered her first love, but twice in nineteen years, and that was only from a distance. She knew if she saw Martin again, stood close to him, touched his hand, she couldn't let him go. And yet she hadn't spoken a word to him since she was fifteen. But with Martin, time hadn't passed. God help her, she knew it was true.

She shut her eyes now and made Martin fade as she had many times before.

Milton was growing, and new people moved here every day. So many new faces. Though why people came here was a mystery to Esther. One furniture factory had shut down, a piano plant relocated, the small family-run hosiery mills were closing one by one, and no new industries were moving in. Yet people came to the foothills—drawn by the Blue Ridge Mountains—bought land and developed it. The downtown stores were moving to shopping centers—Walmart and Roses Plazas—farmhouses leveled, cornfields dug up and paved. When she thought about the changes in Milton—how unfamiliar the town must suddenly seem to the older citizens—she decided her daddy was right in abandoning himself to T.V. He watched *Wheel of Fortune,* first on one channel and then another, and it made sense.

And all these thoughts because she passed by St. James' church and recalled Richard. He wasn't worth it.

While she drove beyond Main Street and drew closer to Oak Grove Cemetery, she wondered if the dark-haired maintenance worker would be there. She checked her watch and saw that she had time to drive through the cemetery.

It won't take long, she thought. Even if I'm tardy my students will wait. Lately her enthusiasm for teaching had waned, though she couldn't afford to lose her job. Her parents' social security checks wouldn't support three people. As it was, with her salary she bought the groceries, kept the house painted and repaired, and saw that her daddy had a nice Zenith television set. Without children of her own to support and build a bank account for, she focused her spending and attention on her parents. Someone once asked her what she would do someday when her parents weren't in that house with her. She made the idea fade just as she had Martin's face.

She spent some money on herself too. Last summer she financed a new Honda Civic. Her daddy's old Buick sat parked in a garage beside the house, rarely driven, its battery weak from disuse. Her mother had stopped driving years ago.

"What would you do without me?" she'd asked her mother

one Sunday as they sat at the dinner table. Lyla turned her blue eyes on her as she held a bowl of creamed corn in her hands.

"Dip you out some corn here," Lyla said, ignoring the question. "It's some I raised last year," and Esther felt embarrassed for asking the question.

Now she pulled into the cemetery drive, slowly climbed the first hill, and took the right fork. The sun was already bright—thank goodness for the car's air conditioner. She would have to get air conditioning installed at home, too, before the summer was over. Here it was the first day of summer—June 21—and already in the 90's.

At the crest of a second hill she turned left and reached a section of older graves that were marked by flat granite slabs. Some were broken and others chipped by vandals—as revealed in a recent newspaper article. She also noticed that few graves in the entire cemetery were decorated by flowers. Weren't there dozens of wreaths here on Memorial Day? That was less than a month ago. Maybe the families had come to remove them. Or maybe the maintenance workers had cleaned the graves.

Today there were also fewer miniature flags on the veterans' graves.

As she took a U-turn and started down the hill past a row of mimosa trees at a group of World War I graves, she saw him. His dark naked back was turned to her. He leaned into a tangle of vines at the base of a fence-lined family plot. She looked away at first, not aware she'd stopped her car. But her eyes turned to him again. He moved the weedeater slowly from side to side, swaying slightly himself. Despite his strong build, the muscles in his shoulders and arms taut with the weight of the machine, he looked graceful. She watched him.

He must lift weights or something, she decided. Maybe he went to an exercise gym. This idea repulsed her. She didn't like the type of man who went to health clubs to meet women.

But she couldn't help watching him.

Before he turned to look at her, she forced her eyes from him and took her foot off the brake.

Stupid, she thought, to come here. And she headed down the winding hills.

Nearing the front entrance, she saw the yellow-haired man leaning against a brick gatepost. When she passed through the entranceway, she glanced at him, and he winked. She quickly pulled into the highway. She couldn't believe it. Men from her childhood winked at women. Did men still flirt that way?

I hope he forgets my face, she thought.

On her drive to the college, she realized she hadn't even thought about Sandy's grave.

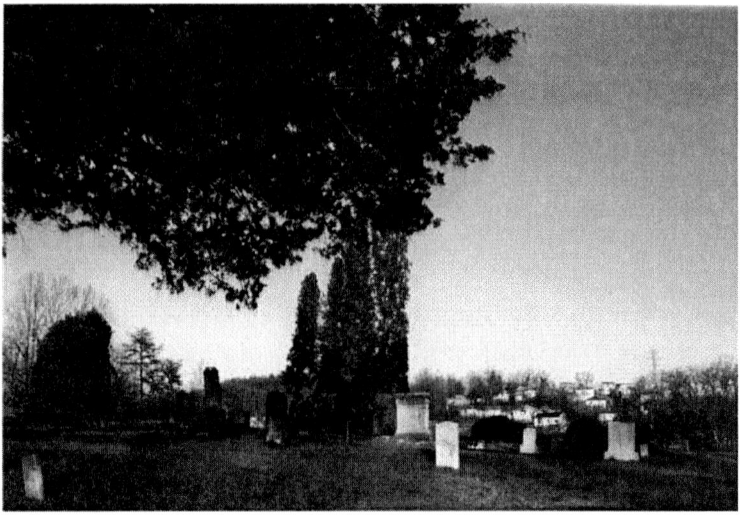

2

In bed that night, in those moments between wakefulness and sleep, she thought about the dark-haired man at the cemetery. And she thought about Martin.

Years ago, at the end of their date, Martin held her in the moonlight on her parents' front porch, her back braced against a support post. He pressed his body against her, and when he kissed her mouth and her throat, she sensed his excitement and she pushed him away.

No, Martin, she warned. *Daddy'll see us.*

Please, Esther, he said and took her face in his hands and kissed her, his mouth sweet and spicy from his Clove chewing gum, his tongue finding her tongue. She didn't fully understand the hardness she felt as he pressed his pelvis against her, but she knew it was his desire that caused it, and she believed that his desire was his love for her. She wanted to lead him into the back yard and lie down with him in the dewy grass beneath the elm tree where even moonlight couldn't intrude. There she would let his body, sweet with the fragrance of *British Sterling* cologne, cover her. Maybe in the darkness their lovemaking would be all right. But despite her yearning for him, she pushed him away. Her mother had convinced her that if she allowed Martin to go too far, he would lose respect for her and her reputation would be ruined.

And now these nineteen years later, she lay in bed and desired Martin again. Nights like this, she forgot there'd ever been a husband whom she'd shared a bed with. Tonight she wished she could have Martin beside her and say, *It's all right now, Martin. I don't mind.*

But Martin was surely long married now, somewhere out there with children, maybe a grandchild. He would be forty, his hair starting to gray, his desire spent on a wife and a life of hard work.

She'd heard he owned a furniture repair shop in the county, but she wasn't sure where. She couldn't imagine his hands stained and calloused. They had always been clean and soft, his fingernails manicured. She recalled his neat black hair, parted on the side, his face closely shaved and fragrant. She often thought of his hazel brown eyes, the color of dark honey; the long eyelashes; the dimple in his chin. *Too pretty for a boy*, her mother said. *Like Lew Ayres.*

Why did I let him go? she wondered, but she didn't want to remember and spoil the memory.

Would he sound the same? She couldn't remember his voice. And yet she knew she would recognize it in an instant if he spoke to her again. He would know her voice too.

"I wouldn't have let you marry him," her mother said when the subject once came up, "even if he'd behaved himself. I wasn't crazy about Richard, but at least he come from a good family. Martin wouldn't have give you nothing but a hard time. There'd always been women running after him, and you know it. He did his share of running after them too, as I recall. I needed my head examined for letting you go out with him in the first place."

She knew her mother was right. But a memory could take any form you wanted. She chose to leave out the hurtful parts. What did she have to lose now?

Her mother seemed to have forgotten that it was Martin, along with her daddy, who helped her walk into the church for Sandy's funeral. She and Martin hadn't been dating long, yet he insisted on being with the family during their tragedy. Martin held one arm, her daddy the other, and Lyla could still scarcely walk down the church aisle. At the end of the funeral when the preacher called the family forward to say goodbye before the casket lid was closed forever, Lyla almost collapsed.

She had been heavily sedated then and would stay that way

for the next few days. But soon she put away the sedatives and was Lyla again, and Martin's support at the funeral didn't change her mind about him.

Seeing the man at the cemetery had brought all these feelings for Martin to the surface again. Yet there were only vague physical similarities: although both men had black hair, Martin's had a glimmer of chestnut in the sunlight. The cemetery man was tall, maybe six feet; Martin was small, scarcely taller than her five feet six inches. The cemetery worker looked sweaty, hardly as immaculate as Martin, though she'd seen the man only during his work hours, so it wasn't a fair judgment.

In any case, seeing the man as he trimmed vines stirred her memories of Martin.

She lay and thought about this until she fell asleep.

When she awoke early the next morning, she wanted to get up immediately. Hunger gripped her stomach, and she stretched her legs and her back and listened to her mother rattling pans in the kitchen. Her daddy's snoring reached her too and she smiled. These sounds of family comforted her.

When she came into the kitchen she saw her mother stooped over the electric stove, her faded brown hair still rolled in bobby pins. Esther wanted to reach and pat her shoulder, sheltered in the worn terry housecoat—her favorite blue one, though Esther had bought her a new pink one for Mother's Day—but something held her hand back.

"Why you up already?" Lyla said and stirred a skillet of bacon gravy. "Did I wake you up?"

"I heard you, but I was awake anyway. I smelled bacon cooking. Did you sleep any last night?" She knew her mother rarely slept over four hours a night. Lyla said it must be all she needed, though Esther noticed how she often stopped in the garden to lean on her hoe.

"I come in the front room and watched a movie on TNT. Wasn't much good—Jane Russell. I never liked her; she was plastic, a female Elvis Presley."

"You like Elvis."

"Not in female form. She's turned out awful looking."

"So did Elvis."

Lyla stirred the bacon gravy and then tapped the spoon against the edge of the skillet.

"I wish I could sleep more," she said finally. "I don't know what's wrong with me."

"Too much on your mind."

"I reckon. Even when I'm asleep, I ain't resting. Last night, I dreamed we went on a picnic—you and me and Arthur and Sandy—and Sandy put his hand on a snake. We was at a picnic area on the Parkway. I don't know if you remember the one we used to go to. It was off the road with woods behind it and little grills and cement tables. In my dream Sandy was a little boy. You was the same age as you are now, which don't make sense."

"Dreams mix up things," Esther said, uncomfortable with the conversation.

"He was going to get a drink of water at one of them creek rock fountains there, and he yelled, 'Mother, a snake's bit my hand.' I said, 'Arthur, go and kill it,' and Arthur said it was against the law to kill a snake on the Parkway, and he just sat there eating his hotdog."

"What did I do?" Esther asked.

"I don't remember much about you in the dream except that you was sitting at the table beside Arthur."

They stood at the stove for a minute and Lyla looked at her.

"I woke up and for a minute I thought, Did Sandy get bit by a snake there sometime? It was like him to pick up a snake. He wasn't afraid of nothing. And Arthur acting that way. Why you reckon he didn't help Sandy?"

"It's just a dream, Mother."

"But I'm sure Sandy never got bit by a snake."

"Don't worry about it."

"But it seemed so real."

"Dreams do seem real sometimes," she said to her mother.

"More than real life," Lyla said and slid her hand into a mit pot holder. She carried the heavy skillet of gravy to the kitchen table, where she set it on an iron trivet.

Esther didn't like to talk about Sandy. The subject had been silenced for so long. Her daddy never discussed him. But now was an opportunity to bring up something she'd wanted to ask.

"Didn't we take some flowers to Sandy's grave a few weeks ago? I was thinking we did one Sunday in May."

"Mother's Day," Lyla said and sat in a straight chair at the table.

"That's right."

"Arthur give me a basket of plastic geraniums, and I took it to Sandy."

"Nobody's gone to pick it up then?" she asked and Lyla shot her a peculiar look.

"Pick it up? You mean me and Arthur? You know you can't get your daddy to drive anywhere."

"I just noticed a lot of the flowers were gone from the graves at Oak Grove."

"Not Sandy's."

"No, I didn't see his grave. But I thought I'd drive out there and check today. You think the maintenance workers might remove the wreaths if the families don't?"

"Them wreaths belong to the dead. I know some of these new cemeteries don't allow any flowers except in little vases built into the grave marker, but I never knowed of Oak Grove taking Sandy's flowers away. They've always let us keep a wreath or something there. Why, I've seen baskets and wreaths out at Pleasant Gardens Church Cemetery that must have been forty years old—faded plastic roses and dingy white carnations. Nobody dared touch them."

"Well, I just wondered. I thought I'd go by and check on it today. I might be home a little late this afternoon."

"Don't be too late," Lyla said, as was her habit.

She sat in her office at the technical college and thought about how she could discreetly see the dark-haired maintenance worker again. Her brother was there, so why did she need an excuse?

And yet the yellow-haired man gave her a look yesterday as if he read her intentions. Who cared what he thought, though? And yet she did care. The idea of chasing after a man embarrassed her.

But I want to see him, she thought.

Later that day, her hands sweated as she gripped the steering wheel and stopped at the signal light, within sight of Oak Grove. To her right was the cotton mill where her daddy had spent more than half of his life. So strange that the mill was in clear sight of the cemetery. Her daddy used to joke *From the mill to the grave* until his brother Dave was laid to rest there.

Beyond the mill were the mill village streets, where rows of frame houses stood on steep inclines, simple shot-gun houses and two-story houses once made available for mill workers and their families. Martin had lived in one of those houses, though he never worked in the mill while she knew him.

"I don't want you marrying him and moving into that house," Lyla once said, though she'd never actually seen Martin's family home—a small, but neat white house, with a tidy front yard and sloping pasture behind. "Arthur pulled us out of that."

With cotton mill wages, she might have responded to her mother. But she admitted she preferred their own quiet neighborhood, miles beyond the cotton mill and city limits.

Mainly her mother and daddy had wanted her to protect her

reputation, get an education, and marry into the middle class, which she did.

"If only Richard had been Baptist," Lyla lamented. If only he had loved me, Esther thought.

Now she pulled into the cemetery drive, looking for a man who could only be poor. But her mother wouldn't know.

She drove immediately to the section where Sandy's grave lay and parked on the edge of the road. Beyond this section, down a steep bank were railroad tracks. She looked down there and saw a lone man walking the crossties. She felt a little uneasy being in this part of the cemetery by herself, but she knew that vandals usually struck at night, and she'd come here by herself before.

She walked around the tombstone but saw no geraniums. She was not surprised. A few weeds grew at the base of the stone—he needed his weedeater here, she thought—and when she reached to pull these weeds, a striped lizard scurried out and then slithered into a hole. Her heart jumped, and she jerked her hand back. Something twisted inside her. Did the lizard have a nest beneath the ground? Dear Lord.

The grave had sunk but the grass on top was closely mown. At least they kept the grass neat, she thought. As she ran her hand over the stone's rippled top, she heard a puttering sound approaching her.

Looking around, she saw the yellow-haired man driving a three-wheeled City of Milton vehicle.

"Howdy, ma'am," he said and tipped an invisible hat. He hadn't washed his hair yet, she could tell; it was parted in the middle and pulled tight behind his head in a ponytail. His eyes were dark brown, an odd contrast to his light hair, and his skin was sunburnt. He jerked his head aside and spat and pushed his tongue into his cheek. "Excuse me, ma'am," he said and patted the snuff can in his tee shirt pocket.

She nodded and looked away. She wondered if he

remembered the wink he gave her yesterday.

"Is this here family?" he asked and pointed to Sandy's grave. He strained to see the engraving on the stone. "Not a husband, I hope."

"No," she said and looked at him.

"That's good, I guess," he said and laughed. His laugh seemed more boyish than rude. He must be in his late-twenties, she thought, though his shabby clothes and hair made him seem older. She could tell he was simple-minded.

"He's my brother," she said.

"Oh," he said and after a minute, "I got one of them, too."

She looked toward the railroad tracks and at the woods beyond them. Maybe she shouldn't have come here alone. She looked at her watch.

"Like I said, I got a brother. You might a-seen him here. He seen you."

"What?" she said. "What did you say?"

"My brother. Adopted-wise. His mama raised me."

"Oh," she said and nodded.

"I say, he seen you."

"Listen," she said, backing toward her car, "there was a flower basket brought to this grave a few weeks back, and it's gone now. Do you know what happened to it?" She stood straighter now and changed her tone to the one she took with unruly students.

"You a teacher or lady lawyer or something?" he asked and stared at her.

She didn't know what to say.

"Oh, I could tell by that pantsuit you're wearing. Ain't you hot out here in that?" He studied her and said, "Me and my brother was talking and we decided you must be important. He likes your car. That set you back some, he said. Where you buy that kind?"

"Morganton," she said and looked beyond him to see if

anyone else were around. They were alone. "Do you know anything about the flowers or should I call somebody else?"

"I ain't a flower man, ma'am; I just cut grass. You could talk to my brother. He's the caretaker, and he's worked here since March. I just started last month. I can go get him. He's out at the trailer over yonder," he said and pointed to an indistinct place.

"That's not necessary," she said and opened her car door. "I'll call someone about it."

"It's just on the other side of the cemetery," he said. "He won't mind, I guarantee you that."

"Don't bother," she said, her face flushed. Couldn't he take no for an answer?

Before she sat in the driver's seat and closed the door, she heard him say, "Teacher, I'd wager. I had a few of them once."

Pity them, she thought.

"Teacher?" he asked. He wouldn't be satisfied until she answered him, so she nodded her head. "I was right then," he said and grinned. "I can read people pretty good."

Before she pulled away from the curb, he tapped her passenger window and she had to reach to roll it down.

"Not junior high school," he said and grinned. "I know for a fact the junior high school's out for the summer. What is it then? College? Do they run in the summer?"

"Something like that," she said.

He laughed at his perception and she saw him nodding and mouthing words as she drove away. She decided then and there he had mental problems and she'd better avoid him.

When she pulled from the main entrance, she glanced up a side road adjacent to the cemetery and caught a glimpse of a white trailer. It had a banistered front deck and lattice underpinning. So that's where he lives, she thought. A weedeater was propped against the front steps.

And he's impressed by my car, she thought, anxious to get out of there.

3

At home that evening while her mother worked in her garden, Esther called the Public Works Director, who told her no decorated grave at Oak Grove should have been stripped of all flowers. After a burial service, he said, all flowers could remain for ten days, and after holidays two or three weeks might pass before the city personnel removed the wreaths.

"But we always give the family the first chance to take them away," he said. "Then we leave one or two baskets or wreaths because we know families don't like a bare grave."

"So if we put a basket on a grave on Mother's Day, it should still be there?"

"Unless you removed it, ma'am."

"Then I don't understand."

"We advertise in the paper just before mowing season—about the first of March—and tell people they need to remove any flowers they don't want discarded. But like I said, we never take all the flowers to the landfill. It's touchy business. Some folks don't like us handling any of their flowers."

"But do you think a maintenance worker or a caretaker might mess with them?"

"Mowing's all the men are paid to do."

"Well, then, somebody has stolen my brother's flowers."

"I'm sorry, ma'am, but it wasn't us. You get some real weirdos coming into cemeteries at times. Oak Grove's no exception."

This news of the flowers' disappearance would be hard to break to her mother, but maybe the subject of Sandy's flowers wouldn't come up.

She went to the kitchen and looked out the picture window at her mother. The cucumbers had started coming in and Lyla stood gathering them in a straw basket. Lately her garden seemed her only enjoyment—just like her mother before her, who had been found dead between her rows of corn.

"Mother," she yelled as she stepped onto the back stoop, "Do you want to run to Asheville tonight?" There she might find a new pair of jeans. Her old ones were too ragged or had bell-bottomed legs or were hip-huggers, all outdated. It seemed more appropriate to dress casually when she went to talk to the caretaker. Since his brother had probably filled him in on their conversation, he would know she was a teacher and would assume she didn't work on Saturday. She didn't want him to think she was dressing up for him.

Would his brother be there? Was the caretaker married? If so, would his wife be suspicious of her coming to talk to him?

But this was business. Her visit would concern her brother's grave, and after all, he was the cemetery caretaker.

She would need some new Keds, too. It's funny that she hadn't worn sneakers since her feeble attempts at playing tennis with Richard. Maybe that's why the smell of the sporting goods store in the Asheville Mall, with its new leather shoes and expensive clothes, made her turn away when she passed it.

Tonight she would buy what she needed at Belk's.

She would buy her mother's supper at the Piccadilly cafeteria and buy her daddy a bag of cashews at Sears. The nuts would still be warm when she brought them to him tonight so that he could eat them while watching *20/20*.

In the mall after they ate, Lyla said she'd sit on the bench outside the Piccadilly while Esther did her shopping.

"I wanted you to help me pick out some clothes," Esther said.

"I don't want people seeing my hands," her mother said and looked at her nails. "You can't get the dirt out once it's in there. I ain't fit to be seen in public."

"You're fine, Mother. C'mon, I need you."

"Well, I don't know why we couldn't have waited till

tomorrow morning. This crowd makes me nervous."

"They won't bother us. Let's go before the stores close."

They walked into Belk's department store, by the glittering cosmetic counters, the mirrored petitions, and elegant mannequin displays. Lyla stopped at a female mannequin that reclined on a beach towel. Her wavy red hair spread over white shoulders, and her bikini revealed swelling breasts and a flat white belly.

"That's vulgar," Lyla said and studied the mannequin. "A woman who would wear that couldn't blame a man for nothing. They should be ashamed putting that out in the open. And look at that position she's in."

The mannequin lay with one knee bent, and the long fingers of her right hand rested on her collarbone. Her lips were parted to expose straight white teeth; her long-lashed blue eyes were narrowly opened.

"Looks like she's waiting for a man to crawl on top of her."

"Mother," Esther scolded and laughed, looking to see if anyone had heard. "You know, Mother," she said in a lowered voice, "I had a bikini once that was as skimpy as that. Remember the little white one with blue flowers? You bought it for me at Burand's Department Store in Milton. I'd just lost my baby fat and I think you wanted to show my new figure off. I was wearing it at the Catawba Springs swimming pool when Martin asked me out for the first time."

"Well, that's why he never had but one thing on his mind," Lyla said. "I should've had my head examined to buy you such a thing in the first place."

"All the girls wore bikinis then. You never saw a one-piece bathing suit. Only older women wore them, along with bathing caps. I was no different from other girls my age."

"I'm glad you outgrew all that."

"Let's go," she said and walked ahead of her mother.

As they looked through the jeans, she pushed the pairs, one

by one, across the rack. She couldn't focus on the sizes or styles.

"I don't know if people should outgrow some things," she said. She had to say it.

"What you talking about?" her mother said, adjusting her reading glasses as she peered at price tags.

"Why can't a woman my age be interested in sex? I'm still alive, you know."

"Why would you be interested in sex? You ain't married anymore. I thought that was a problem for you and Richard anyway. You told me you didn't like it."

"With Richard. All he wanted was a child, or I should say all he and his parents wanted. He didn't want me."

"It's just as well," Lyla said. "You can live without sex. Plenty of married couples do."

"I can believe that," she said. "But maybe I don't want to live without it," she said.

"Since when?" Lyla asked and looked at her. Her stern tone of voice and blue stare stirred something in Esther she'd almost forgotten. A judgment had been cast her way, the same kind of threat that had scared her away from Martin, though she wanted him so much.

"Never mind," she said and looked at the jeans.

The next morning she carried her radio into the bathroom and tuned in a soft rock station, turned on the taps and let the steaming water fill the bathtub as she sat on the toilet seat and filed her nails.

Later, soaping her body with Ivory soap, her mother's favorite, she wondered if she were making a mistake to go to the caretaker's trailer.

"Dang trailer," she could hear her daddy saying as if he knew of her intentions. Since a developer had bought a pasture down the street from their house and set up a trailer park, her daddy said he didn't care about going outside. "Someday they'll tear down this house and put a trailer here."

"Not as long as I'm here," she said.

"Is that so?" he said.

So she wouldn't dare tell her daddy where she was going. Anyone who lived in a trailer was suspect. It wasn't that he was against the poor—he himself grew up poor in the Depression, was a self-proclaimed yellow dog Democrat, and revered FDR because he strived to help the working man—her daddy just thought people could *do* better. One day they had driven by the trailer park and a young man sat in an aluminum chair in his yard, holding a pistol.

"See that?" her daddy said. "He's looking for somebody to shoot. This didn't use to be that kind of a neighborhood. You watch him when you go out, Esther."

"He just target practices against a bank, Daddy. I've seen him doing that. He's okay. I taught him at the college last year."

"Is that why he grins at you that way?" her mother asked from the back seat. "I wouldn't want a student of mine giving me that kind of look. It's rude."

"He's just friendly," she said. "And I think he works for the Police Department now. We ought to be glad he's on the street."

"Him and his pack of dogs," her daddy said.

What bothered her most about what her daddy said was that deep down she agreed with him. When she saw the caretaker's trailer, the first thing she thought was *Why did he settle for this?* If he thought so highly of her car—it set her back, he said—he must not have much money of his own. *Why not?*

She lay in the soapy, hot bath water and closed her eyes. The song "To Love Somebody" began playing on the radio, and she opened her eyes. Funny how a song could take you back twenty years.

It was a Saturday evening and she and Martin sat in his car at the drive-in theater. The movie had not begun yet. She was fourteen, Martin was twenty, and the rusted speaker that he'd hooked across his car window played "To Love Somebody." It was their third date and she'd told her parents that Martin was taking her to the town theater to see a Kurt Russell Disney film. Instead he headed west and pulled into the Pleasant Gardens Drive-In Theater. Here the parking area was a series of washed out, dusty trenches, separated by speaker posts. Ahead was a giant dingy white screen and to the side a small cinderblock concession building.

No respectable couple went to the drive-in theater, her mother would tell her later.

But that night Martin and she sat in the dusk and before the movie began, the speaker scratchily played popular music.

He hadn't touched her yet. The first two dates were meetings at her house, evenings in the front porch swing, her parents close by to call her in before ten o'clock.

Tonight he wore a short-sleeved white shirt, dress pants, and cologne, and she wore a mini skirt, sleeveless blouse, and new sandals. Her arms and legs were tan from mornings at the swimming pool, and her honey blond hair had platinum highlights from the sun and chlorine.

They sat in his car and listened to the music. Neither spoke.

Then "To Love Somebody" began playing and she felt Martin's eyes on her and her heart ticked. She was afraid to look at him. When she finally turned her face to him, he said, "Come here." He reached his hand to her, helping her scoot to his side.

He put his arm around her shoulders, pulled her close, and said, "Are you glad you came?" and she could only nod *yes*. Even at that moment, she wanted more of him, his protection and love.

When the dusk turned to darkness and car horns urged the movie to begin, a flickering of images at the beginning of the film reel came onto the screen and then the movie *Thunder Road* began.

Only then, under the seclusion of darkness, while other

lovers necked in old pickup trucks and beat-up cars, did he turn and lift her chin and cover her mouth with his. Then he touched her cheek, gently like a brother, and said, "You look beautiful."

And he kissed her deeply.

Later she walked through the dark to the restroom, housed in a narrow block building near the concession building. When she entered, the stench of urine and excrement took her breath. In the cool stall, she balanced, careful not to let her skin touch the black toilet seat. When she stood and flushed the toilet, something caught her eye. On the back of the stained door were written the words *Martin Faulkner fu—'s whores*. Though some of the verb had been scratched out, she knew what it meant and her heart sank.

When she opened the car door, Martin said, "What's wrong, Babe?" She shook her head and he reached to touch her cheek. When he felt her tears, he pulled her close and said, "Has something hurt you, Esther?" But she could only cry and hope the words she'd read on the bathroom stall door were a lie.

Now in the bath water, she felt her throat constrict, and she closed her eyes and wished the song had never played on the radio.

She didn't like to lie to her parents and had rarely done so. Her mother's eyes could read her soul and she felt helpless in their scrutiny. But she couldn't tell her parents everything, especially this.

Sitting in her bedroom, brushing and blow drying her hair, she looked at her reflection in the vanity mirror. The Dutch girl decals that her mother had stuck there when Esther was twelve were still in the corners of the mirror.

The question had already come up, of course. Why was she buying new blue jeans all of a sudden? And weren't they too tight? How could that be comfortable?

"I need some younger clothes, Mother," she'd said. "I can't

go around in polyester all the time. And I need some new shorts, too."

"Shorts?"

"C'mon, Mother, they sell them. We both need us some shorts. I always wore them when I was growing up. So did you back then, I remember."

"That was pedal pushers," Lyla said. "You can do what you want."

The jeans really were tighter than she'd like, and she tugged at the legs to loosen them at the crotch. She didn't want to give the wrong impression, especially to that sort of man. What if his wife answered the door? She didn't want trouble with a woman over a man. Not again.

Can't a woman talk to a man without everybody getting the wrong idea? she thought. Milton was the worst place in the world for people jumping to the wrong conclusions.

She hadn't dated since her divorce. An administrator at the college had asked her out, and Lyla thought that was okay.

"What would we do?" she asked.

"Well," Lyla said, "you could go to Crabtree Meadows on a picnic or tour the Biltmore Estate in Asheville—that's educational. An educated man like that would know of some cultural activities. Bring him here and I'll cook dinner for you. Arthur could show him his record collection. That'd do Arthur good to have a man to talk to. There's plenty to do."

"I guess," she said, wishing she'd not brought it up.

"Or you could take him to church, or we all could go out to Andrew's Geyser in Old Fort. I've not seen that geyser in years. I reckon it's still there. Arthur used to ride us up there some Sunday afternoons when you and Sandy was little. We'd have a picnic lunch of beans and meatloaf biscuits. You remember?"

"Vaguely," she said. She knew she'd had dreams through the years about a water fountain. In the dream she and Sandy had climbed a wrought iron fence to get to the gushing water. Once inside, they danced around in the cold spray and splashed each other. But the fountain in the dream was probably the Indian arrowhead fountain, a pioneer monument in Old Fort, a town in their county that they drove through on their way to Asheville.

"Why date a man you're not attracted to?" she'd asked.

"You don't have to date nobody," Lyla said. "But I'd hate to see you alone someday. Since it didn't work out with Richard."

"I was alone with him."

"No, you wasn't. But you will be alone someday, and that worries me. I'm not saying marriage is the best way, but it's about all a woman has to depend on."

"I wouldn't mind having a lover who I could see when I wanted to." She knew she was poking a hornet's nest.

"You don't want no such situation," Lyla said. "Unless you want people to call you a whore."

The last word stung her, and she dropped the subject.

At her vanity she now opened a bottle of *Wind Song* perfume and held the bottle's mouth to her nose. The citrus fragrance filled her senses. No, she decided and screwed the bottle cap back on. He might get the wrong idea. Even when she went to work she avoided wearing perfume, for some man might think she wore it for him.

Elsewhere in the house was a gold rectangular box that held a purse-sized glass cylinder of *Joy* perfume. It was the last gift she received from Martin on her fifteenth birthday, and at the time it hadn't meant a thing. But she'd kept it stored inside a cedar chest of mementos, hidden in an upstairs bedroom, tucked beneath layers of blankets, unknown even to her mother.

As she sat at the vanity, Lyla called to her and tapped on the bedroom door.

"You don't have to knock, Mother," she said.

"You never know what's happening in here," Lyla said, and she wondered what her mother meant.

"Here, let me brush your hair," Lyla said and pulled up a

chair and sat behind her. She drew the brush through Esther's shoulder-length hair, from crown to shoulders, and Esther felt her stop and lift some strands with her other hand.

"What are you doing?"

"I don't see a gray hair yet. You're lucky your hair is as light colored as it is; gray won't ever show much."

"You don't have much gray yourself, Mother," she said and looked at her mother's reflection in the mirror.

"Hold your head still," Lyla said and started brushing again.

"That feels good," she said and closed her eyes.

"I brushed my mama's hair like this," Lyla said. "Her hair was so thick, I'd have to part it in sections and brush it a section at a time. It was the prettiest color, a dark chestnut, and had only a little gray at the cowlick. Sandy had that same cowlick."

"Do I have it?" Esther asked and lifted up her bangs to see her hairline.

"No, yours is more of a widow's peak."

"Oh," she said and studied her reflection. "Where did I get blond hair? Sandy's was brown and so is yours. Wasn't Daddy's hair dark when he was young?" His scant hair was silver now, but she'd seen old photographs.

"It was dark and had a natural wave in it. When he was younger, he'd stand in front of the bathroom mirror and massage Brylcreem in it and comb it. He'd take such pains, you'd think he was courting."

"I wish I could have known him then. That doesn't sound like Daddy."

"That ain't him now." Lyla continued brushing her hair and she enjoyed how the bristles tingled her scalp. This was a rare moment of touch between her and her mother. She closed her eyes.

"I've heard tell my daddy's older sister was blond and fair complected," Lyla said and stirred Esther from her reverie. "She died before I was born. She wasn't but eighteen when she died."

"What killed her?"

"She was trapped in a house during the 1916 flood. There was a mudslide behind the house that caused a staircase inside to collapse, and she got pinned in and drowned. Nobody could get to her in time. That flood's what brought Daddy's family to Milton in the first place. They'd farmed in Rutherford County till their farm was washed away. After that, they all went into the mills here in Milton."

"What was his sister's name?"

"Malinda Grant. She's buried in Rutherford County beside the Montford Cove Baptist Church. You remember, Arthur used to take us there to the cemetery on Decoration Day."

"Why don't we go anymore?" she asked.

"Oh, Arthur gets impatient. Last time we went out there to Montford Cove Cemetery, he sat in the car while I decorated the graves. So I don't bother him about it anymore."

"I'd take you," she offered.

"It's hard enough to keep up one grave," Lyla said and laid the hairbrush on the vanity.

It's hard all right, she thought, when someone steals the flowers. She hoped her mother didn't read her thoughts.

"Do you need anything from the store?" she asked and kept her eyes from her mother's face. "I'm going into town."

"I know you're going," Lyla said and smoothed her apron. "That's why you bought new clothes." She said it matter-of-factly, no accusation in her tone.

While her mother walked out of the room, Esther said, "I won't be gone long." She regretted she felt the need to say it.

4

She stood at the trailer door and heard a T.V. playing inside, so she knew they were out of bed by now. After she knocked, she looked at the corner of the deck and saw a potted fern in an iron stand; on the other side was a similar fern. Were those here yesterday? The ferns were scraggy, with few stems and yellowish leaves, and clearly needed some Miracle Grow, but they did give the place a homey look. She had given her mother two hanging baskets of potted ferns for Mother's Day and was pleased when Lyla hung the baskets on the front porch. She wondered if her daddy was disappointed that Lyla took his gift of geraniums to the cemetery.

Maybe the ferns on this deck just needed watering, she thought. You'd think the two men who lived here would know how to take care of plants, though. After all, they took care of the cemetery grounds. Her mother's ferns never looked this forlorn, even in the heat. But Lyla took her watering can onto the front porch every morning and gave the baskets a good soaking.

The ferns here might signal a woman's presence. It didn't seem likely that a man would have anything floral like this, though you never knew. She looked for other feminine signs.

The deck boards were gray and cracked, needing a coat of tinted water sealant, and the trailer's metal siding looked dingy, rusty in places. Close up, the trailer didn't look as neat as it had appeared from a distance. But wind chimes suspended from the deck's overhang caught her eye. The wind chimes featured brightly painted chickens that hung in varying levels. She imagined if the wind blew, the wooden chickens would clack together to sound like a chicken clucking. Her mother would like something like this on her porch.

While she studied the chickens, someone said, "Howdy," and she looked down to see a child's face behind the screen of a storm door. She hadn't heard the front door open.

The boy's plump face was smooth and tanned, his nose sprinkled with dark freckles; his brown hair was close-cropped, and his eyes a yellow hazel. In his left ear lobe was a diamond stud. She couldn't help staring. Who would let a boy his age get his ear pierced? Even Richard, at his rebellious stage, wouldn't have approved of that.

"Howdy," the boy said again and opened the storm door with his knee.

He wasn't much shorter than she, but a good twenty pounds heavier already. He looked nothing like the yellow-haired man or the caretaker as far as she could tell. Maybe he was a younger foster brother, but probably a son. "You the teacher?" he asked.

She nodded and said, "I'm looking for the caretaker." The boy's steady eyes waited for more information. "The caretaker?" she repeated.

"Okay," he said, tossing his head, and pulled his knee back to let the door close.

In a minute she heard the yellow-haired man say, "Howdy, ma'am," and he stepped out onto the deck. His hair was hanging down around his face onto his bare shoulders and chest, his tight blue jeans were zipped but unbuttoned, and he stood barefoot, as if he'd jumped out of bed to come to the door. "You wanting to see Davis Lee?"

She couldn't speak. She could only manage to lift her palm as if in some feeble supplication. He answered quickly, "Davis Lee's who you want. I'll get him."

What's wrong with me? she asked herself. What am I doing here?

In a minute she heard a man's voice inside the house saying, "Cut down that T.V.," and then the boy's voice answering. Then she heard no sounds at all.

She waited on the deck, looking at the wind chimes, her back to the front door. When she turned, he stood watching her.

"My brother Jeff said you wanted me," he said, stepping out onto the deck. He was several inches taller than she, six feet probably. His dark hair, combed back from his forehead, was wet as if he'd just showered. A sprig of loose hair fell over his eyebrow, and he combed it back with his fingers. His face was broad, his cheekbones well defined, and his eyes—so dark she could barely see the pupils—looked surprised. The dark stubble that shadowed his lip and dimpled chin suggested he hadn't shaved in his shower.

"I didn't get you up?" she said, though it was obvious she did. She clutched her purse at her side. What an idiot she was, coming here, getting this man out of bed on a Saturday morning. He must wonder, Who is this woman and what does she want?

"Sometimes I sleep late on Saturday," he said and stared at her.

"I'm sorry," she said and stepped back. "I heard the T.V. and assumed you'd be up."

"Oh," he said and glanced behind him. "That's Jim and Jeff's cartoons. Sometimes they'll sit in front of the T.V. till noon. You met my boy Jim?"

"Yes," she said and tried to think of something to say about the boy. He was cute. A big boy. Why in the world did he have his ear pierced? Better to say nothing, she decided.

He stood and watched her. She waited for him to say *What can I do for you?* But he didn't seem to care one way or the other.

"You want a cup of coffee? I ain't had mine yet. Jeff's got it brewing if you'd like some."

"You probably wonder why I'm here."

"Cemetery business, I reckon. Unless you're a Jehovah's Witness."

"No," she said and laughed lightly. Just a back-slid Baptist, she thought, realizing her heart was tapping and her mind getting mushy. "I don't want to bother you. I just wanted to ask about the flowers at the cemetery—"

"You ain't no bother. Say you want some coffee?" He cracked open the door. "Come in the house."

"Oh, no," she said. "I can't stay." She hadn't expected this courtesy, though maybe a cemetery caretaker was supposed to act this way to the public. It just seemed odd to her. And why would he think she'd enter a strange man's trailer? He could be a murderer for all she knew. Didn't strange things happen in cemeteries? Vandals had smashed gravestones. An escaped Tennessee convict had hid out at Oak Grove. Milton was not immune to weird events: forty-year-old murders unsolved; unidentified bodies pulled from Lake James. No, she wouldn't enter this man's house. And in any case, her mother would think she was not only crazy, but also cheap to step inside his door.

But the man's voice was kind, though his eyes were guarded as if he suspected her too.

"Well, if you won't come in, will you have a cup of coffee with me out here? We can just sit on the porch." She didn't see any chairs to sit in.

"Well," she said after a minute, "I guess I could." She was more of a tea drinker, but he seemed to want company and she needed to talk to him about the flower basket.

He went inside and in a minute his son brought out two wooden straight chairs. The boy went back in without speaking to her. He came out again with a T.V. tray stand and set it up in front of the chairs. Again, he left without speaking. She knew these chores were interrupting his cartoons.

In a few more minutes the caretaker came out, holding an orange plastic tray, like the ones at Hardees, that held two cups of coffee, some packs of creamers and sugar, and a Krispy Kreme doughnut box. He set the tray on the tray stand. He pointed to a chair and told her to sit in it, and he sat in the other chair.

"You like doughnuts?" he said and held the box to her.

She didn't have the heart to tell him she'd eaten breakfast hours earlier, so she reached inside the box and pulled out a glazed doughnut.

"Jeff got these at Winn-Dixie. He does our grocery shopping."

"So you all live together?"

"You mean Jim, too?" he said and bit into a doughnut with strong white teeth. He chewed and shook his head *no*. "I get Jim some weekends. His mama has him most of the time."

So she didn't live here, Esther thought.

"You like your doughnut?" he said and looked at it in her hand. "We go through two or three boxes of these a week. Nobody here can cook too good."

Esther thought of a childhood warning she often heard from her paternal grandmother: *Don't eat anything off the floor or you'll get T.B.* She wondered now how clean these men's kitchen was, noticing the man's hands as she took a bite of the doughnut. His hands were clean, the fingernails of his long fingers trimmed and smooth, not ragged and stained like she might have expected. She glanced toward the highway and wondered if anyone she knew had passed by, someone from the college or worse a member of her mother's church.

He saw her glance and said, "I've seen you come to the cemetery. Jeff says your brother's there. I'm sorry to hear that."

So he did recognize her. She nodded and chewed the doughnut.

His eyes widened and he pushed the box toward her. "Get you another one," he said. "These things grow on you."

When she shook her head and held her hand up, trying to get the bite swallowed, he said, "Jeff says you're a professor."

"Well, no, I'm an instructor. Technical college," she said and glanced at her watch. "Say, listen," she said and stood. He looked up at her and then stood too. "I don't want to hold you up. I just came to ask about the flowers on my brother's grave—"

"Sanford Arthur Robertson, born 1953 died 1970. He was the Sunshine of Our Home," she heard recited from inside the storm door. The gravestone epitaph spoken that way stunned her. The words had always seemed her family's private property. She looked toward the voice.

"Hey," the caretaker said and turned quickly to face the screen, "you shut that up." He went inside the trailer and she heard his angry voice and Jeff's, a pitch higher, though she couldn't make out either man's words.

He came back outside, this time closing the trailer's main entrance door behind him. "I'm sorry for that," he said, blood rising in his face. "He didn't mean nothing by it, it's just something he does—learning the engravings by heart—he's been doing it since he started working here. I don't know why. It's some kind of hobby of his. But I'm sorry he picked your brother's words."

All she could do was nod *yes* to say it was all right.

"At times he's smart as a whip, but other times I don't know. There's a wildness in him. Jim's got more sense and he's not but twelve. Course Jim's had to grow up fast—you know this situation with his mama and me."

She didn't know, of course, and wasn't too sure she wanted to know the details. He stared at her with dark eyes until she had to look away. He seemed to be reading more in her visit here than an inquiry about her brother's flowers.

"I'm taking up your time," he said and she said, "No, I'm taking up your Saturday morning with your son. I just wanted to know who might have moved my brother's flowers."

"I don't know," he said. "But I'll be on the lookout for thieves. Me and Jeff both."

"I would appreciate that," she said, ready to leave. She took an obligatory sip of coffee and thanked him for the refreshments.

"Thank you for honoring us," he said and bowed slightly.

His words and gesture seemed odd for a caretaker and she wondered if he were being sarcastic.

"And your name's Davis Lee?" she asked as she turned to leave.

"Yes, ma'am," he said and nodded to her. She waited for him to ask her name but he didn't.

"Come back and see us," he said after a minute and turned to go inside.

When she reached her car, she looked to see if he or Jeff were watching from behind a window. She thought she saw Jeff's face.

Driving home, she rubbed her fingers together and worried she'd gotten the doughnut glaze on the steering wheel. She reached behind her and pulled a tissue from the box in the back seat.

As much as she tried, she couldn't wipe the stickiness from her hands.

Later that afternoon she sat in the front porch swing to read one of her literature assignments. But Tennyson's poem about the Lady of Shalott, who lost her life for love, made her want to close her eyes and rest. She set the book aside and laid her head against the swing chain. Down the street, dogs barked, and closer was the chirping and whistling of birds. Across the street a child banged on a galvanized tub, saying words she couldn't make out; and from somewhere came the high-pitched whir of a weedeater. Its low hiss as it lapped weeds and its higher-pitched buzz like a giant bumblebee lulled her. A breeze laced with the apple scent of sweet bulb blossoms lifted her hair.

She swung and listened.

If she concentrated, she could imagine Sandy sitting beside her in the swing, pushing with his long legs, making the swing arc too high, too high, until she begged him to stop.

"Pretend we're on a Ferris wheel," he'd say and throw his

shaggy head back and laugh. "Now we're falling, Blondie, and nothing can stop us." And the loose chain ends slapped the support chains and his laughter filled the air.

"Stop it, Sandy," she yelled, but her begging made him laugh harder. There was no stopping him.

He looked at her with wicked green eyes and sunburnt face and said, "What'll you give me?"

"I ain't giving you nothing," she said, locked beside him.

"Well then, Blondie, I'll swing us to the stars and you'll come flying down on a meteor."

"I'll bite you," she said and grasped his skinny arm.

"No meat on my bones," he said and kicked the porch with his heels. "Tonight you come to my room and scratch my back fifty times and I'll set you free."

"That ain't fair, Sandy," she said, tired of his control.

"Well, in that case, Blondie, we'll go to the stars—" But before he could push with his toes, she jumped from the swing, landed on her knees, and ran in the house.

That night she sneaked upstairs to his room and sat on the bed beside him and rubbed his freckled shoulders.

"You're not such a bad kid," he said and after a while his breathing slowed. She stroked a few minutes longer. Moonlight through the window lit his face, his closed eyes, and she didn't know how you could hate somebody one minute and love him so much the next.

It might be simpler, she decided, just to put another basket of flowers on Sandy's grave. That way, she'd be able to tell her mother that some flowers were there, and she could also test the caretaker to see that he'd watch for thieves.

Since her visit to his trailer on Saturday, she'd not seen him out working. But she had tried to keep her eyes on the road when she passed the cemetery, going back and forth to work. No need in his thinking she was trying to see him as she drove by. And she sensed sarcasm in his words when she left him and his bowing like a gentleman—what was that about?

But he had begun to talk about his marriage and his son, as if he wanted to confide in her. Still, wasn't that the oldest come-on in the book? The administrator at the college who'd pursued her had started with, "I can't talk to my wife. We never could talk. You're easy to talk to—" All she'd done was listen while he rambled on.

But there was no physical tug she felt by the administrator's words or looks. He wore expensive shirts and tweed blazers, belonged to a country club, and drove a new Volvo that Davis Lee would really like. But she could not imagine his body close to hers, his mouth on hers. His pale blue eyes and boyish good looks didn't interest her.

He was divorced now, but she didn't care.

Sex with someone today would be an adjustment anyway. Eight years had passed since she'd lain beside a man, and Richard had been her only lover. His hands moved mechanically over her shoulders and breasts, as if he didn't quite know where to put them. *Here*, she'd said and directed his hand to bring her pleasure, and had pulled him closer to press differently against her body, but his focus was on himself so that he hardly realized what she was doing.

She wanted him to kiss her ear and her throat and when he'd nearly reached his pleasure, she whispered *Wait, Richard, wait*, so that she could join him in the moment. But he couldn't wait, and she lost the chance, as she always did.

And then his mother got involved. "Let's put a pillow under your hips, Esther," Richard said when he prepared to make love to her; "it'll help conception." Esther knew these were his mother's promptings. "No, Esther, stay under me. It won't work if you're on top." And afterwards, "Don't run to the bathroom, Esther. Keep the semen in for a while."

But all the medical encyclopedia techniques his mother

advised and the sexual positions they tried, often at the expense of her comfort, didn't help conception or their marriage. She'd heard women say they knew the moment they conceived: the penetration had been deeper or the orgasm more spectacular or the love felt between the two more profound. Esther never had the feeling that any goal had been reached, and in time, the disappointment made the efforts seem pointless. And anyway it wasn't any fun to make love to Richard. She doubted he'd ever truly enjoyed it either.

She knew Richard's new wife had given him something back for his efforts. They had a daughter, and who knows, they might have more children yet. She hoped his wife was a good listener. It's what he had liked best in *her* during their courtship. He might even feel a genuine attraction for the new wife. The kind of desire she and Martin once had, though it hadn't been enough to build on.

And now this stranger, Davis Lee, seemed to want her to listen.

Wreaths of artificial roses and carnations lined the florist wall, and fluted metal baskets of plastic flowers crowded the floor. On the glass-topped counter sat silk arrangements in conch- and rabbit-shaped vases and in ceramic baby shoes, pink and blue. She heard voices in the back room, but saw no one in the main shop. She walked to a tall refrigerator and looked through the glass door at the long-stemmed red roses and gladiolas and lilies. On the wall behind the main counter hung a calendar displaying this month's date *June 1990* that had most of the day blocks X-ed out. The calendar also featured a picture of Milton Funeral Home with its banistered front porch and swing. *Serving the people of Milton since 1910*, it read. Come to think of it, this florist smelled just like the funeral home. She rang the bell on the counter. *Come on*, she thought, the stifling atmosphere making her queasy, and finally a woman wearing a green apron came from the back room. She held a pair of scissors in one hand and a long-stemmed rose in the other.

Esther told her she needed a basket of plastic geraniums and pointed to an arrangement displayed in the shop's front window.

"Them's left from Mother's Day," the woman said. "Red will be popular next week, too, for the Fourth of July. Do you need a card for that basket?"

"No, just the flowers," she said and paid the woman. Once outside in the sunlight and cooler air, she breathed deeply to rid herself of the funeral home smell.

Julia Nunnally Duncan

5

She took the basket to the cemetery. The Saturday morning traffic was heavier than usual, with travelers heading south to the interstate and west to the mountains. She pulled off the highway and drove to Sandy's grave.

A few other cars were parked alongside graves, and people had placed flowers throughout the cemetery. Red, white, and blue flag wreaths stood by some veterans' headstones. Tomorrow more people would come, and next Wednesday, after the Fourth of July parade in town, the local VFW group would decorate the veterans' graves with miniature American flags.

She set the basket in front of the stone and took a rag from her pocket and dusted the letters of Sandy's name. Her mother would probably want to come to the parade next week, which was fine with her. They might as well do something to pass the time, since she would be on vacation leave from the college for a few days. Maybe they could get her daddy to come too, though she doubted it. He preferred watching parades on T.V.

The sun seemed to drill a beam into her head, and she went to her car and put on the royal blue straw hat she'd bought in Asheville last Friday night. She felt a little self-conscious in it, but her mother said it brought out the color of her eyes and would prevent sun stroke, so she bought it. It matched the cotton sundress she wore today.

Maybe I'll roll my hair for the parade, she thought and inspected the strands that lay across her shoulders. Her hair had been longer once, but in recent years she'd kept it shoulder length and cut straight at the ends, with the bangs trimmed at her eyebrows. Richard had preferred her hair this length, thought it was neater and less "countrified" than when it hung to her waist. So she'd kept it this way, mostly out of habit.

But there was Martin, on the other hand. That night at the

drive-in, he held her and spoke softly, touching her face and caressing her hair.

"I love your hair," he said and though at first she thought he was going to say "I love you," she wasn't disappointed. For she knew these more intimate words would come soon, and she would wait for them, so she could answer him with the same words.

He often caressed her hair, the way someone might caress your shoulder, and nestled his face into her neck when he held her. "Your hair smells good," he said. "I could drown in it." When they lay on her bed on Sunday afternoons, her mother occasionally knocking on the door to remind them of her presence, he leaned over her and kissed the ends of her hair.

One Sunday while they sat in the porch swing, he said, "When we make love, I'll spread your hair like a fan across the pillow, it's so beautiful."

She wanted him then, she told him, but she was afraid.

"No, we'll wait," he said, and added they'd better not be alone in her bedroom anymore.

Later that day her mother told her that her daddy had had a talk with Martin in the driveway before he came to the house. And she told Esther they were worried about her and Martin getting too *cozy*. "Your daddy knows how boys are," she said. "They'll go too far if you let 'em."

She and Martin didn't go into her bedroom to be alone after that, but she felt intuitively that someday they would make love.

Now she thought as she looked at her hair, too short to spread like a fan across a pillow, that your intuitions didn't always prove true.

She stood at Sandy's grave and as she turned to leave, an elderly woman, whom she'd seen standing at a nearby grave, came toward her. The woman was dressed as if for church or town, with a matching pink skirt and jacket. Her high heels made her walk unsteadily on the uneven ground.

The woman smiled and glanced at Sandy's stone and then at her.

"My son brought me here today," the woman said and nodded toward a man who stood smoking beside a station wagon. "I came to see my husband's new stone."

"Oh, I'm sorry," Esther said.

"No, he's been dead for twenty years. Somebody smashed his tombstone and we had to replace it."

"That's terrible," she said and backed closer to her car. The sun grew hotter by the minute. She wondered how the woman could stand a long-sleeved jacket.

"Idn't it, though?" the woman said and stared at Esther. "That's a real pretty hat," she said. "You don't see many young girls wearing hats." The woman apparently thought she was younger than she was. People often made that mistake. Adjusting her own black velvet pillbox hat, the woman waited for Esther's response.

"I like hats," she told the woman. "Especially when the sun's hot like this. It's really too hot to stand out here over a minute or two."

The woman looked at her until Esther smiled out of politeness.

"Haven't I seen you on T.V.?" the woman asked.

Esther laughed. "T.V.?" she said. Then she realized what the woman was thinking about. Last summer the college had made a two-minute T.V. commercial that aired several times on a local cable station. She was cast as the narrator—chosen by her admiring administrator—and said some words about the college's curriculum programs as she walked through the college library. Several students also spoke rehearsed lines about their experiences at Milton Technical College.

"I could have sworn my daddy was the only one who would remember that commercial," she said. He had thought it an honor that the public would equate his daughter with higher learning.

"Who's your daddy?" the woman said.

"Arthur Robertson," she said and looked at her car. She really didn't want to get personal with this woman.

"Arthur Robertson," the woman repeated. "I knew an Arthur Robertson who lived on Second Street—just up there," she said and pointed toward the cotton mill village. "But that's been forty years ago. My husband and I both worked in the mill. I knew an Arthur Robertson. That idn't his stone there?" she said and stooped to get a closer look.

"No, that's my brother," she said. "Daddy's still living." The woman had obviously known her daddy, but Esther didn't want to pursue the memory. "Well, I need to go by the trade lot and then get home," she said and turned to her car.

"Hey, Missy?" the woman said as Esther opened her car door. "I wanted to tell you to be careful here by yourself. I don't come here without my son."

"There's a caretaker who lives nearby," Esther said. "He watches out for things here."

"Didn't watch out for Archie's stone," the woman said. "But we've called the law to look into that," she added.

"I don't blame you," she said and thought of her brother's stolen basket. She had seen no sign of Davis Lee earlier today when she passed his trailer. Probably he was still in bed.

Before she started her car, she watched the woman and saw that she had returned safely to her son. The woman stood and talked to him and pointed at Sandy's stone and then at her. The son looked toward her and then motioned to the station wagon as if he wanted to leave.

That's the way her daddy had acted years ago when he brought them to see Sandy's grave. He rested his foot on the car bumper and peered at the railroad tracks. When a train rumbled by, he followed each car with his eyes and watched the caboose go out of sight. While she and her mother set flowers on the grave or pulled weeds, her daddy kept his eyes turned away. What they were doing seemed none of his affair. He just wanted them to do their business so they could get on home.

The trade lot pavilion, an enclosed area of wooden stalls where people sold produce, handicrafts, hardware, new and used clothes, and chickens and goats, was crowded as a carnival on Saturdays from early morning until afternoon. When she walked through at eleven a.m., people were stirring, the dirt floor already boot-tracked and spotted with wads of discarded chewing tobacco. She smelled burning grease from the hamburger grill at the concession stand and buttered popcorn from a vendor. The fermented aroma of ripe cantaloupes, sliced and drawing flies, filled the air.

She went to the stand and ordered a Diet Coke and sipped it as she walked from stall to stall. A display of music boxes caught her attention, in particular a miniature porcelain Victrola.

"That's a genuine antique," said the woman who sat in a folding chair behind the display. Before Esther could answer, the woman picked up the music box and wound the key on the bottom. "Do you know that tune?" She held the music box out to Esther.

At first Esther didn't recognize the faint melody.

"I found that music box at a estate sale in Savannah, Georgia. A old woman had that in her family for years."

"How old is it?" Esther asked and took the music box in both hands.

"Why, I'd say it dates from the First World War, anyway. My mama had one of them Gramophones when I was little. We ruined it by winding it up too tight, though. The horn on it was wood with flowers painted on it. Prettiest thing you ever saw. I wish you could see it."

Esther rewound the music box and held it to her ear to distinguish the tune. She listened to the melody twice before she set down the box and said, "Well, thank you."

As she walked away, the woman said, "I'll take $25.00. I can't go any lower for a antique like that."

The melody was one she hadn't heard in a while. "Lara's Theme," from the late '60's film *Dr. Zhivago,* still tinkled from the music box while she walked away. She couldn't help smiling, thinking the woman would probably sell it as an antique to someone. Who knows—maybe the woman really believed it was an antique.

"You like music boxes?" a voice asked from across the dusty pavilion, and she glanced behind her to see the caretaker's brother Jeff leaned against a wooden support post.

"Hello," she said and didn't see his brother nearby. She touched her hat self-consciously and wished she'd left it in the car.

"Pretty hat," he said and she dropped her hand.

He looked different now, and she stared at him for a minute. Then she saw. He sensed her thoughts and touched his head.

"I cut my hair," he said and laughed. His teeth were surprisingly white against his crimson face.

She didn't respond and people walked back and forth between them. He looked at his work boots, shabby as his faded jeans, and waited until no one separated them.

"Cut it with a straight razor," he said and shook his head as if his action amazed even him. He pulled a bone-handled razor from his back pocket and flipped it open, exposing the shiny blade. "See?" he said, then closed it and stuck in back in his pocket.

Couldn't he afford a barber shop? she wondered, but knew money probably had nothing to do with it.

"Davis Lee says I look like Rod Stewart. He thinks I'm crazy."

"He does?" she said, and she couldn't tell if he meant it as a joke.

"I was going more for the Steve McQueen look. Jim approves, though."

"Davis Lee's son?"

"Yeah. He ain't with us this weekend. He's with his mama. He comes here to the trade lot with me on Saturday when he's with us. He ain't with us this weekend."

He looked at his boots again and laughed.

She looked at the dirt floor, unsure what to say next.

He looked at her and said, "Say you like music boxes?"

She crossed the floor to stand in front of him so people wouldn't have to keep saying *Excuse me* as they passed between her and Jeff.

"I make music boxes," he said.

"You *make* them?" she asked.

"I do," he said and tilted back his shaggy head. "I order the musical workings from a catalog, and then I saw out the box and whittle designs on it with my pocket knife," he said and dug the knife from his jeans pocket. He held it up. "Case," he said and pushed it back into the tight pocket. "I think it's the best make, but Davis Lee carries a Boker."

"Does he whittle, too?" she said, but what she really wanted to know was whether or not Davis Lee was divorced. Maybe that answer would come up in the conversation.

"No," he said. "He might carve his initials on something, but he don't whittle."

"Well, I need to find my mother a new cast iron skillet. I better be going," she said and backed away from him.

"Don't run off," he said.

"Well, I'll see you," she said and suddenly felt sorry for him. He stood there and looked at her.

As she turned to leave he said, "Davis Lee *wants* to see you again. He told me so."

She didn't say anything, but felt heat in her face. She kept her back to him, pretending not to have heard.

"Bye, *pro*-fessor," he said and laughed, and when she walked away, she still heard him laughing.

"I'll have to burn the finish off this pan before I use it," Lyla said when Esther handed her the heavy skillet.

"I talked to a couple of people today," Esther said as her mother coated the skillet with shortening. They stood in the kitchen at the electric stove.

"I ain't talked to nobody but the scarecrow," Lyla said and slid the skillet onto the preheated oven rack. She wiped her hands on her apron and looked at Esther. "You ought to wear that hat," she said. "It's becoming on you. I never had the face for a hat."

"I've been complimented on it twice today."

"A compliment never did nobody any harm. If it's sincere."

"I believe these compliments today were sincere. One of the people was a total stranger and one I know slightly, but he's basically a stranger. I mean, it's odd that strangers would talk to me and compliment me that way."

"It used to be nobody was a stranger in Milton," Lyla said. "Everybody knowed everybody—farm people, town people. Like a big family. It ain't that way n'more."

She sounded tired when she said it.

"Mother, one of them I talked to said she knew Daddy. I didn't ask her name, but she looked kind of fancy. But she said she and her husband had worked in the mill."

"Who?" Lyla said suddenly and stared at her. "Where'd you talk to her?"

She hadn't wanted to mention going to the cemetery today.

"Oak Grove," she said. "I stopped there for a minute on my way to the trade lot."

"Was she a old woman?" Lyla asked.

"Maybe a little older than Daddy," she answered. "It was hard to tell. Like I said, she was dressed kind of fancy with a

Jackie Kennedy hat."

"Arthur knowed a lot of women in the mill. They'd buy him Christmas presents and make him cakes. One even had the nerve to bring him a bottle of wine for his birthday."

"One of them gave Daddy wine?" She'd never known her daddy to drink wine. Her mother had forbidden alcohol in their house as long as she remembered, especially after Sandy's accident.

"That was before you was born. I put my foot down that time. You know she had to get that wine from a bootlegger. There was a family of bootleggers that lived on one of the mill hills back then."

"Bootleggers?"

"That was one reason I wanted us to move out of the mill village. Bootleggers deserve to be shot," she said.

"This woman I talked to today seemed like a lady," she said. "She wore a dress suit and high heels. Like somebody going to teach Sunday School."

"Time and money can make anybody seem proper, but what they are inside don't change."

"I guess not," she said. Was her mother jealous? She wouldn't have mentioned the woman if she'd expected this response.

"Your daddy was a good looking man in his day," Lyla said. "You've seen pictures in my scrapbook."

It had been a while since Esther had looked at these World War II pictures of her daddy, a handsome uniformed twenty-year-old.

"Yes, he *was* good looking," she said, recalling his dark hair and pleasant grin.

"We was all good looking then," Lyla said and stooped to get the skillet out of the oven. Esther noticed the hem of her mother's housedress unraveled on one side, the cotton material too rotten to mend.

Later that evening she started to ask her daddy about the woman in the pillbox hat, but when she saw him engrossed in the Discovery Channel, she decided not to disturb him. And her mother might hear their conversation and get upset again.

But she lay in bed that night and thought about the woman's question *That isn't his stone there?* The time would come when his stone would stand there near his son's.

And then there was Jeff's remark about Davis Lee wanting to see her again.

There would be no sleep tonight.

6

She hadn't prayed in a while, but a Sunday morning seemed the appropriate time. If she couldn't go to church with her mother—and she wasn't ready for that—she could show God that she was still here, needed His advice, could use His help, and was grateful no one had died in the night.

For years after Sandy's death, she awoke early mornings and dreaded what the day might bring, recalling too vividly an unexpected phone call, the scream of a heartbroken mother, the cursing of a despondent father.

Thank you, Lord, that I don't have another brother to be killed on Coxes Creek Road. And forgive him again, Lord, for drinking and have mercy on his soul.

She found herself saying these words again and wondering how on earth she'd gone so long not saying them. Had God forgotten about her as she had Him? Did her daddy ever pray? Years before, she'd heard him in the front room at night, when he thought she and her mother had fallen asleep. She'd heard his words spoken to God, his voice hoarse like a preacher's in a fever of sermon, but it seemed he was accusing God of a sin rather than asking forgiveness for his own sins.

But that was long ago.

This morning she wanted to tell God about her yearning for something: the tug she'd felt for Martin all these years that had left her feeling empty around other men, until she'd seen the man trimming weeds at the cemetery. And wasn't this yearning a sin—maybe the greatest one, at least in her mother's eyes? For she would never marry this man Davis Lee. At best she would only desire him as she had desired Martin, and he, too, would surely disappoint her in the end.

But, Lord, how could you stop desire? While you were alive, how could you fend off something in your brain and your body and even deeper in your soul that pulled at you when you saw a man like Davis Lee? Her mother would say you could live without sex, and yes, people did—she herself had for eight years—but wouldn't there always be that tug if the right man came along?

When her mother had spoken of her daddy combing his dark, wavy hair at the bathroom mirror, Esther sensed something different in her mother's voice. Was it nostalgia? For a moment her mother was watching him again in front of that mirror. But the next instant her heart turned cold as she came to the present. Yet her mother would always feel heat in the memory of her young husband, as she herself did in memories of Martin.

No, you couldn't stop desire, whether it was proper or not.

Deciding this, she said *Amen*, not sure it had been a prayer, and threw back the bed covers.

In the kitchen her mother sorted through dry pinto beans she would later boil for dinner. In a ritual she practiced every Sunday, she picked out the withered and brown ones and the occasional rocks, which she discarded into a separate pot. After the sorting, Lyla washed the good beans in a colander and put them in a pot of cold water to cook on the stove for three and a half hours. While Lyla was at church, Esther would add a slice of fat back to season them as they boiled.

"Was there ever a Sunday when we didn't eat beans?" Esther asked her mother as she sat across from her at the table and peeled potatoes. Lyla had dug them from her garden the evening before and had pulled onions, too, for their dinner today.

"When Arthur went to the hospital with his gall bladder," Lyla said. "I think we must have gone over to Asheville on a Sunday to see him because we had trouble finding a restaurant open. You remember us going to Memorial Mission?"

"I was twelve," she said and recalled her daddy asking her to hand him a Dixie cup of water on a side table. In the room another patient lay in his bed behind a dividing curtain, and she could hear his family talking to him. "On the way home, we stopped and ate at that little motel cafe in Black Mountain. You couldn't find a McDonald's or Hardees then. Remember?"

"I remember something funny," Lyla said and stopped sorting beans. "Arthur had took out a life insurance policy a few months before that and was telling us it was worth $20,000. When he said that, you got excited and said, 'We'll be rich, Daddy. I can get a horse.' He laughed and laughed at that because you wanted him to die so you could get a horse."

"I didn't want him to die. I didn't understand he had to die for us to get the money. I told him that afterwards when he explained it to me. I wish everybody would forget that."

"Well, he got a kick out of it anyway," Lyla said and went back to her beans.

"So, that Sunday was the only time we didn't eat pinto beans?"

"Well, when your uncle Dave died, we went over to his house and ate the dinner people had brought."

"On the mill hill?" she asked. At that time, she had recently married Richard and had attended only the funeral.

"That was ten years ago, but he died on a Thursday and was buried on a Saturday, so that wouldn't have affected our Sunday dinner."

"No," Esther agreed. She thought for a minute and said, "Dave was younger than Daddy, wasn't he?"

"A couple of years," Lyla said. "Seems like a lot of times the younger ones in a family will die first. Wonder why that is?"

"Maybe their genes; who knows?"

Lyla looked at her, not understanding.

"I mean genetic makeup. Survival of the fittest. I don't know."

"Sometimes it seems like the good ones die young and the mean ones live on. I've seen that happen in a lot of families. Sometimes it seems like God takes away the best ones first—"

Her mother's voice faded and her expression grew distant. Esther had seen this look before and knew she was thinking about Sandy. Maybe he *was* the best one in their family. He had been full of life, and even in his school pictures an excitement shone in his green eyes. His smile revealed a mischief that his mother often compared with that of *Dennis the Menace* whom they'd watched on T.V.

But it was mischief and excitement that caused him to get in the car that rainy November evening with his friends, drinking and carousing, and head toward Spruce Pine. The newspaper clipping, taped in a scrapbook upstairs, said the car was going approximately ninety miles per hour when it skidded into the wet curve. An eye witness said the Ford Mustang flipped three times before it landed in a ravine. All four passengers were removed from the wreckage, the article said, and rushed to Spruce Pine Hospital, where they were pronounced dead on arrival.

Taken instantly, by the mercy of God, the preacher said in their front room the next evening, and her daddy said a red car wasn't good for nothing but killing. Anybody that rode in one was asking for trouble.

"I'll finish peeling these potatoes while you get ready for church," Esther said and her mother stood and walked from the room without a word. Had her mother remembered, as she herself suddenly did, that the day of Sandy's funeral was another Sunday when they didn't eat pinto beans?

As always, she dropped her mother off at church, but this morning Lyla lingered in the car and said, "They've been asking about you. You could come to my Sunday School class if that'd make you more comfortable—"

She didn't answer. She shook her head, as she had done all the times before. She knew the church questioned her mother about why she came to church alone, and her mother respected her church family's judgment. But Esther didn't want to go inside with her.

"Maybe sometime I'll go with you, Mother," she said and Lyla looked away and opened the car door. "I'll pick you up after while," she said and Lyla nodded, still not looking at her. She watched her mother, whose shoulders stooped in her navy polka dot dress. She felt the pity her mother wanted to arouse, and thought her mother was pathetic at times, with her stubborness and childlike view of things. But she fought her guilt and looked away.

Members had gathered on the church's front porch: the men leaned against the Corinthian columns and smoked cigarettes; women clustered in groups of three or four to chat. Children chased each other in the grassy churchyard, clutching white New Testaments. Vacation Bible School was behind them now, so they had the full freedom of summer.

Even in her car, through memory, she could smell the mingled blend of cigarette smoke and perfume and could hear their gossip, the men's talk of politics and the women's of church missions and training union. Not much had changed since she herself had played in the churchyard.

As her mother stepped onto the porch, the men turned to nod at her, holding their cigarettes at their sides, and the women smiled and reached to touch her arm. It was good they did this, she thought, for her mother needed people to understand her and share her beliefs. Everybody needed that. She wished she could offer more to her mother.

When she arrived home, she sat on the loveseat in the front room while her daddy sat on the couch. Charles Kuralt's voice thundered into the room and she blinked at the sound. How could he stand the volume so loud?

During a commercial she looked at her daddy, his eyes fixed on the screen, and said, "Well, I got Mother to the church."

He glanced at her and nodded. "That's good," he said.

"Do you want another cup of coffee? I'll get it for you."

"That'd be good."

She liked to wait on her daddy. He seemed to require so little of them. She poured milk into the warm cup and then the strong Luzianne coffee. Gently she placed the hot cup in his hands and sat again across the room from him.

"We ought to go with her some Sunday," she said as he slurped the steaming coffee.

He shook his head.

She said, "No, I don't really want to, either. It'd mean so much to her, though."

"Yeah," he said, and when Charles Kuralt appeared on the screen to say his final words, her daddy said, "He's from North Carolina."

"I know, Daddy," she said and watched T.V. with him for a while.

At dinner the three of them ate, no one speaking.

"It's nice we still have Sunday dinner together," Esther said, breaking the silence, and Lyla nodded. "Some of my younger students say their mothers never cooked a meal on Sundays. I can't imagine that."

"My mama always cooked Sunday dinner," Lyla said and crumbled a biscuit into her beans. Esther handed her a jar of chow chow. "My brothers and sisters and me walked across the railroad tracks to the church and afterwards we'd come home to a big meal. Mama didn't have much to work with, but she'd kill a chicken and dig some new potatoes and tell us to invite the preacher. She probably wanted to go to church herself, but she was too busy at home fixing us dinner. The preacher never turned down the invitation, and I'd be lucky to get a chicken wing after he got through."

"Shame she couldn't go to church," Esther said and glanced at her daddy, who kept his eyes on his plate.

"Her family come first," Lyla said and mashed the beans and biscuit with her fork. When the mixture was right, she took a bite.

"I think we ought to get out and go somewhere this afternoon," Esther said. "I was thinking we might ride on the Parkway. It'll be cool in the mountains. What do y'all think?"

Her mother said she wouldn't mind getting out of the house, and her daddy said the road would be swarming because of the Fourth of July. When she told him most of the travelers had headed for the beach or mountains yesterday and traffic seemed light this morning, he said, "But the Atlanta Braves play this afternoon," and his critical tone made her look at her mother. Lyla shook her head as if to say *Don't beg him*, so she dropped the subject. But before she did, she said, "I just thought we could do something together."

The laurel bloomed on the Parkway, and the air was crisp when Esther rolled down her car window to catch the breeze. Lyla cracked her window and tied a kerchief around her head to keep her hair from blowing.

"It's nice up here," Esther said and suggested they stop somewhere to get an ice cream cone.

"I could use something to drink," Lyla said. "Riding always makes me thirsty."

So they pulled off at a Parkway gift shop, that had a small restaurant and restroom, and went inside. After they sat at a table and drank a Coke, they looked at souvenirs.

"These places always smell like cedar," Lyla said and picked up a miniature cedar chest that had the words *Blue Ridge Parkway* stamped on the lid. "You got one of these, don't you, Esther?" Lyla said and set it back on the shelf.

"Look, Mother," she said and picked up a Mason jar filled with gold honey, "they have sourwood honey. I think I'll buy one for Daddy. He loves sourwood honey, doesn't he?"

"I wouldn't take him a thing. He wouldn't come with us," Lyla said and took the jar in her hand. "I bet this ain't real sourwood honey anyway; probably clover. Looks too light for sourwood."

"Well, look at these little black bears, Mother," she said and picked up a stuffed bear to inspect the price tag. "They look real." When she turned to show it to her mother, she didn't see her.

"Lookee here, Esther," Lyla called from around the corner, and Esther went to find her.

"Now these are cute," Lyla said and pointed to a set of wooden wind chimes that had red chickens suspended from the strings. Several hung on display.

"I've seen wind chimes like this," she said and shook a set to make it rattle. She removed it from its hanger and saw the initials *J.J.* carved on the back of the wooden support piece at the top.

"I wish I had a rooster," Lyla said and stared at the wind chimes. "I miss a rooster crowing of a morning."

"I'll buy you one of these," Esther said, though her mother didn't hear her, still lost in her memory.

At the check-out counter she asked the cashier if she knew who made the chicken wind chimes. The girl told her she'd seen a man bring them to the shop in June, but she didn't know his name. He lived down the mountain in Milton, she knew that much, and maybe the manager could tell her more.

"That's all right," Esther said as the girl put the jar of honey in a bag. She wrapped the wind chimes in brown paper and put it in a separate bag.

On the drive home Lyla said, "You didn't have to buy me them wind chimes. I wasn't hinting."

"Well, I don't mind supporting a local craftsman anyway," she said. "If people'll buy his wind chimes, he'll get more orders from that shop. So we've helped somebody in the bargain."

"I always liked chickens," Lyla said. "Mama called her

chickens by name. *Henrietta* was her pet hen. When her chickens was loose in the yard, they'd hear Mama's voice and come running like younguns. One time one of 'em drowned after a rain, and she cooked it. None of us younguns would touch it. Funny how we could eat one Mama had killed, but not one that'd drowned. I wish I had me some banties."

"They'd get in somebody's garden and then you'd find them poisoned."

"Or shot," Lyla said and leaned her head against the car window.

"Well, at least now you have some wooden chickens," Esther said.

Later when she hung the wind chimes from a nail on the front porch, between her mother's baskets of petunias, she wondered if Jeff sold his music boxes too.

She'd never noticed Jeff's hands, though she'd made a point to look at his brother's hands. Davis Lee's tanned fingers were long, the fingernails rounded on the tips. His hands and arms were smooth, with a light covering of dark hair, and his chest was smooth, too. She noticed his face had only a slight growth of beard, on the lip and dimpled chin; she doubted he shaved his cheeks.

The initials *J.J.* on the wind chimes puzzled her, though she knew they were Jeff's. She wouldn't mind asking Jeff what the second *J* stood for. At least then she'd know Davis Lee's full name.

Davis Lee was a peculiar name, she thought, but she liked it. His son Jim was nice-looking, so the boy's mother was most likely attractive too.

I wonder if I know her? she thought, for she'd taught so many people in the community. Her classes were filled with students of all ages and situations: housewives, future nurses, electricians and auto mechanics, recent high school graduates who would eventually transfer to local four-year colleges;

mostly working class people who wanted to improve their lives but couldn't afford to spend much money on an education.

Even *he* could be my student someday. The thought intrigued her. In the past she'd taught male students whom she'd been mildly attracted to: a young man who complimented her boldly in class and nicknamed her *Bo Derek*; a lonely older man who confided about his divorce and cried in her office. But she'd taught none who caused her to lose sleep.

The feeling Davis Lee stirred in her was different. She hoped he would never be her student, for her feelings would be hard to keep secret.

7

People had lined both sides of Main Street by ten a.m., waiting for the Fourth of July parade. When she and Lyla arrived, they stood in front of Milton Funeral Home, in the shade of a magnolia tree. She'd worn a new pair of shorts, a sleeveless blouse, and her blue hat. Lyla wore a floral print cotton dress.

Before the parade began, they heard the high-pitched voice of a preacher, and Esther said she wanted to walk down to the courthouse to see what was happening. Lyla said she'd sit in the swing on the funeral home's front porch and wait on her.

She walked down the street and saw a few people gathered, listening to the boy preacher. He stood on the courthouse lawn and waved his Bible above his head, quoting the Scriptures, some of the words mispronounced in his deep Southern accent.

"Go home, youngun," a man in overalls yelled and turned to his friend, who stood with his arms crossed over his belly. The two men laughed at the boy.

"Pay them no attention, Son," the boy's daddy said and wiped his own brow with a handkerchief. Like the boy, the man wore a dark suit and tie.

The boy preached, calling the listeners "Pharisees" and "whoremongers," and a few in the crowd listened intently to his sermon. She watched the boy shouting to the cloudless sky, his eyes rarely meeting the eyes of his listeners. He was cute in his preacher's suit, looking so solemn and sincere. But when he lifted his Bible and looked directly at her to say, "Repent, Jezebel, for your sins are as scarlet as blood," and his daddy nodded a hearty, "Amen," she looked at her bare legs, too white for the season, and felt mortified. Hoping no one noticed the boy's focus on her, she turned to leave. She almost stepped on Jeff, who had stood behind her. He held a soft drink can in his hand.

"That's a wild preacher there," he said.

"Oh, hello," she said and looked back at the boy.

"Don't worry, I've heard him call women 'whoremongers' and shout 'Jezebel' at old ladies who were flattered by the title. He ain't learned the meaning of the words he uses. His daddy tells him what to say."

"Oh," she said and nodded.

"I heard he makes that boy handle snakes, too," Jeff said and looked at her. "I ain't no friend of the rattlesnake. Copperhead, neither, for that matter."

She laughed when he said this and he laughed too. He turned his head and spat in the can. He wiped his mouth with the back of his forefinger.

"We seen you up here, and I thought I'd say howdy."

"Who?" she said, wondering where Davis Lee stood. She looked across the street at the crowd there and down toward the railroad overpass.

"We're all here today," he said and pointed toward the hardware store.

She looked and saw Davis Lee standing there, smoking a cigarette, and Jim beside him. A short, blond-haired woman stood with her hands on Jim's shoulders. She didn't look familiar.

"Oh, I see," she said and he said, "Brenda didn't come with Davis Lee. She brought Jim and seen us here."

She looked at him. He seemed to be reading her mind and must have seen some disappointment in her face. She hoped she wasn't that transparent.

"My mother's with me," she said to change the subject. "She's waiting at the funeral home."

He laughed and she looked at him and said, "What?"

"Just her waiting at the funeral home sounded funny," he said. He stood so close she smelled the minty snuff that he held in his cheek.

"I guess it did," she said and smiled. Even though she didn't really know this person Jeff, with his wild hair and odd sense of humor, she liked him.

"I better get back up there, or Mother'll think I've deserted her," she said.

"Yeah, I know what you mean," he said.

He kept looking at her as if he wanted to say something. She waited too.

"You mind me asking you something?" he said.

"What?" she said. She hoped it wasn't anything too personal.

"What's your name? We was just wondering."

"Esther Robertson."

"Then you ain't married?"

"What?" she said.

"Your brother's name's Robertson, too. So you must not be married."

"Well, not anymore," she said.

He laughed and looked toward the hardware store. She glanced, too, and saw Davis Lee looking at her. She looked away.

"Is the initial of your last name *J*?" she asked and he said, "Yeah. For *Johnson*. How'd you know that?"

"I bought one of your wind chimes on the Parkway Sunday. I saw your initials on it. It's hanging on our front porch now."

"What d'you know," he said and stared at her with dark eyes.

"It's nice handiwork," she said and he kept staring. It almost seemed he wasn't focusing on her, but lost in another thought.

"Davis Lee said he hoped we'd see you today," he said and glanced toward his brother again.

"He might not want you telling me that," she said and heard a distant siren. She looked at her watch and noticed the boy had stopped preaching.

"He didn't expect Brenda to hang around him or he wouldn't have come," he said.

She didn't know what to say, and he said, "He asked me if I

thought you'd be here today, and I told him I reckon you would. You might even be in the parade: Miss Milton or something. He said he wouldn't be surprised, you was so pretty—"

"Goodness," she said, shaking her head. His bluntness threw her off guard.

"—He said you was even prettier than you was on T.V."

"He saw that commercial?" She couldn't believe so many people had actually watched and remembered it.

"We all seen it," he said. "Davis Lee said when you come to the trailer he knowed you looked familiar. Then he remembered where he'd seen you before. He said, 'Ain't that something, us seeing her on T.V., and then here she is at the front door.' He said he wished he could have taped the commercial. But we don't have a VCR."

"Oh," she said, her face hot. She looked toward the funeral home and saw that her mother had come to the sidewalk and was looking for her.

"I've got to go, Jeff," she said. "Mother'll come and get me."

As she started to go, he said, "You coming to the fireworks tonight?"

"I don't know," she said. "I hadn't thought about it."

"Well, we was just wondering," he said and glanced down the street. Davis Lee was looking at them.

"I may try to," she said and felt her heart ticking. Was he setting up a date for her and his brother?

"I'll tell him," he said and started to walk away as the Milton Police Department car came down Main Street with its blue light flashing. He turned and said, "Davis Lee'll be here at nine." At this, she turned to go join her mother.

When she reached the funeral home, Lyla stood at the wrought iron fence that surrounded the yard.

"Was that a student you was talking to?"

"No. Why?" she asked. She could tell by her mother's tone that she disapproved.

"He looked rough. I got tired standing here by myself," Lyla said. Her face was flushed from the summer heat.

"I didn't mean to take so long," she said. "That man's a maintenance worker at Oak Grove. He's brother of the caretaker there. He's the one who whittled your chicken wind chimes."

"Is that why you bought 'em?" Lyla said and studied her.

"No, I bought the wind chimes to please you. But it's nice to have something handmade by someone you know."

"You don't know him."

"Well, yes, I do, Mother, a little. I've talked to him around town. He seems like a nice man."

"You never told me about him."

"What was there to tell?"

"He looks like a hoodlum."

"He looks like most everybody around here," she said.

"I wouldn't stand on the street and talk to a man like that for a hour," Lyla said. "He might get the wrong impression."

"It wasn't an hour," she said.

"And people might get the wrong impression," Lyla added.

"I'm a teacher; I talk to men like that for a living," she said. "Nobody thinks anything of it." She looked up the street to see the uniformed NJROTC marchers coming.

"I wouldn't be too sure about that," Lyla said and squinted at the advancing procession. In the distance the strains of *Yankee Doodle Dandy* could be heard from the high school marching band.

"Let's try to enjoy the parade," she said and thought about Davis Lee standing at the hardware store. The crowd blocked her view, but she knew he was there.

As the Grand Marshal's car drove by, Lyla asked what the yelling at the courthouse had been about.

"It was a boy preaching about Jezebels and whoremongers," she said. "As if a child could understand those things."

"Out of the mouth of babes—" Lyla said.

"Now you sound like a preacher, Mother. Everybody's a preacher around here."

"A preacher never did nobody any harm," Lyla said and Esther knew these words were meant for her.

After the parade they went to the cemetery. Veterans' graves were decorated again with miniature flags, and Sandy's geraniums were still at his stone.

"I ought to bring some of my dahlias," Lyla said. "Mama loved dahlias—-they did so good for her."

"Your flowers do well, too, Mother," Esther said and fanned herself with her hat. Her mother had talked a lot about her mama lately. She herself didn't remember much about her maternal grandmama, except for fleeting images of a woman hoeing barefoot in her vegetable garden. She also recalled a screened in back porch with a wash basin and a back yard with chicken coops and flowers everywhere. She was five when her grandmama died.

"Her hands were big and strong as a man's," Lyla had said many times. Lyla's hands weren't so large, but were rough from digging in the soil and pulling weeds. Esther's hands were smooth, and she took pains to keep her fingernails well groomed.

She looked at her hand, the outstretched palm, and Lyla asked what she was doing.

"Studying my hands," she said.

"I've seen Arthur do the same thing."

She thought about Davis Lee's fingers, long and tan.

"Sandy's hands were freckled, you remember?" Lyla said.

When Esther thought about it, she nodded. "His face was freckled too, like Alfalfa's."

Esther remembered the early mornings before school when she and Sandy watched the *Little Rascals* on T.V. in the front room. She squeezed beside him in the easy chair that rested near the Seigler oil heater, while her mother baked breakfast biscuits in the kitchen.

"Wear my hat, Mother," she said and lost the memory. "It's too hot for you out here."

"Let's go now," Lyla said and put her hand on the gravestone for support as she turned and started toward the car.

Riding home, Esther asked her mother if she'd enjoyed the parade.

"There was only two First World War veterans in that car," Lyla said. "Did you notice?"

"Yes," she said, recalling the two white-haired men who waved from a Model T. "I guess there was a time when Confederate veterans marched in the parade."

"I reckon," Lyla said and looked out her window at the passing landscape.

"It was a pretty morning for a parade," she said.

"Hot," Lyla said.

"But it'll be cool tonight for the fireworks."

"I got cucumbers to put up tonight," Lyla said. "But you go on if you want to."

"I think I will," Esther said.

That evening she bathed and washed her hair, squeezing a lemon into the rinse water to give her hair a fresh scent. At the vanity mirror in her bedroom she applied mascara and lip gloss and touched *Wind Song* perfume to her throat. She inhaled the citrus fragrance and wondered if her parents would notice it as she passed through the house. She took a tissue and dabbed at her throat to absorb some of the scent.

She put on her new blue jeans, a white Oxford blouse, white socks, and her new white sneakers. She brushed her hair. It was growing longer and would soon drape her breasts again.

Before she left she looked into the kitchen, where her

mother stood at the stove, leaning over a boiling pot filled with Mason jars.

"I'll be home around eleven."

"You lock your car doors," Lyla said. "I don't know if you ought to go out tonight."

"It'll be daylight till nearly nine," she said. "I drive home from work at night."

"Not that late, though. And there'll be a different crowd out tonight," Lyla said, keeping her concentration on her jars. She took her canning seriously.

"Just people and their kids watching the fireworks," Esther said.

"You be careful."

When she passed through the front room, she told her daddy bye. He raised his hand and nodded, his eyes focused on the T.V. screen.

When she arrived in town at the Recreation Center's baseball field where the fireworks display would be held, she saw that people had already gathered on the bleachers and others sat on blankets on the grassy banks. In the dusk, she sat on the grass and listened to distant bluegrass music that drifted from the Main Street dance. In a few minutes, as the sky darkened and the music died, the ballfield was surrounded by people: old men in overalls; teenaged couples holding hands, some girls wearing short shorts and brief tops that exposed their navels; children who ran barefoot and stirred up dust. The smell of hotdogs and popcorn from vendors filled the air, and uniformed VFW volunteers walked around handing out red paper poppies and asking for donations. She took a poppy and rolled the stem in her fingers. *In Flanders fields the poppies blow*...her daddy recited to her when she was a child.

While she thought about the poem, trying to remember the words, she sensed someone standing behind her.

"Esther?" he said and she turned to look up at him. "You

mind if I sit next to you?"

"No, I don't mind," she said, and he sat cross-legged on the grass beside her.

"I'm Davis Lee Johnson," he said.

"I know," she said.

"I didn't know if you'd remember me," he said and looked at her. Sitting so close to him, she only now noticed how tanned his skin was, how dark his eyes and eyelashes were. He might have been a Gypsy.

"I remember," she said, wondering if he'd forgotten how they'd stolen glances at each other earlier in the day.

"How have you been?" she asked, not knowing what else to say.

"All right, I reckon."

They sat for a minute, neither speaking.

"I been watching out for vandals," he said to break the silence, "but I ain't seen nothing suspicious."

"I was out there today," she said and he raised his eyebrows.

"I didn't see you," he said.

"My mother and I went there after the parade. I wanted to check and see if the new basket I'd put there was still there."

"It *was*, wasn't it?" he asked.

"Yes," she said, noticing the concern in his voice. "I just wanted to make sure."

"Jeff and me've been working on the back side of the cemetery, near the railroad tracks, and a couple of other men have been mowing near the highway. I've tried to keep an eye on your brother's grave."

"We appreciate that," she said and looked at her knees. She wondered if he'd noticed that her jeans and shoes were new. Maybe it was too dark to tell. Could he smell the perfume she wore?

She had the sneaking feeling that he had watched for her to come, just as she'd hoped to see him. His brother Jeff had set it up, after all. She was glad now her mother had chosen to stay home.

The first firework rocket exploded—a spray of white lights—and the crowd applauded. She and Davis Lee looked at the sky and he whistled. She glanced at him.

"That's something, ain't it?" he said, his eyes still on the sky. "How you reckon they do that?" He said it more to himself than to her.

"I don't know," she said. "Where's your son tonight?" she asked, then thought the question might be too personal. "I mean, this is something children love. Look over there," she said, pointing to a toddler in overalls who rode piggyback on his father's shoulders. She and Davis Lee watched him, and when the next firework rocket burst into streamers of red and green light, the boy held his ears and squealed, joy and bewilderment on his face as he kicked his father's chest.

"Jim's mama has him tonight," he said and looked at her.

She glanced at him and said, "Oh," and looked at the sky again.

"You have any younguns? My brother Jeff said you'd been married."

"No," she said. "I don't have any children."

"It's a responsibility," he said and took a pack of Camel cigarettes from his shirt pocket. He tapped out one and put it in his mouth. "You mind if I smoke, Esther?" he said around the cigarette and she shook her head.

He pulled a pack of matches from his jeans and lit the cigarette. He sucked deeply and turned his head to exhale the smoke and held the cigarette to his side, away from her, cupped in his hand.

She sat beside him and watched the fireworks, the crowd cheering and sighing. When he leaned to talk to her, she caught a whiff of spicy cologne and wondered if he'd worn it for her. The night air was crisp, and the falling florescent cinders whispered around them. A dry cinder fell on her head and she jerked and said, "Oh," and he said, "Here, I'll get it," and he picked it from her hair.

"See, it won't hurt you," he said and held it to her in his white palm.

"I'd hate to catch on fire," she said.

He laughed and said, "I'd put you out." He stubbed his cigarette in the grass and pulled a pack of Dentyne chewing gum from his jeans pocket. He offered her a piece. She took one, and he unwrapped a piece and put it in his mouth.

"Fireworks are pretty, but they ain't the stars," he said and gazed at the black sky. He shook his head.

"No, I guess not," she said.

They sat quiet for a while, watching the fireworks.

"Jeff tends to run his mouth," he said and looked at her. "I don't know what he said to you today. I know it seems strange me asking you here tonight."

So he did consider this a date, she thought, and wondered what he must think of her.

"I'd noticed you coming out to the cemetery, and then when you left the trailer that day I said, 'I won't talk to her again' because it seemed that's the way you wanted it. But I had the feeling we'd see each other again. I said to myself, 'If she comes here tonight, I'll talk to her,' and so here we are. I'm glad for it, too."

"So am I," she said, surprised by her own honesty. Maybe the darkness gave her courage.

"I don't know what Jeff might've said to you. I hope it didn't offend you."

"No," she said and looked at him. "He just talked."

"He's good at that," Davis Lee said.

They sat silent for the rest of the fireworks, and as the rockets exploded and hissed above them, he leaned against her and their arms touched. She held her breath when this happened, but didn't move. How long it had been since another person's touch had affected her this way.

The last firework display was a series of bursting pompons of light—green, red, purple—and the people cheered and applauded. She'd never seen so many people gathered in Milton before.

As the crowd dispersed into the darkness, heading to the town's parking lots, she and Davis Lee walked with others to the Recreation Center parking lot where her car waited. She stumbled on gravel, and he caught her arm before she fell.

"Thank you," she said. "I can't see well in the dark," she apologized, and she held to his arm for support. She felt the heat of his body as she clung to him.

"I'm glad you come," he said when they'd reached her car. He stood behind her as she unlocked her car door.

"Do you have a car here?"

"Naw," he said. "I'll get home, but I appreciate you worrying. Like my brother says 'a man always has this,'" and he lifted his right thumb.

"Hitchhiking?" she asked and almost laughed. Could he be serious?

He shrugged off the question, as if he didn't want to bother with it.

"I got a feeling we'll talk again, but I don't know how you feel," he said when she sat in her car. He stood looking down at her. "I think I know, but I ain't sure."

"We can talk," she said.

"Do you have a phone number where I can call you?" he asked. She started to give him her home number, but thought about her mother answering the phone.

"Here's my office number," she said, pulling a business card from her wallet and handing it to him:

Esther Robertson, English Instructor
Milton Technical College....

He held the card in front of his face, scanned it in the light of the street lamp, and said, "Oh."

Suddenly she felt like a teacher avoiding a student's advances.

"I'll be there next week, after the holiday," she said, and he nodded and stuck the card in his shirt pocket.

"After you come to the house, I remembered you was a college teacher," he said. "You make a good commercial." And he shut her door and started to walk away.

She rolled down the window and said, "Davis Lee, I enjoyed tonight."

He looked around and said, "Be careful driving home, Esther," and headed into the darkness.

Driving home, she thought about this evening, how unreal it seemed. Her window was still rolled down, letting the night air rush over her face. She tossed out her chewing gum, its cinnamon taste still sweet in her mouth.

8

The next few nights she lay in bed and wondered why she didn't just give him her home phone number. What was the worst that could happen? Even if her mother answered the phone, she could tell her it was cemetery business the caretaker was calling about, something about removing the flowers after holidays. It would be a lie, but at least she'd be able to talk to Davis Lee.

She could call him at his trailer. Though his name wasn't listed in the phone book— she'd looked—she could call the Public Works Director and he'd surely have Davis Lee's number. She could tell the director she was calling for Milton Technical College about a workshop that might interest the cemetery caretaker. That would be easy enough.

But he would call her soon, she told herself, and she lay in the dark and thought about his face.

He was handsome, no question about it, and that came with problems in itself. Would he be vain about his looks? Would there be women from the past and present pursuing him? What type of women was he accustomed to being pursued by? And there was the wife Brenda. That would be a story in itself. How attached were Davis Lee and Brenda now? In time, she suspected, all her questions would be answered. But was she ready for the answers?

First, though, he would have to call her.

As soon as she thought this, she felt ashamed.

I won't run after a man, she thought. What must he think about me coming to the fireworks? We're not teenagers, for goodness sakes. I'm thirty-four, and he must be in his thirties, too. We both should have lives by now. Not crippled lives, though, like they both seemed to have.

It was obvious she'd expected Davis Lee to come to the fireworks and had hoped to sit with him. Her mother would die to think she'd turned down the college administrator yet plotted to spend an evening with the cemetery caretaker.

"I got a feeling we'll talk again," he had said and she thought then *Yes, despite everything, we will*. It might be fate or God's will or whatever you wanted to call it, but it seemed clear to her that from the moment she saw him in the cemetery's shadows, leaned over the weedeater, she would talk to him, know him, lie beside him if she allowed it to go that far.

The time would come inevitably, when she would have to make that decision, as she had done with Martin and then with Richard. But with Richard, there was no question. Their long evenings of philosophical talk—Confucius and *I Ching*—had satiated any need he felt. Always talk. He burned out his sexual energy with talk and tennis, and there was nothing left for her.

Not that she'd felt any special need for him during their courtship. He didn't hold her close in the moonlight; she never felt the press of his groin against her. She may have stroked his hair in his darkened car, but the texture was coarse and didn't ask for her caress.

Only after they married did she feel the sexual need she'd known with Martin and had almost forgotten. But then she was like Tantalus, always grasping for something she couldn't reach. Her mother had commented once about drinking liquor: "If you take a drink of whiskey and like it, sooner or later you'll want the whole bottle. And mark my word you'll end up emptying it. Better not taste it in the first place."

This advice applied to sex, too, she thought. During their marriage, Richard touched her just enough to make her want it all, but never offered her more than a taste. And in time he stopped offering even that. And it wasn't just the physical act itself that mattered. It was himself he never gave. Like a miser, he protected his emotions. Even in lovemaking, he kept his eyes open and fought being lost in the orgasm. Of course, he couldn't stop it, but when she grasped his arms and called his name, wanting to join him in his pleasure, he looked at her as if he didn't know her. He was ashamed, she believed, of his pleasure, and she felt like a thief when she tried to find hers.

Then when he became fixated on fatherhood, she felt he was robbing her. His lovemaking was clinical, calculated. She wasn't even a part of it, and they both knew it. His mother watched them from the walls—*Do it this way, Richard. The medical book says*.... Richard listened to her voice and ignored his wife.

Maybe from the first time she saw Richard standing on Main Street in front of his father's insurance agency, she knew that what she wanted from him was different from what she'd wanted from Martin. She passed by and he glanced at her with cool blue eyes, as if to say, "Speak to me if you want to. I don't care," and she couldn't help grinning at his aloofness. His effort to seem detached amused her.

He had the middle class boy's polished look with his white tennis outfit, but his ponytail and earring were a smirk at his parents' social status. His arms and legs were lean, muscular, richly tanned, and covered with a golden down. After she passed him, her mother said, "Who was that boy?"

"I don't care," she said and kept walking.

Lyla looked back and said, "He turned to look at you, Esther."

"Who cares?"

"If he'd get a haircut, he'd be right cute," Lyla said. "He must be well-to-do. Did you see how neat he was dressed?"

"He's a snob," she said. "His daddy owns an insurance agency, and he thinks he owns the town. He's a show off."

"I saw you grinning at each other," Lyla said and looked at her. "Maybe he wants to ask you out."

"Who cares?" she repeated.

But despite herself she liked the arrogance in his eyes.

Martin's light brown eyes had been forlorn at times and his conversations filled with memories of mill life and hard times, though he'd never worked in the cotton mill himself. Martin's job while she knew him was bag boy at the Winn-Dixie supermarket in town, where she'd first met him when he rolled their grocery cart to the car and helped her daddy put the grocery bags into the trunk. He called her daddy *sir* and impressed him with his good manners and neat appearance.

Though Martin knew nothing of mill work from personal experience, he'd seen his daddy come home from the cotton mill to lie down on the bed, too weary to eat supper, and he'd watched his mama drink beer into the evenings until she was too drunk to cook for them. Martin would make himself a peanut butter sandwich, he said, until he was old enough to work and could buy his meals at the Kentucky Fried Chicken nearby. While Esther and he sat on his parents' front porch at night, in sight of the illuminated mill clock, he told her he was saving his money so he could buy them a home of their own someday.

Later Richard's icy blue gaze was like a fresh breeze, and she found herself walking by his father's agency on Friday evenings, until they talked and found out they would attend college together. And for a while, she forgot Martin's sad eyes.

A week after the fireworks, she was back at work and sat in her office looking at the Phone-O-Gram memorandum that had been taped to her door.

The name of the caller *Davis Lee Johnson* looked strange written in the switchboard receptionist's handwriting. She scanned the memo to see if the message boxes had been checked: *Please return the call* or *Will call again*. No check marks had been inserted in either. But he'd left his phone number, so he wanted her to call him back.

The call came at nine a.m.—hours before she would arrive—and now her watch read four-thirty p.m. She sat behind her desk and glanced at the phone. If she called now, he might still be in the cemetery working, but at least she could say she tried.

When Day Is Done

Earlier this evening when she'd driven to work, she passed the cemetery but kept her eyes focused ahead. She'd wanted to look for him, but wouldn't let herself. She'd thought about him for a week, recalled his attractive face, quiet voice, the spicy aroma of his cologne, but mostly the way he'd caught her when she stumbled in the dark and then allowed her to hold his arm so she wouldn't fall. Yet she challenged herself to be disinterested. I can take him or leave him, she told herself.

She punched the numbers and waited. Her heart was speeding and her hand trembled as she pressed the receiver to her ear. How shameful to be so nervous, she thought. On the third ring (she would have waited only two more) a voice answered, "Howdy, there, what can I do for you?" She heard a T.V. in the background.

"Jeff?" she said.

"Yes, ma'am," he answered, a smile in his voice. It must please him to get a phone call from a woman, she thought.

"Yes, Jeff," she said, raising her voice to a formal pitch, the tone she took with students trying to get too personal, "this is Esther Robertson. I'm returning a call from your brother. Is he in?"

"Well, I can sure get him," Jeff said and she said, "Listen, if he's not close by—"

"I'll get him," he insisted. "Davis Lee'd kill me if I didn't." She heard him laughing in the distance after he set down the receiver.

She sat and stared at a poster of D.H. Lawrence tacked to a bulletin board and wondered if Davis Lee would call her back if they were accidentally disconnected. She was tempted to hang up as she listened to the sound of the Flintstones' voices over the line. How could a grown man watch cartoons? This is ridiculous, she thought, and shook her head.

Then she heard men's voices in the background, the T.V. quieten, and a breathless, "Hello, Esther." He breathed heavily and she said, "Davis Lee, I'm sorry. I think I've called you at a bad time."

"I'm a little out of breath is all. I didn't want to keep you hanging. I was about finished working anyway. Jeff took off early was why he was here. I'm glad he was."

"I thought I'd call before my class starts," she said and wondered what else she might say.

"I'm glad you did," he said. "Did you try calling earlier?"

"No," she said. A minute lapsed and she said, "But I just got your message."

"Oh," he said. Then he said, "Say, I was wondering if we might do something together sometime, I mean go to a movie or something. I don't know what teachers like to do—"

"I don't either," she said and laughed. He didn't answer and she said, "We like what normal people do."

"Esther, I didn't mean nothing by saying that about teachers."

She waited for him to say more and wished they could start the conversation over again. When he didn't speak she said, "I know, Davis Lee."

After more silence, he said, "Would you want to do something with me sometime?"

"Yes, I would like that," she said slowly so he wouldn't mistake her reaction.

She heard a release of breath or a laugh—she couldn't tell which—and suddenly she felt sorry for him. He must have been more nervous during this conversation than she was.

Yet she felt uneasy at his expectations. What would her parents think if Davis Lee came calling at their door? They were no more prepared for her to start courting than she was, especially with Davis Lee.

"When could I call on you?" he asked.

"Maybe a Saturday?" she said.

"Night?" he said and the idea seemed bold the way he said it.

"I guess," she said.

"Let's see," he said, "I'll have to find out about getting my car out of the shop—"

"That's okay," she said. "I can pick you up. That might be better anyway."

He didn't question this last remark. He couldn't know that she would prefer to introduce him to her parents after she'd prepared them better.

They set it up for two Saturdays later. The distance of the date made her appear less eager, she thought, and he didn't seem disappointed. It would give him time, he said, to get prepared. She imagined this meant to save money for movie tickets, a meal.

It would give them both time to back out, she thought.

But they didn't. She checked her faculty mail slot each day and found no messages from him there nor any taped to her office door. She didn't call him. When she passed the cemetery, she didn't look that way, not even to acknowledge Sandy's presence there. If she were to see Davis Lee in his sweaty tee shirt or the dingy orange vest the workmen sometimes wore, she might back out. So she didn't look.

It had been so long since she had prepared for a real date, she didn't know where to start. As she rummaged through her closet, eliminating dresses and skirt suits—too formal, for would he even own dress clothes?—she kept thinking of the fireworks and the way Davis Lee had leaned against her, their arms touching. She smelled his cologne that night—yes, he'd worn it for her—and it permeated her thoughts.

It reminded her of her daddy's *Old Spice* aftershave. She went into the bathroom and opened the medicine cabinet. On a shelf where her daddy kept his shaving items, a dusty white bottle of *Old Spice* sat, and she opened the bottle and held it to her nose. The aroma was still there.

She sniffed the aftershave and put it back in its dust. Someday she would help her mother thoroughly clean the house. Too much dust had settled around them.

At her vanity mirror she applied mascara and dabbed rose lipstick to her mouth. She thought about Davis Lee's mouth, the way his teeth showed white when he talked. What was his smile like? She didn't believe she'd seen him smile. Jeff seemed to do all the smiling for them.

Martin had been somber like that, his eyes closed as he lifted the strands of her hair and kissed them.

She touched a spot of *Wind Song* perfume to the hollow of her throat. The smell was so faint, Davis Lee wouldn't notice unless he stood very close.

Would he want to kiss her tonight?

Years had passed since she'd kissed a man. Richard never enjoyed kissing her, it seemed, his muscles tense when she took his face in her hands.

"Relax, Richard," she'd told him and pressed her mouth softly to his. But while she closed her eyes and tried to savor his lips, he pulled away quickly, his discomfort apparent. At times like this, she doubted if he'd ever truly loved her.

After the separation when she told her mother about Richard's reaction, she said, "Some men don't need touch; others are born for it. You'd better avoid *them*."

Her mother was probably thinking about Martin when she said it, but still Esther wondered why you'd want someone who didn't want to touch you.

"There's more to life than sex," her mother had added. Heaven knows Esther had proven the truth of this for eight years.

She'd often wondered if Sandy had died a virgin. She doubted it. He loved life too much, and all the weepy high school girls who came to the funeral suggested he'd already enjoyed his share of involvements. Occasionally he'd bring a girl home to meet the family, but none seemed to be a steady girlfriend. She figured he was playing the field.

Years ago she'd asked her mother what sex was like. Mainly she worried about how much it would hurt. She wanted to be forewarned, as she would be Richard's wife the next day.

"It's like drowning, in a way," her mother said as she rolled her hair, a glass of water between her knees. She dipped her fore- and middle fingers into the water and dampened a brown strand of hair between her fingers and thumb, then curled and pinned the hair close to her scalp with a bobby pin.

"That sounds terrible," Esther said. At college she'd heard married students talk about their wedding night, the pain and bloody sheets. Some girls bragged they hadn't waited until their honeymoons.

"Well, it *is* terrible in its way," her mother agreed. "The man gets close to you, and it's like he changes into somebody else."

"You make him sound like Dr. Jekyll and Mr. Hyde," she said.

"Well, in a way that's true. When it happens, he makes sounds."

"Sounds?" she asked. "What do you mean?"

"I don't know how to explain it, Esther," her mother said, now embarrassed by the conversation. "You'll find out soon enough."

Does he grunt? she wondered. Or moan? The love scenes in movies she'd watched as a girl—*Romeo and Juliet*, *Dr. Zhivago*, *Love Story*—were tender. Martin had promised once, "When we make love, I won't hurt you." So she knew pain must be involved, but her mother made it sound like a nightmare.

As it turned out, Richard didn't hurt her, much. She helped him find his way into her, and the discomfort was sharp but short-lived. They muddled their way through the first few times until experience guided them. But by then she found the intimacy joyless, and she knew it left him empty too.

She decided to wear a cotton jumper and long-sleeved blouse, and when she knocked at the trailer door and smoothed her dress tail, she felt like a twelve-year-old girl arriving at a birthday party. The door opened, held wide by Jeff, and she said she'd come to pick up Davis Lee.

"Won't you come in the house?" Jeff asked and grinned at her.

"I'll just wait here, thank you," she said and looked toward the cemetery.

They stood at the door and after a minute Jeff said, "I got you something. You wait here."

He went inside and when he came back out, he held his hands behind his back.

"What?" she said, smiling at his mischief.

Like a magician he jerked his right hand from his back and held a red rose to her. She took it and touched it to her nose. It had the bland non-fragrance of a florist rose, its petals curling as if they'd been too long in the sun.

"*My love's like a red, red rose...*," he said and peered at her. "Ain't that how it goes?"

"You know Robert Burns?" she asked and stroked the petals.

"I read it in Davis Lee's book he got from the library. He walked there yesterday to get it."

"Davis Lee likes poetry?" she asked, surprised that either man would care for poetry. Most of her students were indifferent about literature and especially disliked poetry.

"Takes all kinds," he said and he rested his shaggy head against the door frame.

She looked beyond him inside the darkened front room.

"He's fixing to come," Jeff said. "He tells me you're going to the movies. What you gonna see?"

"*Ghost*, I think," she said. "If it's playing in Asheville."

"Sounds scary," he said and looked sleepy-eyed at her. His lashes were dark, though his hair was pale.

"Well, I think it's a love story mainly," she said and regretted having said it when she saw his eyes narrow as he smiled.

"Oh," he said and nodded.

While they stood and looked at each other, Davis Lee stepped behind Jeff and put his hand on his brother's shoulder. Jeff stepped out of the way and Davis Lee said, "What kind of lies my brother been telling you?" When he noticed the rose, he shot Jeff a questioning look. "You can go back to bed now, Jeff."

He explained to her that Jeff had spent the morning thumbing rides to an afternoon motorcycle race near the South Carolina border and the rest of the day thumbing and walking home.

"Wasn't that dangerous?" she asked. She didn't know which would be worse, the hitchhiking or walking such a long way in summer heat.

"Didn't you know I was born for danger?" Jeff said and laughed. "Ain't no pleasure in safe living."

"You're crazy, Brother," Davis Lee said and shook his head.

When she and Davis Lee stood at her car a few minutes later, he asked where she got the rose.

"Jeff gave it to me," she said.

"Oh," he said and nodded. "That's what I figured. I reckon it was my place to give you one."

"I didn't expect it," she said. "We're not going to a prom."

"That'd be a first for me," he said and opened her car door.

On the drive to Asheville, they didn't talk much. Occasionally she glanced at him, at his hands that rested on his thighs. He wore a Western shirt and jeans and cowboy boots, probably his dress clothes, and the cologne he'd worn earlier. The royal blue shirt made his hair seem even blacker than she'd recalled. She wanted to get a better look at his features: his nose that was slightly hawklike, his shapely mouth, and dimpled chin.

When they reached a road sign that pointed to the Blue Ridge Parkway, he said he bet the air was cooler on the Parkway and when he got his car fixed he'd bring her back here and maybe they could pack a picnic lunch or something.

"I'd like that," she said. "My parents and Sandy and I used to ride on the Parkway a lot when I was little, but we'd always go the Spruce Pine route. Matter of fact, my mother and I went riding on the Parkway near Spruce Pine not long ago."

"My mama lives in Spruce Pine," he said.

Funny she hadn't even imagined his having a mother.

"Esther, what happened to your brother, if you don't mind my asking?"

"He was killed in a car wreck," she said. "He and some boys were on their way to Spruce Pine and they'd been drinking. The driver hadn't had his license long. The car was going about ninety."

Davis Lee whistled and shook his head. "They's some rough driving up that way anyway. Especially in bad weather."

"The weather was bad that evening, rainy and foggy."

He didn't say anything else for a while and then he said, "That must have been hard on your family, losing your brother like that."

"It was," she said. "My mother and daddy won't talk much about it anymore."

It was odd talking to this man about Sandy. He might be close to Sandy's age, though she suspected he was younger. If Sandy had lived, he'd be thirty-seven.

"Was he your only brother? I mean, do you have any other brothers or sisters?"

"No," she said. "He was it."

"That's bad," he said.

"Well, it was good to have him growing up. It'd be awfully lonesome not having a brother or sister when you're little."

"Yeah," he said. "I hate my boy Jim's by himself. But Jeff's more like a brother to him than a uncle."

"I can see that," she said.

"Well, I'm sorry for your loss," he said. "That's about the way it was with my daddy."

"Your daddy died in a car wreck?" she asked and looked at him.

"Naw," he said. "I didn't mean that. My daddy was shot over bootleg whiskey. I don't remember much about it. My mama won't talk about him. That's why she moved back to Spruce Pine. Her people all come from over there, and she says Milton don't hold nothing but heartache."

"I guess not," she said, a little dazed by his revelation. She hoped her mother never caught wind of this. "Do you see your mama often?"

"Not since my transmission broke. That and a bad fuel pump. When my car gets fixed, I'm going to see her. She's getting old."

"I could take you to see her," she offered before she even thought about it.

"Naw, that ain't necessary. I wouldn't want to trouble you. You got better things to do than haul me around—" He looked at her and though he didn't say it, she heard in his look *Don't you?*

"Anyway, Jeff's getting a motorcycle, and I can ride it if I have to."

"I wouldn't mind taking you, really," she said. "My schedule's light this summer. I'm not that busy—just reading and grading a few papers—teacher stuff."

"That's more important than hauling me around."

"I wouldn't say that," she said. "I'll take you to see your mama."

"I'd like for you to meet her," he said.

"Then we'll plan it," she said as they reached Asheville.

"It means a lot to me," he said and smiled. His smile was so unexpected and sincere that she couldn't help smiling back at him. How long had it been since her heart had felt this light?

In the mall theater they sat and waited for the movie to begin while other couples leaned to each other, talking and laughing. A couple in the row ahead openly kissed, though the room had not darkened yet. She glanced at them, self-conscious, and wondered what Davis Lee thought.

He leaned to her, their shoulders touching, and said he'd not been in a movie theater in years. When his face lowered close to hers, she smelled his cologne and the cinnamon aroma of his Dentyne chewing gum. Suddenly she felt she was really on a date.

She wondered if he'd taken his wife to the movies when they dated. Probably so. That's one of the few places young couples went to on Friday or Saturday nights in Milton. She wondered if he might now be thinking of his wife as she was when they were younger. Had he kissed her for the first time in the movie theater?

She thought about Martin and imagined him in the seat beside her, there to watch *Love Story*, as they had done years before in the old downtown Asheville *Imperial*.

But she glanced at Davis Lee, scanned his profile in the dim light, and saw that this was not the boyfriend of her girlhood, but a man she scarcely knew.

As the movie's music started, everyone grew hushed. At one point, during an erotic scene between the main characters Sam and Molly at a potter's wheel, Esther felt embarrassed at the sensuality, yet moved by the couple's affection. She felt Davis Lee's presence close beside her, was always aware of him, never totally immersed in the story. At the end of the movie, as Sam, now a ghost, said goodbye to Molly and walked into the light, Esther glanced at Davis Lee. He looked at her and smiled, as if he'd enjoyed the movie. She smiled, too, pleased that he seemed happy.

Neither said much on the ride home. They stopped for a sandwich in Black Mountain, and later when she pulled into his driveway, he said, "Can you come in for a while, Esther?"

She glanced to see a dim light in the trailer's front room. He saw her glance and said, "Jeff ain't here. And Jim's with his mama. Nobody's here but us."

"I don't think I'd better, Davis Lee," she said. "My parents are expecting me. I don't want them to worry."

"Oh," he said and looked at his hands.

"Davis Lee," she said, and he looked at her. "I have to be honest. I'm just not comfortable yet. It's been so long—"

"You don't have to explain yourself," he said. "I didn't mean to put you on the spot."

His look was so solemn and intense that she thought he might lean to kiss her, but of course he wouldn't now.

"I'll go in, then," he said and turned to open the car door. He hesitated and said, "Esther?"

She waited, thinking he might say they shouldn't see each other again.

"Have you ever loved anybody as much as they did in the movie? I mean, to love somebody beyond death—you believe that's possible?"

The question surprised her. She didn't imagine he'd taken the movie so seriously.

"I've loved somebody," she said.

"Your husband?" he asked.

"I'm not sure," she said. "I don't think he really loved *me*—not like that. But I've been loved, I think. I was so young, though."

"Yeah," he said as if he understood. "I thought I saw you crying during the movie. I thought maybe you'd lost somebody like she did."

Had she cried? Maybe she had tears in her eyes at the end,

but she didn't think he'd noticed.

"I did lose somebody, but not to death."

"You lost your brother," he said and looked ahead through the windshield into the night. Scant moonlight lit the evening, and the streetlights were blocked by tall white pines. The cemetery stretched into deeper darkness. "I shouldn't have brought that up."

"No, it's all right," she said. "Sandy's been gone a while. I can talk about it."

But they didn't. And after a silence, she said, "I've not loved anybody romantically in a long time."

He sat quiet, still focused on the night.

"But you've not forgot him, have you?" he said and looked at her.

"No."

"That's his ghost still hanging around," he said.

"I guess so."

He thought for a moment and said, "You think you can ever love anybody else?"

"I hope so," she said. "I don't want to always be alone."

"Naw," he said. "I wouldn't want that either."

She didn't know if his last words applied to her or him.

He opened his door and said, "I enjoyed this evening, Esther. Thank you for spending time with me."

His words seemed so formal and final that she said, "Davis Lee, do you want to go see your mama tomorrow?"

"You still want to do that?" he said.

"Of course. I said I wanted to."

"Well then, I'll call her tonight. She'll want to cook Sunday dinner for us. But don't dress up. Not for Mama. She wouldn't want that."

So they would spend tomorrow together. How easy it would have been to end it tonight, drive away and forget any of this had happened.

But it was too late for that now.

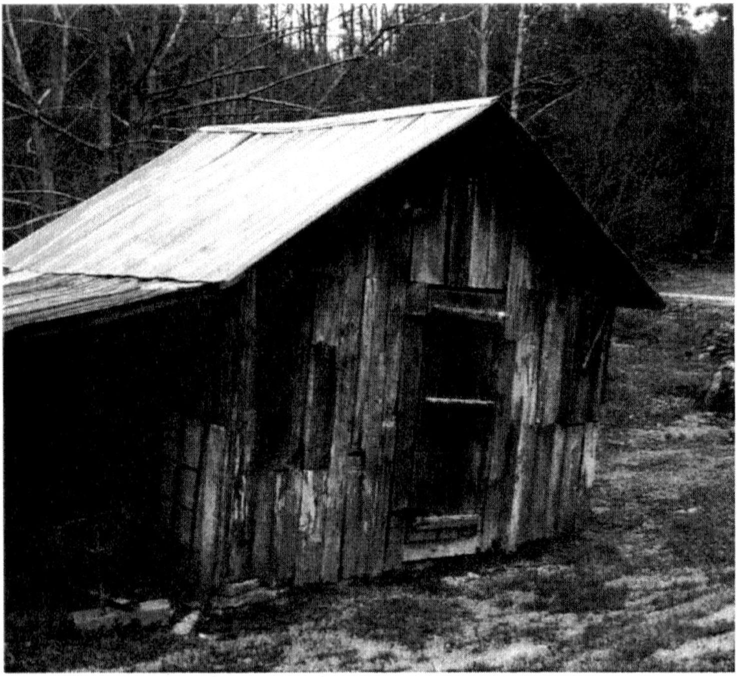

Of course her mother was angry at her. That night Esther had gone to her room and hadn't offered an explanation of where or with whom she'd been. Then the next morning she had to ask Lyla to get another ride home from church and that's what started it.

"You're going back out again," Lyla said as she washed the beans for dinner. The statement was an accusation that couldn't be denied.

"Yes, I am, Mother," she said, her own voice as tolerant as possible.

"Well, I guess you won't be eating with us again today. Arthur missed you at supper yesterday evening, and I told him I didn't know who you was spending time with, you'd tell us when you wanted to—"

"Daddy never cares whether I eat supper here or not," she said, bothered by her mother's bringing her daddy into it. "What did he say?"

"It ain't what he said. He kept going out on the front porch, looking down the street. I wouldn't think you'd want to worry him that way."

"I wasn't meaning to worry anybody, Mother. Why do you try to make me feel guilty?"

She knew there was no answer to this problem except for her to apologize for going out at all. But she couldn't do that, for she wasn't sorry.

"You could at least bring him in to meet us, Esther. He'd respect you more for that."

"I'm not fourteen, Mother," she said. "I don't know why you make me feel that way. It's not right."

"You ain't ashamed of us? Is it some man you work with who you're ashamed to introduce to us? We're not that shabby, you know."

"I would never be ashamed of you or Daddy," she said. "How can you say that? He's not a man I work with; I can't even imagine—"

"Then you're ashamed of *him*."

"Mother, *this* is the reason I don't bring a man here. You'd worry him to death. Can't I go out without having to explain? Why do I have to make excuses?"

"I thought you didn't care about dating."

"I didn't." *Until now*, she thought. "I've put in the proper period of mourning. It's been seven years, and I think a year's standard procedure."

"So you're not eating dinner with us?"

"No, I'm eating dinner somewhere else."

"With this man you was talking to at the parade?"

"What man?" Then she realized her mother meant Jeff. "No, not that man. As a matter of fact, it's his brother and their mama I'll be eating dinner with. She lives in Spruce Pine."

"You're riding to Spruce Pine with him?"

"No, I'm driving him."

"Well, you can tell Arthur you're not eating dinner with us, because I don't have the heart to."

"Mother," she said, shaking her head. "Daddy doesn't care."

"You better stick by your family," Lyla said. "They're all you've got."

"I do stick by you. You know that."

But her mother didn't answer. She had hardened her face and frowned into the colander of beans. What else was there to say? Esther thought, and she left her mother at the kitchen sink.

On the ride to Davis Lee's trailer, she wondered what sort of woman his mama would be. He'd said his daddy got shot over bootleg whiskey, which wasn't much of a recommendation. But he might have said anything—his daddy was on the chain gang or his daddy worked in the carnival—it wouldn't have made any difference now. She didn't sleep last night for thinking of his face when he said "But you've not forgot him, have you?"

How clearly he recognized her feelings about Martin, though she'd not breathed a word about him. But it wasn't Martin she wanted to see now.

She wanted to be with Davis Lee. There, she'd admitted it, and even her guilt over missing Sunday dinner with her parents was overshadowed by her anxiousness to be with him.

How long had it been since she'd felt this craving to see someone?

How could she hide her feelings? She must, though. Was he divorced? She knew he and his wife had separated, but that didn't prove anything. Had she stooped so low as to pursue a man who still had a wife? If he weren't divorced, did he intend to get divorced? Too many questions.

But in any case she would see him today, and that was enough. A few minutes in his company would ease her restlessness. And to spend time with him in another town, to forget for a while who they were—who wouldn't want that?

When she pulled up to his trailer, she saw that he waited on the porch. She stopped the car, and he came straightway to her. So he's glad to see me, she thought.

You look as good as I remember, she thought and glanced at him as he slid into the passenger seat. He was dressed neatly with a red-checked Western shirt, faded jeans, and cowboy boots. His hair was combed back from his brow, but a sprig had fallen over his eyebrow. He brushed it back with his tanned hand.

On the ride to Spruce Pine he looked out his window.

"You don't see many working farms anymore," he said and pointed to a dairy farm in the distance. Cows grazed on the rocky hillside.

"I guess not," she said.

That spoken, they were quiet again, and she didn't know

what to say. She turned on the stereo and pushed in a cassette.

When music filled the car, he leaned forward in his seat as if to hear the sound better.

"Do you like that?" she asked and he nodded, still listening.

After a few minutes he said, "I like fiddle music. Always have. But I reckon that's a violin. My granddaddy taught me to play fiddle music when I was younger than Jim."

"You play the fiddle?" she asked. How much she didn't know about him. "I'd love to hear you play sometime."

"Oh, I ain't good enough at it to play for nobody. I ain't picked up a fiddle in a long time."

"I bet you're good at it," she said.

"Naw," he said and shook his head, still listening to the music.

"What is that music?" he asked and she handed him the cassette case.

"Tartini," she said. "It's a violin concerto. The largo movement."

He looked at her as if he didn't understand.

"Slow movement," she said.

"It's a pretty tune," he said and studied the plastic case and then handed it back to her. "Little twists and turns in it, but pretty. Sad like the mountain tunes Granddaddy used to play."

"It's my favorite music," she said.

"It is?" he asked, and they listened until the concerto was over. When she turned the stereo off, he said, "Would you mind if I borrow that cassette sometime?"

"Of course not," she said. "You can take it today, if you want to. I'm glad you like it."

When they reached the town, she told him he'd have to direct her. It wasn't her territory.

"Mama's happy we're coming," he said.

"I'm kind of nervous about meeting her," she said.

"Ain't no reason for that," he said. "She's nobody to be

nervous for."

Off the main highway, they drove down a long dirt road, where the gravel made her car slide, and the potholes and washed out gullies jostled them until she slowed and crept along.

"You got good shock absorbers," he said, apparently not joking. She wondered what bad ones would be like.

Finally, in the shade of a gnarled willow, the house appeared: a tall, peeling farmhouse, the banister-enclosed front porch bare except for a swing. She pulled into a dusty spot in front, where he told her to park.

"This was my grandmama's house," he said, and she stepped out and dusted her jeans as if the place had shed its age on her.

She surveyed the house, the gabled upper story, the vine-covered posts and rotting rose arbors. Behind the house ran a creek that hissed; beyond that stood pine and hemlock woods, and farther still loomed dark mountains. The air was cool and bitter with galax.

She stared and wondered how lonely it would be to live so close to the mountains where few people knew you were alive except family like Davis Lee.

"Does your mama live here by herself?" she asked and Davis Lee tapped a cigarette from a pack. He lit it and blew the smoke over his shoulder.

"She likes it here," he said. "Didn't like the town. She'll probably tell you about it."

"It's quiet," she said and listened to the silence, broken only by the tree limbs' creaking and the water's hissing that was like a whispering. The sound reminded her of the fireworks cinders as they fell to earth. She thought of the way he had picked the cinder from her hair.

"I wouldn't mind living here," he said. He looked beyond the house, into the shadowy mountains.

"It's peaceful," she said, and as she watched him, a voice called from the house.

"Davis Lee, bring your girlfriend in the house."

She caught only a glimpse of the dark-haired figure that turned in the door, and Davis Lee said, "You want to go in?" She wondered what he'd told his mama to make her call her his *girlfriend*.

The front room was large and smelled of mildew and dust. She scanned the room: the floral-patterned mohair couch and chairs were barespotted and dressed with yellowed linen antimacassars; the floor lamp's fringed shade was dingy and dark-spotted. A faded rug covered the unfinished hardwood floors, and a small-screened television set like the one she remembered from her childhood sat on the floor. She doubted it worked.

"Have a seat right there," the woman said and pointed to the couch.

She and Davis Lee sat together while his mama sat in a chair across the room. She was a tall woman, perhaps sixty years old, dressed in a shirt waist cotton dress, an apron, and loafers. Her shoulder-length hair was still dark, only lightly streaked by grey, and she wore bright red lipstick and rouge on her cheeks. Esther saw much of Davis Lee in her: the sensuous mouth, expressive brown eyes, and dimpled chin. In years past she might have been mistaken for Ava Gardner.

But she looked more mountain woman than movie star now. Her jawline sagged and her eyes were more hollow than striking. Her voice was raspy, and the butt-filled cut glass ashtray that rested on the table beside her chair suggested she smoked heavily. She clasped her large hands across her bare knees, and Esther noticed the gold wedding band on her ring finger.

"How've you been, Mama?" Davis Lee asked.

"I won't complain," she said and laughed until the rasp turned into a rattling cough. It took a few minutes for her to recover her breath. Maybe emphysema, Esther thought, like her uncle Dave.

"Where was you when I called you last night? I let the phone ring eight times before you answered."

"I was peeling apples on the back porch," she said and looked at Esther and laughed. Her laugh was as quick and pointless as Jeff's.

"I was worried," he said and glanced at Esther. She looked at him and then at his mama.

"I got dinner ready," his mama said, changing the subject, and she motioned for them to follow her.

Davis Lee stepped over to the filled ashtray and stubbed his cigarette into it. He let Esther follow behind his mama into the dining room, and they sat at a long table covered by a linen cloth, stained and repaired in places, its lace border hanging nearly to the linoleum floor.

During the meal neither Davis Lee nor his mama spoke, and when Esther said a word or two, they glanced at her with interest, but didn't respond. Both kept their faces close to their plates and spooned their navy beans and mashed potatoes into their mouths without raising their heads. It reminded her of the sincere way her daddy ate, as if it were his last meal. Her mother had said that's the way country people ate, though Lyla had come from as poor a family and didn't eat that way.

After their meal of beans, potatoes, and cornbread, along with sweet milk to drink, they finished their meal with applesauce cake.

"Let's go out back and sit," his mama said when they'd put their forks down, and they went to a mossy clearing close to the creek where a green metal chair and glider waited beneath a hemlock tree. "This is the coolest spot in Spruce Pine," his mama said and laughed.

Davis Lee and she sat in the glider and his mama in the chair facing them, and he started to light a cigarette.

"I want you to quit that," his mama said.

He looked at her, the cigarette lying on his bottom lip. He took it out of his mouth and said, "Mama, ain't that the pot calling the kettle black?"

"It is, Son," she said. "But you got a life to live yet."

"I reckon you're right, Mama," he said and crumpled the cigarette in his hand and stuck it in his pocket. "But you might heed the same advice."

Esther couldn't tell if his tone were embarrassed or angry or indifferent. He looked at the creek, leaned back, rested his clasped hands on his belt buckle, and stretched out his long legs, crossing the right boot over the left as if he had settled for a nap.

"I can live without it," he said as if he'd thought it over and made his decision.

While they sat in the shade, she listened to Davis Lee's mama talking to him, about her apple trees and her canning; the yellow jackets that seemed worse this summer; the black snake that had crawled into the house through a chimney crack and had to be chased out with a broom.

None of this talk involved her. She felt distant from Davis Lee though they had seemed so close in the theater last evening and then in the dark car. Today they hadn't shared a smile or even spoken more than a few words. He seemed distracted, and suddenly she felt empty inside and forlorn. What had she hoped would happen?

Maybe they should go home and forget it.

No sooner than she thought this, the woman said, "Davis Lee told me you're a teacher. What grade you teach?"

"Oh, it's a technical college," she said. "You know, adults, not children. I teach English."

"Lordy," the woman said and laughed. "I ain't never been any good at that. I wasn't much good at school, what little time I stayed there."

"I wasn't either, Mama," Davis Lee added.

"Why, that ain't true, Son. You used to come home and say verses you'd learned at school; I still remember one: *I wandered lonely as a cloud*.... It never made sense to me, but you had it all by heart. Such a little feller recitin' such words—"

"That's the poem about daffodils, isn't it?" Esther asked Davis Lee.

"We always called them March flowers," he said. "Grandmama must have planted them here. Come mid-March, it looks like a blanket of yellow bells has been spread outside."

"They'll come up year after year," Esther said. "I've seen patches growing in a field and know a homeplace must have stood there sometime. Daddy says when you see the March flowers blooming, spring's around the corner. But sometimes it'll snow on the March flowers, and that's pretty."

"I've saw it do that here many a time," his mama said, nodding.

So Davis Lee likes Burns and Wordsworth, Esther thought, *and* Tartini. How unexpected.

"You still in the graveyard business?" his mama asked him.

"I reckon I am."

"How about Jeff?" she asked, her tone deeper. She leaned forward to hear his answer.

"Same," he said.

"There's a drifter for you," his mama said and leaned back again with a sigh. "You met him, I reckon," she said to Esther.

"Oh, yes."

"You been watching after him, ain't you?" his mama asked Davis Lee, who shot her a surprised look.

"I always have, Mama. You know that."

"How's the boy?" she said, her voice softer.

"Jim? Growing like a weed. I'll bring him over one day when he's with me."

"That ain't often, I reckon."

"No, ma'am," Davis Lee said.

They sat in silence and Davis Lee's mama said it was time for her to go in the house and rest a spell. A big meal always took something out of her.

"Why don't you take Esther to see your place in the laurels?"

"You go on in the house and lay down for a while, Mama," he said.

She left them and he turned to Esther. "You want to see it?"

"Sure," she said, not sure what she was agreeing to see.

She followed him to the creek, where he took her hand to help her maneuver over the slick, moss-covered rocks, and into the woods, through tangles of low hanging pines, until they reached a clearing of flowering laurels where stood a whitewashed cabin.

"My granddaddy built this cabin for my grandmama and brought her here when they got married. It was their first homeplace before Granddaddy built the main house. I spent many a summer day out here when I was a youngun," he said and told her to follow him. "I reckon it was a kind of playhouse for me then. But I ain't been here myself in a while."

"Was that the granddaddy who taught you to play the fiddle?" she asked.

"He was a smart man," Davis Lee said.

He had to kick the door open and pry vines to open it wide enough for them to enter.

Inside the front room were a wooden table that held a kerosene lamp; a wide iron bed, covered in a ragged patchwork quilt; and a white telescope mounted on a tripod that stood in front of a bare window.

"Look at that telescope," she said and went to it. "Can you see much through this?" she asked, leaning to look through the eyepiece.

"With a clear night and a steady hand," he said and came to stand beside her. He lifted the end of the telescope and pointed it to the window.

"I always wanted a telescope," she said and laughed. "I wanted to see the rings of Saturn."

"It was the stars for me," he said and looked at her. "The

constellations: Orion and the Big Dipper. The Seven Sisters. That's what I looked for."

"So when was that?" she asked.

"Oh, probably twenty-five years ago when I was about ten," he said. "When I'd come and stay with Grandmama and Granddaddy."

So you're thirty-five, she thought. A year older than I am.

"And then we moved here to Spruce Pine after my daddy died when I was fifteen. By then Grandmama and Granddaddy had both passed on. I liked to stay in this cabin by myself. But then Jeff come along and I didn't have time to do much on my own. He was a wild one when we first got him. Mama handed him over to me, and I've had him ever since."

She recalled Jeff had told her he was adopted.

She looked around the room and went to sit on the tall bed. It sank with her, the boxsprings jingling, and she patted it. A fine mist of dust rose.

"Feather mattresses," he said and came to sit beside her. He sank too and she smiled.

"See here where I scratched my initials in the headboard?"

She looked closely and sure enough there were the initials *D.L.J.* etched on the iron headboard.

"I've spent many a night dreaming in this bed," he said and looked at her.

"What did you dream about, Davis Lee?" she said.

"Oh, the stars and my daddy being shot—but that's a nightmare, I guess."

"I know what you mean," she said.

"I guess you do, Esther, with your brother."

"Yes."

He watched her closely and said, "*Esther*—that's such a pretty name."

"Thank you," she said, flushing at his steady gaze.

"It means 'a star.'"

"I'd forgotten that," she said and smiled.

His face looked so somber that she reached to touch his cheek. She couldn't help doing it, for he seemed like a boy, lonely and hopeless.

He pressed his cheek into her hand and closed his eyes. For a moment he left his eyes closed, his black eyelashes so long, and she held his cheek. His face was warm, as the blood had risen in it. When he opened his eyes he reached and pulled her close to him, pressed his face in her hair. His body's heat and the scent of his cologne filled her senses.

"Esther," he said, his voice low and intimate, and she felt her heart beating. To hear him speak her name this way was sweeter than she could have imagined. She held him and listened to his breathing. "I've wanted to hold you," he said, his voice almost a whisper.

They sat embraced until he relaxed his hold, and she knew the spell had been broken. Before he pulled away, he turned his face to her and pressed his lips into her cheek.

"We better go now," he said. He stood and took her hand.

Walking to her car, they held hands and she said, "Hadn't you better tell your mama we're leaving?"

"No need," he said. "She's resting now. She knows we'll be back sometime."

She glanced back at the house and farther to the woods, where his cabin stood hidden in the laurels.

When Day Is Done

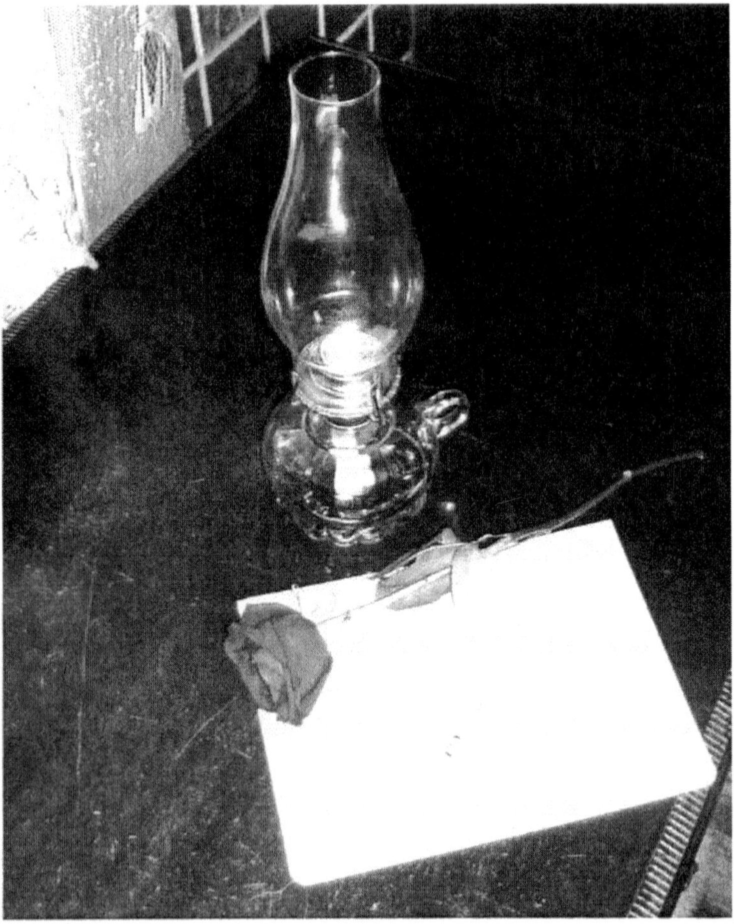

10

She had to talk to somebody about him, to recall the way he spoke her name and the way his cheek rested in her hand as if she held his life there. His closed eyes, the long dark lashes, his face in her hair when he held her for the first time—it was all too much to keep inside.

She had no women friends she could confide in. At work, she was a loner and didn't go out for lunch with her colleagues. Other than the administrator who had pursued her, she had no one at the college who seemed to want her company. Her only confidant was her mother, and through the next week she dropped hints to Lyla about her Sunday with Davis Lee.

"Did you know my name means 'a star'?" she asked.

"No," her mother said. "I named you after a queen in the Bible who saved her people from harm. To me *Esther* meant loyalty."

She dropped the subject.

Another evening she said, "How long did you know Daddy before you knew you loved him?"

Lyla stopped mopping the kitchen floor and said, "Arthur come to my mama's house and courted me there for months before he dared to ask me to ride in his car. My mama wouldn't have allowed me to go out with him until our family knowed him and his family and approved of them. It wasn't just a matter of love. I wouldn't have dreamed of going against my mama's wishes."

"Do you think that helped your marriage?" While she asked this, she heard the *Wheel of Fortune* theme blaring from the front room.

"Arthur respected me and my mama," Lyla said and slapped the floor with the mop, splashing dingy water on Esther's legs. "A man's respect meant something then."

"I don't doubt it, Mother," she said, wiping the water that

had specked her shorts.

Lyla mopped furiously and said under her breath, "I thank the Lord I never disappointed my mama or caused her any grief. I thank the Lord for that. That means something when you get old."

"I've never meant to cause you grief, Mother," she said and her mother looked at her with agitated blue eyes.

"Then why do you sneak around behind our backs? Are you ashamed of us?"

"Mother, I told you I'm not ashamed of you. How can you think that?"

"If you can't bring that man here to your parents' house, then either you're ashamed of us or him. What's wrong with him—is he a married man?"

Her mother stared at her, her brow dotted with sweat. She shouldn't have to mop floors in this heat, Esther thought, ashamed of herself for letting her mother do the housework.

"I know he's separated," she said. "I can find out if he's divorced."

"I would if I was you. There's nothing much worse than being caught in adultery."

"I'm not committing adultery," she said. *Not yet, anyway*, she thought and turned so her mother wouldn't see her face when she thought it.

She would call Davis Lee and invite him to her house to meet her parents, she decided. It was time. She had gotten a glimpse of his childhood, had seen a personal side of him, and he should do the same with her. Her mother might like him, after all; he was quiet and serious and handsome. The last attribute might be a problem, though, as her mother equated a handsome man with a faithless one. Still, she couldn't help but be impressed by his sober manner.

She would call and invite him. But when should she bring

him to her house? Next weekend, if she could wait that long to see him. But she must wait. They both needed time to think about what had passed between them in the cabin.

Yet she had thought of little else but him. Now she wished she'd given him her home phone number—how foolish not to have.

She dialed his number. If he answered she would say, "Davis Lee, I like your name too. When I say it, I think of stars and moonlight and everything beautiful about the night."

But he didn't answer. No one did, and she kept calling until Thursday evening when Jeff answered and she said, "I need to speak to Davis Lee." Her need was great. She must hear his voice to reassure her he still wanted to see her again.

"He ain't here," Jeff said. "He's been gone this week—took off Monday, said he had some thinking to do. I ain't heard from him since, but I reckon he's at Mama's."

"How did he get there?" she asked.

"Likely thumbed. They's plenty of people that drive back and forth to Spruce Pine every day. Wouldn't be hard to thumb a ride."

"Oh," she said, not sure where to go from there.

"It's best he's gone," Jeff said in a confidential tone. "When he has thinking to do, he ain't fit to live with. He's gone to the woods. He does that when something's on his mind. Me, I take to the road."

"How long will he stay, do you know?"

"He'll be back, Esther," Jeff said. "Jim's supposed to stay with us this weekend, so he'll have to come back. I can give you Mama's number if you want to call him there."

"Oh, no," she said quickly. "I won't bother him."

"You can come here and see me," he said, his voice brighter. She could hear the smile in his voice. "I got something I want to show you. Something I bought me yesterday."

"What?" she asked.

"I was gonna surprise you, but I'll tell you it's the finest motorcycle ever built. I'm gonna ride it to New Orleans next year to the Mardi gras. I been saving my money, and I'm going, you watch me—"

Esther couldn't follow his rush of words. She was so disappointed that Davis Lee wasn't at home. She'd taken comfort that at least he was close by, in the same town as she. Though Spruce Pine was only a thirty minute drive away, it seemed another continent now.

"—I loved my Yamaha Enduro, but you can't beat a Triumph. They's some who'll try to fool you with that talk about Harley-Davidsons. Man, I wouldn't trade my Bonneville for all the Harley-Davidsons in the county. You wait till I pull up in the French Quarter on my Bonne'—"

Finally she broke in and told him she needed to go; she'd see his motorcycle when Davis Lee got back. If he spoke to Davis Lee, tell him she'd called.

"You get ready for a real ride," he said. "I guarantee it'll be the best motorcycle ride you ever had. I ain't Steve McQueen, but I'm damn close."

She didn't admit to him that she'd never been on a motorcycle in her life.

After she hung up, she felt hollow inside. He'd gone back to the cabin without her.

The next morning at the college she checked her faculty mail slot and found a letter addressed to her, postmarked Spruce Pine. The penciled handwriting on the envelope was small and neat, printed rather than cursive. Her hand trembled as she stuck the letter in her book bag, and she rushed to her office to read it. She shut the office door behind her and sat, taking a breath.

She tore the envelope's flap open and pulled the folded letter out. Unfolding the notebook paper, wide-ruled like a schoolchild would use, she raced through the words, from page to page. Then she reread it slowly to savor each word:

Wednesday night

Dear Esther,

I am writing this by lamplight because the cabin has no electricity. It's something I might add someday. But I like lamplight. It makes me feel like my granddaddy must have felt when he sat here as a young man.

I write this letter because I been thinking about you since Sunday and I believe you been thinking about me.

It seems like I always had a sense about such things. I've seen times when I would be standing up on the hill cleaning around a grave and think, I wonder where Esther is now? and I'd look to see you down on the highway. Even that first time I saw you on T.V., I thought, I will meet her someday. And then there you was at my front door.

I brought my old tape recorder up here and I been listening to your violin music. When I hear it I think about you and the time we heard it together. Anytime I hear it from now on I will think about you.

Last night I dreamed about you. In the night when I woke up from the dream I went outside and stood in the dark. The moon was hid by clouds so it was pitch black.

But do you know I could see your face and hear your voice? Your voice seemed familiar to me from the first time I heard it and I don't think I could ever forget it now.

In my dream we was both younguns. I don't remember much else, except that you was crying. I recall thinking in the dream I want to make her stop crying, but how can I? I don't even know her. When I woke up I wanted to tell you my dream but of course you wasn't here. So I'm writing this letter to tell you.

I'm here at the cabin to clear my mind. Sunday caused me to start thinking about many things. I've talked to Mama about you. She asks what Robertson you are and thinks she knows your people. She asked me what your daddy's name was but I didn't know. She asked me two or three times what your daddy's name was.

Will I see you again? I hope you will want to see me again.

The lamp is burning low so I will say goodnight. I'm hoping that I will dream about you again tonight and that it will be a happy dream.

Davis Lee Johnson

Oh, Davis Lee, she thought, and took another deep breath, now ready to put the letter away. She folded it and tucked it back into its envelope. She sat quiet at her desk and thought about his words. Never had she received such a letter and how unexpected to get one from him. How long it must have taken him to compose what he wanted to say and then to meticulously print the words on the paper. She could see erasure smudges here and there, as if he'd reconsidered a word or a phrase and changed it. He wanted to be sure she understood exactly what he felt. And she believed she did.

His words were poetry to her, more lovely than Burns. She imagined him writing at the wooden table, the kerosene lamp casting a flickering yellow light on the paper, his face bent over it. He might have lifted his head, his eyes closed, to contemplate his next words. In her mind she held that image of his closed eyes, just as she had stored in her memory the image of his face cupped in her hand, his eyes closed, his eyelashes so long.

She had felt so close to him at that moment in the cabin, as if she had known him always. Touching him had seemed completely right.

On Monday morning he had called the college and left a message for her that he was home and wanted to see her. When she read the memo on Monday evening, she wondered how urgent his voice had sounded to the receptionist and also knew gossip could start over such a call.

But she didn't care particularly what anyone thought. She had been divorced for seven years, and you couldn't build a scandal over two divorced people spending time together.

It would be too late to see him after work that night, she thought, but the next evening after class, on her drive home, she slowed as she approached Davis Lee's trailer. A motorcycle stood parked in the driveway, and a line of clothes stretched across the porch from post to post: jeans, tee shirts, the blue Western shirt Davis Lee had worn to the movies, and a week's worth of men's underwear. This sight embarrassed her, especially the underwear hanging out for any driver or pedestrian to see. Surely there was a better way to dry these clothes; a back yard clothesline would have been more discreet and less tacky. Maybe men wouldn't see it that way.

She pulled in behind the motorcycle. Stepping onto the porch, she ducked under the clothesline and knocked on the storm door. Jeff appeared and held open the door. "Howdy, come in the house," he said.

"I don't want to bother you, Jeff. I'll just stay out here," she said. "Could you get Davis Lee for me?"

"Why, you ain't no bother," he said and stepped outside himself. "You'll have to excuse my washing. Brenda usually takes our clothes to the Laundromat on Mondays, but she didn't show up yesterday, so I washed them myself. In the kitchen sink," he added and laughed. "Made a mess, but you can't haul clothes anywhere on a motorcycle." He stepped off the porch and said, "Lookee here, I wanna show you what I was telling you about."

She followed him back down to the driveway. Why would Davis Lee's ex-wife still wash their clothes? she wondered.

Jeff stood next to the motorcycle and patted the long black seat. A black helmet was propped there.

"What d'you think of it?" he said. "Ever seen anything as mean as this?" He patted the green gas tank and ran his fingers over the name *Triumph* embossed in chrome. His hands were small, the fingernails chewed and ragged as his hair, but his fingers stroked the motorcycle as tenderly as they might a woman's body.

"It's nice, Jeff," she said and glanced to see Davis Lee inside the storm door.

She heard him call her name and she said, "Hello, Davis Lee."

He stepped out on the porch and asked what she was doing, and Jeff laughed and said, "I'm gonna take her for a real ride."

"No," she said and looked at Davis Lee for help.

"Naw, Jeff," Davis Lee said. "You ain't taking her nowhere. Why don't you go in the house and make us all a cup of coffee. You want a cup, Esther?" he asked and she said, "I don't mind."

"Well, I didn't know we wanted coffee or I would've made it anyway," Jeff said in a miffed tone. He stuck his hands in his jeans pockets and shrugged his shoulders as if submitting to fate. "I'll get it," he said and took a last look at his motorcycle.

"Thanks, Brother," Davis Lee said and patted his shoulder as he passed by.

"You want to come in the house, Esther?" Davis Lee said, and before she answered he said, "Or sit out here? There's a breeze stirring. I'll just get these clothes out of our way."

"Are they dry?" she said.

He nodded and unpinned the clothes quickly and piled them in his arm. "I'll be back out in a minute and bring chairs."

When he came back out with the straight chairs, he said, "I'm sorry you had to see our laundry flying. Ain't much of a sight for company to see."

"It's all right, Davis Lee," she said and stood watching him. Someway his formality wasn't what she'd expected. But she, too, felt awkward seeing him again though it's all she'd wanted.

They sat facing each other and he reached and brushed her arm with his hand.

"Did you get my letter?" he asked.

"Yes," she said. If only she could tell him how the letter moved her. "I got it."

"I hope you could read it," he said. "I can't write too good. Ain't had much practice."

"I could read it," she said.

They sat quiet and he looked at the knees of his jeans and picked at a frayed spot.

"It was sweet of you to send it, Davis Lee."

"I just kept thinking about you," he said. "And dreaming. I felt close to you there."

He pulled his chair closer, so that their knees touched.

"It's a pretty place," she said.

"You think so, Esther?"

"Yes," she said. "It's peaceful. I can see why you wanted to go there to clear your mind."

"I had to, Esther," he said.

She heard sounds of dishes rattling from inside. She wanted to ask Davis Lee about Brenda, but he said, "Jeff's tearing up Jack in there. He's like a human tornado sometimes. He already flooded the kitchen floor today with his clothes washing. But usually he's helpful to have around. He's awful good with Jim. Second to Brenda, Jeff means the most to Jim."

Hearing him say the woman's name so casually made her heart sink.

"Brenda's Jim's mama?" she said as if she didn't know.

"Yeah." Then he added, "I been meaning to talk to you about her, Esther."

"Jeff said she usually does your laundry," she said and he looked at her.

"Jeff's talked to you about Brenda?"

"Several times," she said.

"I swear," he said and looked toward the front door.

"I've wondered about her," she said.

"I don't blame you, Esther."

"I've wondered if she's still your wife."

"Not like you mean," he said.

She looked at him as if to say *What does that mean?*

"We ain't divorced," he said. "It ain't because I don't want it."

So he wasn't divorced, she thought. She'd known it all along.

He started to speak, hesitated, and shook his head.

"Davis Lee," she said, "I don't feel right about seeing a married man."

"I know that," he said. "I wanted to talk to you about it when we was at the cabin and then again in the letter, but I was afraid."

"I can understand that."

"Can you, Esther?"

"I mean, I can understand why you'd be afraid to talk to me about it. But I don't understand the situation."

She waited for him to say something, but he just looked at her.

"It seems dishonest," she said, "to be married if you don't want to be."

"I talked to Brenda a couple of days ago," he said, "when she picked up Jim. She still comes around here. Jeff even spends the night over there with her and Jim. That's where he was the night we got back from the movies. But I couldn't tell you that. I was afraid you'd tell me to get lost. And I couldn't blame you."

It suddenly occurred to her that Brenda might have picked him up after the fireworks display their first evening together. How else would he have gotten home? She doubted he always hitchhiked when he needed a ride, as he had suggested that night. If Brenda had taken him home, what else might have happened between them that night? Or had happened since then? The idea of his being married to another woman, as close as she herself had felt to him at the cabin, made her feel ill. Surely he wouldn't sneak and see his wife on the side. Had he told his wife about her and their visit to the cabin? Maybe he was sneaking behind his wife's back and seeing *her*. She didn't know what to think.

"Why does she wash your clothes?" She had to ask him. She couldn't imagine doing any favors for Richard, especially intimate ones, nor imagine his ever having allowed her to. He wouldn't speak to her today if he saw her on Main Street. When he was finished with her, he was finished.

"She won't do that anymore," he said. "When I talked to her Sunday, I told her she's got to stop coming here, except to drop Jim off or pick him up. I told Jeff he's got to stop spending time with her."

"Does Jeff like her?"

"Not like you mean," he said. "Jeff's like a limb on a white pine tree. He moves as the breeze blows him and he don't ask questions. I ain't knowed of him to ever be involved with a woman, and he's almost thirty. He stays over at Brenda's for Jim's sake, I reckon. I'm sure that's all. He's as much a youngun as Jim."

"Do you want doughnuts?" Jeff called from the doorway, and she suspected he'd been listening.

"You can bring some out later," Davis Lee said and went to close the front door.

"I told her I wanted a divorce," he said, sitting again. "We ain't lived together in two years and that's long enough."

"If you've not lived together in two years, what's stopped you from getting a divorce before now?"

"Money, I reckon, has been part of it. But Brenda's held out hope we could work things out."

"Have you held out hope?"

"I never had much hope one way or the other where Brenda was concerned. It ain't much of a excuse, but it never mattered much to me whether or not we was divorced. So long as I didn't have to live with her."

"Does it matter now?"

"That's the thing, Esther. I can see it does now. But before, I never figured on meeting *you*."

"Except when you saw me on T.V.," she said and smiled.

"What a pretty smile you have," he said. "I like to see you smile."

"I like to see you smile, too," she said.

"Sometimes it's hard," he said.

"Yes, it is," she agreed.

They heard Jeff bumping the front door from the inside, and Davis Lee went to open it.

Jeff stood holding a tray with two steaming coffee cups, creamers and sugar packs, and a box of doughnuts.

"Let me help you, Brother," Davis Lee said and took the tray from Jeff's grasp.

Jeff went back inside and came out with the T.V. tray stand.

"You going to join us?" Davis Lee asked and set the tray on the stand.

"Not this evening," Jeff said and headed off the porch. "I'll let the road keep me company." He strapped on the black helmet, mounted the motorcycle, and then cranked the motor. Its roar surprised her.

"You be careful, Brother," Davis Lee yelled as Jeff spun out of the driveway.

They both watched as he pulled out onto the highway and listened to the higher-pitched squeal of his acceleration.

Then all was quiet again.

"I tried to talk him out of getting that motorcycle," Davis Lee said. "It's too powerful for him. Crazy as he is anyway."

He shook his head.

"He thinks he's Evel Kneivel," he added. "When he was sixteen, he wrecked on a motorcycle and like to killed himself. I think it affected his reason."

"What happened?"

"Crazy thing was riding up Coxes Creek Road and tried to do a wheely—"

"What?"

"Raise the motorcycle up on the back tire—"

"On Coxes Creek Road?" she asked, knowing how steep and winding that mountain road was, what an easy road for any reckless driver to be killed on.

"—and he flipped his Yamaha and broke himself up pretty bad. The ambulance took him to the Spruce Pine hospital and then he was sent to Memorial Mission in Asheville. When they released him, he was laid up at home for weeks. That was the end of school for him. I think it was as hard on Mama as it was on him. But I think she's about washed her hands of him now."

"I've never met anybody like him," she said.

"God never made nobody else like him," Davis Lee said. "But I don't know what I'd do without him."

"I like him, too," she said.

"I bet you wonder what you've got yourself into with this family," he said and smiled.

"See, it's not that hard," she said.

"What?"

"To smile."

"Not with you around."

An occasional car passed as they sat and talked, and the breeze picked up and whistled through the pines.

"I've got to go," she said. "It'll be dusk soon."

"Your parents'll be worried about you?" he asked and before she could suspect sarcasm, he said, "I can't blame them if they worry."

"My daddy might call the Sheriff if I'm not there for supper."

"I won't hold you, then," he said.

"They worry too much," she said and wished she didn't feel so compelled to leave. When might she just be able to say, *I can stay as long as you want me to.*

"I worry about you too, Esther. That's the effect you have on people."

He lowered his head and then looked up at her, and his face looked weary, as if he'd labored too long in the summer sun. Then he held his hand to her. She took it, and they sat holding hands. At this moment she forgot all her earlier concern over his wife and all the doubt she'd felt about his wanting to see her again. They were one again, as they had been in the cabin, like a spell had been cast on them to make everything else unimportant.

"I can't forget Sunday," he said and looked at her tenderly.

"I can't either," she said.

They were quiet then, at peace holding each other's hand.

"It'll be dark soon," he said finally and stood. "I'll walk you to your car."

At the car, he opened the door for her and watched her get in.

"Davis Lee," she said before she started the car, "do you still love your wife?"

"I never one time told her I loved her," he said. "Jim's why we got married."

How strange to hear him say this. How could a man live with a woman, have a child with her, and never say he loved her? How cruel. Yet she had rarely said those words to Richard, despite their supposedly intimate moments, especially after he stopped saying them to her. So maybe it wasn't so unreasonable not to utter the words. She had never heard her mother and daddy say those words to each other.

"But she loves you," Esther said. "If she still comes around and hopes you can work things out—"

"I reckon," he said.

"That's a problem, Davis Lee," she said and looked up at him.

"Does that mean you don't want to see me again?" he said.

"I don't know what I want," she said. How strange that a few minutes ago she had held his hand and felt only peace. Then she had known exactly what she wanted. But as the evening dimmed, so did her mind.

"Esther, she ain't been a wife to me in years. A real wife." She knew he meant sexually, and this comforted her. She wondered what the Church and her mother would say about this. If a man wanted out of a marriage and had not loved his wife—emotionally or carnally—in years, was it wrong for him to be drawn to another woman? Was the legal part so important?

"It's just that I can't stop thinking about you," he said. "This past week I tried to. For your sake, I tried. But I couldn't."

"Don't try," she said. "Okay, Davis Lee? Let's not worry about it now. I'm glad you think about me."

He leaned down to her and she saw by his troubled face that her words didn't relieve him. Maybe he didn't believe her.

She waited for him to speak, and when he didn't, she said, "You can tell your mama my daddy's name is Arthur." She started her car. "Arthur Robertson."

"Can we tell her together?" he said.

"When?"

"This coming Saturday?"

"Yes," she said. "Saturday."

"All right, then," he said, closed her door, and turned to go back to the trailer.

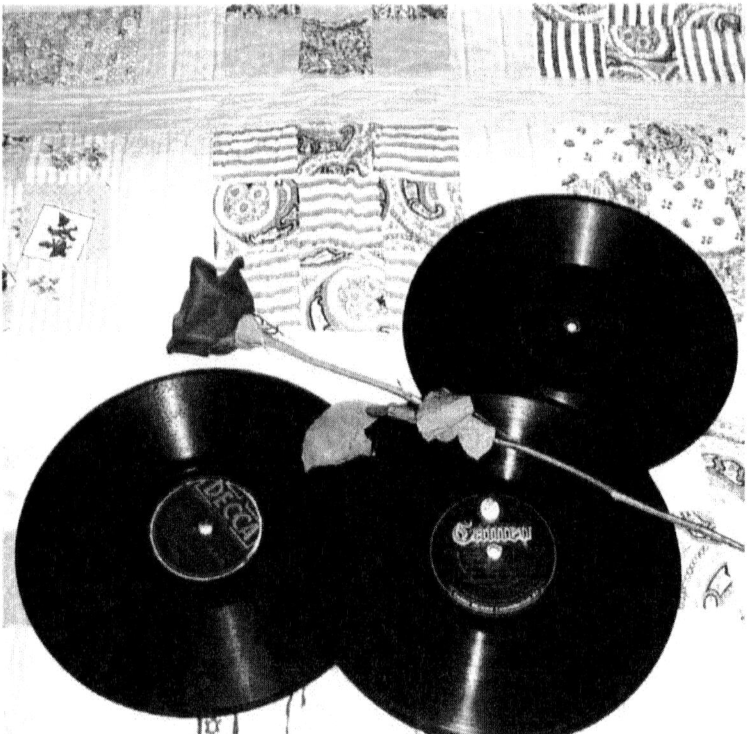
DECCA

11

Saturday afternoon she went outside to say goodbye to her mother, who knelt picking weeds from her dahlia patch.

"Mother, it might be late this evening when I get home," she said and Lyla wiped her brow, a clump of weeds in her fist.

"Too late for supper, I reckon," Lyla said and returned to her work. She'd been preoccupied with work lately, and Esther assumed she was holding a grudge against her.

"I might bring him for dinner tomorrow," she said and Lyla looked up.

"You might take him to church," Lyla said.

"I don't know about that," she said. "Maybe I'll go with you some Sunday."

"You wouldn't be any worse off for it," Lyla said and tossed the weeds into a pile nearby. Now she tugged at the tough grass that bordered her flower bed.

"You need a weedeater," Esther said.

"Mama never used one," Lyla said. "I couldn't work one. That takes a man, and Arthur won't leave the T.V. long enough to do it. It's all I can do to keep the yard mowed."

"I've told you I'd mow, Mother, but you never liked the way I did it. And you retired Daddy from it by shaming him."

"He run over my tulips."

"But the petals had started falling off by then."

Lyla shook her head and tightened her lips over her teeth so that a dimple creased her cheek.

"Well, Mother, the point is I don't like you mowing in this heat. I could get Davis Lee to come; he's a professional groundkeeper—"

"Davis Lee? Is that his name? I never heard of any Lees around here."

"Well, his full name's Davis Lee Johnson."

"Johnson," she said disdainfully, the heavy way her daddy

might have said *Hoover* or *Nixon*. To Esther the name *Johnson* was as lilting as an evening breeze.

"He's the caretaker at Oak Grove Cemetery. He's a hard worker, too. He's taken care of his brother for years; that tells me a lot."

"And he's married, ain't he?"

She sighed. She knew it would come back to this. Why even try to talk to her mother about him?

"He's getting a divorce," she said. It didn't seem exactly untrue, though when she said it, her voice wavered. If someone had spoken it to her this way, she wouldn't have believed it either.

"Don't tell your daddy."

"I don't see why it would have to come up."

"Well, your daddy don't say much, but it would hurt him to see his daughter running around with a married man."

"Running around?" she said and almost laughed. "Is that what I'm doing?" Is that what people would call it?

"Listen," she said, trying to compose herself, "he's a good man. He's a good father to his son and he's good to his mother. I don't think anything else really matters."

"So there's a youngun involved."

"Yes, he has a son," she said.

"He's trouble," her mother said. "You ought to know better."

"He's not trouble to me," she said. Suddenly it seemed she was trying to convince herself.

"Not yet, maybe, but mark my word."

"Are you saying you don't want me to bring him here tomorrow? If you're going to make him uncomfortable or something—"

"You might as well bring him," Lyla said. "Hiding him ain't doing nobody any good."

So I've been hiding him, she thought.

While they rode to Spruce Pine, she thought, *Well, here we are together again, Davis Lee Johnson.* And she realized only now how much she'd missed his company in the long days since they'd been together on Tuesday. She wondered if they would hold hands today. Would he pull her close to him again?

When they stood on his mama's porch, he held the door open for her. The breeze lifted his hair that curled on his white collar and carried the woodsy scent of his cologne.

It seemed he grew more appealing to her every time she saw him. Was it because she needed him a little more each time?

"We'll stop in here for a few minutes," he said and touched her back as he stood behind her in the doorway. He moved his hand to her shoulder and rested it there while they entered the front room.

His mama invited them into the dining room where the table was set with white dessert plates, ornamented with a rose pattern; napkins and forks; and green goblets. A tall coconut cake rested on a glass stand.

"You younguns sit down and I'll cut the cake," his mama said and sliced each of them a thick, snowy wedge. She poured creamy buttermilk into the goblets. After she sat, they began eating.

"This is so good," Esther said, licking the sugary icing from her lips. "The cake and coconut are so moist."

"It's my mama's recipe. But I cheat and use Baker's coconut," she said and laughed. "Mama shredded her own. I don't know where you'd find fresh coconuts this time of year. Mama always made her coconut cakes at Christmas."

A centerpiece of gold and orange marigolds in a green quart Mason jar emitted a faint bitter smell. Esther reached and touched one of the marigolds. "How pretty, Mrs. Johnson," she said. "I want you to look how big the flower heads are."

"You call me Cora," the woman said. This was the first time her name had been mentioned. It hadn't occurred to Esther to ask Davis Lee what his mama's first name was. "Them come from last year's marigold seeds. I never throw away good seeds. I got a bag of Mama's seeds stored upstairs. I need to get 'em out and see if they'll grow."

"Mama don't waste nothing," Davis Lee said and took a drink of buttermilk. When he set the goblet down, he had a drop of buttermilk on his chin. She smiled and touched her chin. When he saw this, he took his napkin and wiped his chin.

"Cora, I left my mother working in her dahlias."

Cora nodded, her eyes on her plate. After she'd chewed her last bite of cake, she scraped the remaining crumbs into a little heap and pressed her fork into it. She put this morsel in her mouth and finished her milk.

"I used to raise dahlias," Cora said and wiped her mouth with her napkin, now stained by red lipstick. "Davis Lee will remember—in front of our house on Third Street."

"I remember, Mama."

"I had them bordering the walk. Zinnias, too. Snails was bad to get 'em, though. I'd line my zinnia bed with ashes from the wood stove and seemed like the snails would find their way through. I got tired of fighting the snails."

"We have snails too," Esther said. She'd seen her mother sprinkle Snarl in her dahlia bed, and it seemed to help.

"Carter never cared much for flowers along the walk, said it made cutting the grass too hard."

Esther assumed Carter was Davis Lee's daddy.

"That sounds like my daddy," she said. Cora didn't seem to hear her, being focused on finishing her buttermilk. When she put her goblet down on the table, Esther noticed the lipstick stain on the rim.

"I did most of the grass cutting," Davis Lee said.

"You did, Son," his mama said, "and you were a help to me. A boy can't learn that kind of work too soon. I reckon you let Jim help you around the house when he's there."

"Jeff keeps him busy," Davis Lee said and looked at Esther. She smiled at him and to her surprise, he returned her smile.

"He's with his mama today, I reckon," Cora said and Davis Lee looked at his plate.

"You say you lived on Third Street?" Esther said, to change the subject. "Where?"

"Down in Milton," she said. "That's before we moved to Spruce Pine."

"Is that near the cotton mill?" Esther asked.

"Right near the cemetery."

"Really?" she said. "My daddy and mother lived near there, too. My daddy worked at the mill. That's been years ago, though. We don't live there now."

"I never had much use for the place," Cora said "except I did raise some pretty flowers there. You don't get much sunlight here. It's shadows most of the time. 'Course marigolds will grow anywhere."

"Mother didn't like the place, either," Esther said.

"I remember we had a big basement where you kept your canning, didn't we, Mama?" Davis Lee said. "And you hung your clothes washing on a line down there, too. I could ride my bicycle in that basement better than in the street."

"It was dangerous in that street," his mama said. "Crowded and steep. Always cars parking in front of the house."

"I don't know how my daddy felt about living there," Esther said, more to herself. "I've never heard him say. But my mother has talked about Second Street."

"Your mama and daddy lived on Second Street?"

"That's what she's been telling you, Mama."

"No," Esther said, "I just said they lived near the cotton mill. But it was Second Street, I'm sure."

"What's your daddy's name?" Cora asked, now looking squarely at her.

"Arthur Robertson," she said.

"Robertson?"

"I told you her name was Robertson, Mama," Davis Lee said, edgy. "Don't you remember?"

"And he lived on Second Street," the woman said, as if to confirm the facts.

"That's what she said, Mama."

Cora stood and began to stack the plates.

"Can I help you, Cora?" Esther said, taking her napkin from her lap. She set it on the table and stood. Their conversation had ended too abruptly.

"No, honey," Cora said, placing the glass cover over the cake. She then began dusting cake crumbs from the tablecloth into her open palm. She dropped them into her apron pocket.

"She likes to do it herself," Davis Lee explained to Esther. "We'll just leave you to your table clearing, Mama."

"It was delicious cake," Esther said, wondering if she'd said something to offend the woman. "And your table looked so nice." Esther suspected Cora had used her best tableware for today. She must have wanted to impress her.

Davis Lee leaned and whispered to her, "She probably needs a smoke. We'll just leave her alone for a while."

"She could smoke in front of me," Esther said as they walked away.

"She thinks you're a lady and wouldn't like it," he said.

"She *thinks* I'm a lady?" she said and smiled.

"She knows it," he added and smiled.

"Are you not smoking today?" she asked, noticing no cigarette pack in his shirt pocket.

"Trying to quit," he said. "But I'm chewing three packs a day," he said and pulled out an opened pack of Dentyne chewing gum from his shirt pocket. He unwrapped a piece, stuck it in his mouth, and offered her a piece. "Naw, I'm giving up smoking sure enough."

"For your mama?" she asked and put the gum in her mouth.

"You don't like it," he said.

"I didn't say anything!" she said and looked at him. She admitted that cigarette smoke affected her breathing—it always had—but she wouldn't have said anything about it.

"You did, darlin'," he said. "I could read it in your face."

When he spoke the word *darlin'*, she looked closely at him. It's the first time he'd spoken such an endearment to her, and he seemed so comfortable saying it.

"Let's go outside, Esther," he said and she followed him out the back door. "I want to show you what I've done."

They headed toward the woods.

Before they reached the cabin, he stopped. "I hope you like it, Esther. I did it as much for you as for myself."

He opened the cabin door, easily this time, no vines binding it, and he stepped aside for her to enter first.

"My goodness," she said when she walked over the threshold and looked around. Lace curtains hung on the window, a colorful linoleum rug covered the wide floorboards, and an oak washstand with a porcelain washbasin stood near the bed. A richly-colored patchwork quilt covered the bed and two embroidered white pillowcases enclosed the pillows.

"Look over here," he said and pointed to the other corner, where an upright cabinet stood. He walked to the cabinet and opened its lid to reveal a turntable and a brass needle-arm. "This here's a phonograph," he said and she leaned over the instrument. On the inside of the lid, behind the turntable was inscribed *Columbia Grafonola*. "Oh, I see," she said and ran her finger across the felt-topped turntable; a faint ringing sound came from the stroke. She lowered her face to whiff the Grafonola's musty, antique smell. Its lid must have been closed for some time to emit this odor.

"Can you play records on it?" she asked.

"It's easy," he said. "See this little arm?" he asked and

grasped a wind-up lever on the phonograph's right side. "You just turn it till it's tight and it makes the machine run without electricity. Ain't that something?"

"My daddy would like this," she said and touched the cracked veneer of the cabinet. "He used to have something similar, by what he's told me. Where in the world did you get it?"

"It was Grandmama's. Granddaddy bought it for her when they started housekeeping here. But it's been upstairs at the other house long as I can remember," Davis Lee said. "Mama said I could move it back here where it belonged."

"Wasn't it hard to bring out here?"

"Hardest part was getting it down the staircase and across the creek, but I got the man that delivers groceries to mama to help me. It don't seem worse for the move."

"No, it's probably relieved to be home," she said.

He looked at her. "That's what I thought, too, Esther," he said.

"How old do you think the Grafonola is?" she asked.

"I reckon about seventy-five years old," he said. "Mama said Granddaddy and Grandmama married in 1915 when Grandmama was fifteen years old."

"That young?" she asked.

"Well, I think Granddaddy was a little older, but not much."

"Who did the patchwork quilt?" she asked and went to the bed. "It looks new."

"It ain't new," he said. "That's my grandmama's work. But Mama had it stored too. I thought you'd like it."

"It's beautiful," she said and lifted an edge to see the stitching underneath. "You can tell no machine touched this. And look at these little remnants of cloth all sewn together," she said, stroking squares of solid red, amber, and aquamarine blue. Other squares featured designs of flower baskets and dogwood blossoms; a rooster was on some. And there were checked and striped patterns throughout. "This is a world in itself," she said, studying the patterns.

She sensed him standing behind her. "It looks like a home now, Davis Lee," she said. She felt his hand touch her back, lightly stroke her hair.

"When I was fixing up this place, I tried to imagine what you'd like," he said. "I'm going to keep working on it."

"I like what you've done, Davis Lee," she said. Sunlight filtered through the curtain's lace and spilled on the rose pattern of the linoleum rug. She knelt and touched a hole in the linoleum and wondered if a woman's shoe heel might have pierced it long ago. She remembered in her girlhood when her own mother wore high heels to church. "I always liked linoleum rugs," she said. "You don't see them much anymore."

"Grandmama had used this one in the other house, but Mama's kept it rolled up and stored upstairs for years. It took some scrubbing to make it shine again."

He sat on the bed and she went to the Grafonola and opened its double cabinet doors. Inside was a record compartment, filled with records.

"You mind if I look at these?" she asked and turned to him.

"You can do anything you want in here," he said.

She leaned and carefully lifted out a stack of records. They were heavy and emitted the phonograph's smell. "These are like my daddy's records," she said. "He used to collect them."

"Them you're holding there are old ones," he said.

"Yes," she said and placed them on the floor. She sat and laid them around her, looking at the labels: *Columbia*, *Vocalian*, *Cameo*. "When I was little, my brother and I would get out Daddy's record books and take the records from their sleeves and stack them and play with them like Sandy's baseball cards. We ended up cracking one every time we did that, they were so brittle," she said, smiling at the memory. "It'd drive Daddy crazy, though he never said anything. Sandy put me up to playing with them."

"You look like a little girl sitting there," Davis Lee said and watched her. "Do you remember a lot about your brother?"

"Well, I remember he always called me *Blondie*. And he was full of mischief. It's a funny thing, Davis Lee," she said and began stacking the records. She returned them to their shelf and went to sit beside him on the bed. "At times I don't remember his face at all. But then all of a sudden I'll remember a detail. The other day I remembered that one of his front teeth was chipped. He chipped it just before he died, so we don't have pictures that would show it. I dreamed about him and in the dream he smiled and I noticed the chip. The next morning I asked Mother if his tooth had really been chipped and she said Yes, he'd done it practicing basketball. She said she'd not thought about it in years, but at the time she'd fussed at him for being reckless."

"Ain't it odd," he said, "that you'd dream something you'd forgot about." He looked at her solemnly as if he were trying to recall something himself.

"Dreams can be odd," she agreed.

"So you broke your daddy's records?" he said, his face suddenly bright, a smile playing on his lips.

"Well, a few," she said. "But I promise I won't break yours."

"Esther," he said, "what do your mama and daddy think about you seeing me? I reckon you've told them."

"To be honest, Davis Lee, I'm not sure. Well, especially with my daddy. They need to meet you. Then they'd understand. It's hard on them because I've not dated in so long."

"I ain't either."

"I'm afraid they've begun to think of me as a girl again, and that's starting to get on my nerves."

"I can see why they'd think of you as a girl. You look young."

"Well, I don't know about that," she said. She patted the patchwork quilt and noticed no dust rising from the mattresses underneath. He must have dragged them outside and beat them with a broom. She'd seen her mother clean rugs that way.

Though it was still early in the evening, it seemed late. "I bet it's dark in here at night," she said. "I mean when you go to bed."

"Pitch dark," he said, "unless they's a full moon. When it's a new moon, or a cloudy sky, you can't see your hand in front of you."

"Or somebody in bed beside you."

He looked at her.

"I ain't never laid with anybody in this bed, Esther."

"I didn't mean—"

"You can't help but wonder, Esther. I'd do the same if I was you."

"It'd be strange to sleep with somebody again," she said, lost in a memory of Richard, forgetting for a moment who she was telling this to. Her last nights in bed with Richard were cold, lonely, neither speaking to the other, their backs turned to each other. *This is not a marriage*, she thought as she lay there so separate from Richard. *We don't even know each other.* Soon after that she moved back home with her parents, and eventually Richard sued her for divorce. She always imagined his mother, who considered herself Milton high-society, saying, "You can do better, Richard."

"You can lay next to somebody and still be alone," he said as if he'd picked up her thoughts. He ran his hand across the patchwork quilt. "Mama said Grandmama made this quilt for her own wedding night. Did you notice the pattern of rings on it?"

"No, I didn't," she said.

He moved the two pillows and underneath were a pattern of interlinked rings.

"These stand for the wedding rings," he said.

"Yes, I see now," she said and instinctively glanced at Davis Lee's left hand that bore no gold band. "It's such pretty work and still in such fine shape. She must have put it back after her wedding night," Esther said. "Maybe as a remembrancer."

He looked at her and she said, "Something to help her remember the night."

He nodded.

"She must have looked forward to her wedding night," Esther said, "to work so hard on the quilt. But she was bound to be afraid." Esther imagined a girl of fifteen waiting for her husband to join her in the bed, the night so dark.

He looked at her.

"Was you afraid, Esther?" he asked her and she looked at him.

"Yes," she said. "I wasn't nearly as young as your grandmama, but Richard was the first man I'd ever been with."

"Same with me and Brenda," he said. "At first it seemed the right thing to do, us both being young and wanting to try things, but later I could see it wasn't right. And I ain't blaming Brenda; I was as willing as she was."

"When you're dating and you love somebody, it's only natural you want to get as close to that person as you can," she said, thinking of Martin. "But it's so easy to get hurt once you give yourself that way. Emotionally hurt, I mean. That's why love's so important. You have to be able to trust someone completely. And that's rare."

"That's the thing. They's got to be that love. And that's where Brenda and me went wrong."

She remembered his saying he'd never told his wife he loved her. And after all was said and done, had she ever really loved Richard?

"At least you got a son out of it," she said.

"That's a fact," he said. "And I ain't saying I regret that. But when you lay with somebody, get that close to another person, love's got to be at the heart of it."

"You're a Romantic, Davis Lee," she said.

He looked at her as if he suspected she'd insulted him.

"I mean like Robert Burns: *And I will luve thee still, my dear,/*

Till a' the seas gang dry."

The blood rose in his face. He didn't say anything for a minute and then, "I thought you was romantic too, Esther," he said.

His eyes searched hers.

"I am, my dear," she said and touched his hand that rested on his lap. She smiled and so did he.

"I feel close to you here, Esther," he said and turned his palm up to grip her hand. His clasp was warm. "That week I come here to think, I laid on this bed and wondered what you was doing. At night I'd dream about you. And I don't hardly know you."

"No," she agreed.

"But then again, I feel like I do know you, Esther. As much as I know anybody."

"You know me as much as *anybody* does," she said. "Except my mother and daddy. But sometimes I think they don't really know me."

"It's like I remember you from the past, too, but I know that ain't possible."

"It's not likely," she said. "Unless we met each other as children."

"That's what I was thinking. Maybe we knowed each other before Mama moved us here."

"Maybe," she said, though she doubted it. Unless they'd lived in the same neighborhood or attended school or church together, they wouldn't have known each other. "But I don't think so, Davis Lee."

"I reckon not," he said. "You just seem familiar."

"It's that silly T.V. commercial," she said. "That started it all."

"Well, then I'm glad for T.V.," he said. "But we don't need one here. We can listen to records if you want to."

He went to the Grafonola, removed a record from the

storage compartment, and placed it on the turntable. He cranked the arm, moved a switch to start the turntable rotating, and then placed the needle arm down onto the record. In a minute a scratchy sound began and then the music started. He opened the wooden louvers below the lid to make the sound louder.

They sat on the bed and listened. He played a concert of records for her: bluegrass and classical and fox trots.

"I'd ask you to dance if I knowed how," he said and she wished he could ask her. Sitting so close to him on the bed and listening to the music, she wanted him to hold her again.

After the fox trot ended, he went to the phonograph. "Well, my arm's tired of winding," he said and put the last record away. He closed the lid and came back to the bed.

"You don't know how much it means to me to have you here," he said and looked at her. "I ain't stopped thinking about you for a minute since I saw you last. All I've wanted to do was bring you back here."

"I've thought about you, too," she said.

He leaned on his elbow and studied her. The room was quiet, shadows growing. Darkness came early in the woods, even while sunlight brightened the civilization beyond the trees. He reached and stroked her bangs, brushing them back from her eyebrows. "Your hair's soft," he said, his voice low. She closed her eyes while he cupped the back of her head and followed the flow of her hair with his hand, stopping to squeeze her shoulder.

"Esther," he said and she opened her eyes. "Will you sit back here with me a few minutes?" he said and propped the feather pillows against the iron headboard. He scooted back there and she joined him, their backs against the pillows.

"But I hate to put my feet on this quilt," she said.

"It don't matter," he said, "but if you'd be more

comfortable with your shoes off—" and he leaned forward and removed his boots to expose clean white socks. He set the boots beside the bed. She removed her sneakers and placed them on the floor on her side. Her white-socked feet looked small beside his.

When they leaned against the pillows, he put his arm around her. She nestled against him, resting her head on his shoulder. A sense of peace passed through her.

"I dreamed of this," he said and pressed his head against hers. Their heads together, she heard his quickened breathing. He turned his face toward her and kissed her temple. She felt the light stubble of his lip and chin.

She, too, had dreamed of this, she admitted to herself. Since the first day she'd seen him working on the grassy slope at the cemetery, she'd wondered who he was and had begun from that moment to look for him every time she passed. At first it was his physical beauty that attracted her, yes—the dark hair and expressive eyes, the tall and tanned physique—a man who in other circumstances might portray Hector or Apollo on stage. But there was more, she knew now. She had sensed from the beginning a somberness in him, a burden that he carried that she wanted to understand better. Maybe she wanted to help him in some way. After all, as an instructor at the technical college, her instinct was to guide people to overcome difficulties.

No, this wasn't it at all. She wanted to be close to him and she knew he wanted this too. It was as simple as that.

She sat forward and reached to touch his face. He watched her as she stroked his high cheekbones and ran her finger over the dimple in his chin, lingering there, and touched his lips. He kissed her finger as it rested on his lips. He pulled his pillow down from the headboard and lay reclined on the bed, not speaking a word. She leaned over him and pressed her lips lightly to his, a kiss of understanding. He took her face in his hands and opened his mouth onto hers and kissed her deeply.

After the kiss, she lay beside him.

"Esther," he said and she heard everything in the word.

"Davis Lee, I'm afraid," she said.

"Darlin', I wouldn't hurt you for nothing."

Wouldn't you, Davis Lee? she thought. Does this mean you love me?

"Can we just lay here for a while, then?" he said and pulled her close, letting her rest her head against his chest. She heard his heart tap, hard and quick, and felt the heat of his body as she nestled against him.

He stroked her forehead with his fingertips, pushing her bangs back, and kissed her eyebrow. She closed her eyes, thinking nothing could hurt either of them now.

While her eyes were closed, she felt him raise himself above her and lower his face to hers, his mouth on hers again. She let the kiss, warm and moist and cinnamony-sweet, carry her into a deeper darkness. She wrapped her arms around him and held him close to her. They lay and held each other.

In time, he sat up and took her hand and pulled her up, too. He kissed her hand.

"You're the most beautiful woman I've ever seen," he said. "I ain't never seen such dark blue eyes," he said, looking deeply into her eyes. "They're like a stormy sky. But around the pupil they's a ring of gold, like sunlight breaking through." And he touched her cheek. "I ain't got a right in the world to say these words to you, but I can't help but say them."

"You have a right, Davis Lee," she said, gratified at his compliment. Through the years she'd received compliments from flirty students and from the administrator at the college, but no compliments had seemed so sincere as Davis Lee's.

"We might ought to go now," he said. "Before it gets any darker in here. Shadows fall early."

They rose and left the cabin. He led her through the woods,

past laurel thickets and fern-covered banks, beneath giant spreading pines and hemlock trees. Before they crossed the creek into his mama's yard, he grasped her shoulders and kissed her again and they embraced each other, their bodies pressed close. She could feel his desire as he pressed into her—he couldn't conceal it—and she didn't pull away from him. The cool air from the creek prickled her skin and made her savor his warmth.

They stopped by his mama's house and went to the screened back porch and he yelled into the door that they were going.

"Can you come in the house before you leave, Davis Lee?" Cora said. "I need to see you for minute."

Esther waited outside while Davis Lee went in.

When he joined her, he took her hand and didn't say anything. He held it tightly until they reached her car.

She could tell by his expression that something was wrong.

"Is your mama all right?" she asked when they got into the car.

"She's worried," he said. "She knows what my feelings are for you, and that troubles her."

"Because you're not divorced?"

"Naw," he said. "Mama ain't religious. None of my family ever was. They ain't put much stock in churches or the law. But Mama sets a lot of store by her family, and she's worried about me."

"Doesn't she approve of me?" Esther asked, surprised. It never occurred to her that Davis Lee's family would have reservations about her; in fact, she had imagined they would be pleased by the association.

"I reckon she thinks your family won't approve of me, is what it is. She don't want me hurt. She asked me if I'd met your family and seems to think you might not want me to meet them."

"I was going to ask you to come for Sunday dinner

tomorrow if you will. My mother wants you to come."

"You mean you already told them about me and they want to meet me, not divorced and all?"

She nodded, a little ashamed of the half-truth.

Yet as they drove home, he didn't say much and she wondered what his mama had said to him. Like the last time they'd left the cabin, they seemed to have left their closeness behind. The spell of sanctuary was broken, and she glanced at his face, wondering when he would ask her to return there with him.

That night she lay in bed and thought about him: his tender expression when she leaned over him and kissed him and the way he took her face in his hands and kissed her deeply. Everything that had happened before seemed to lead up to these moments. And later, beside the creek, when they pressed against each other, his body spoke a secret message.

She wanted him. It seemed the most natural way to show him her love.

She lay in the dark and felt a need so deep she knew she'd never rise from it.

12

The next day at noon she picked up her mother at church, took her home, and then went to pick up Davis Lee.

He stood at the trailer door, wearing a pin striped dress shirt and tie, dark jeans and black loafers, and she couldn't help smiling. He'd told her not to dress up to meet his mama, yet here he was in his Sunday best to meet her parents.

When he opened the car door, she said, "You look so nice, Davis Lee. But you don't have to dress up. Why don't you go back in and put on some comfortable clothes?"

"Naw," he said. "I want to make a good impression, Esther." He nervously ran his hand across his brow.

"Just be yourself, Davis Lee," she said. "That's enough."

"It ain't never been enough before," he said.

"It will be this time," she said. "We'll be having pinto beans and stewed potatoes," she said. "I fixed a banana pudding this morning."

"I bet you're a good cook," he said.

The fact was her mother did most of the cooking. The kitchen was her territory, and she bluntly said nobody's food tasted as good as her own. Esther had to agree. Except for an occasional batch of cookies or a birthday cake that she annually baked for her daddy—a ritual since she was a little girl—Esther had not spent much time in the kitchen. During the two years that she and Richard lived together, in the tiny kitchen of the four-room house they rented, she made grilled cheese sandwiches, packaged pizzas, and Sloppy Joes. On the weekends they ate at Hardees and Western Steer or dressed up and drove to Asheville for a Chinese meal. Richard seemed to prefer these restaurant meals over her attempts at homecooking. In the first weeks of their marriage, she worked one Sunday for hours preparing for him a dinner: pinto beans, meatloaf, biscuits—the food she had grown up with. She set the table and poured him a glass of cold milk.

She watched him chewing the food.

"What kind of beans are these?" he asked.

She assumed everyone would recognize pinto beans. Through all the years of her childhood, into her adolescence, and up until she spent her first Sunday away from home when she left for college, she ate pinto beans. As her mother would remind her later, her daddy's gall bladder surgery when she was twelve disrupted their Sunday routine. And of course Sandy's funeral two years later. But those were rare interruptions.

When she and Richard dated, she brought him home once for a Sunday dinner. She knew her mother cooked beans that day, but maybe Richard didn't put any beans on his plate. She honestly couldn't remember.

"Pinto beans," she answered. "Don't you like them?"

"My family never ate pinto beans," he said. He laughed lightly and said, "My father wouldn't have allowed Mother to cook pinto beans for a meal even if she had wanted to, which I'm sure she never did. I bet Mother's never tasted a pinto bean in her life."

Esther lost her appetite and didn't notice what Richard ate the rest of the meal. She later realized that this meal might have been the start of their marriage's decline. From this point on, she would begin to accumulate in a deep storage place in her soul little reminders that Richard came from a better family.

"Can I sit near you?" Davis Lee asked and stirred her from her thoughts. She looked at him and saw he was grinning.

"No, I'll put you right next to Daddy," she said. His expression changed so quickly that she laughed. "I'm kidding, Davis Lee," she said.

He sat quiet as they drove.

"Don't worry, Davis Lee, they'll like you."

"Are they religious?" he asked and she assumed he was still thinking of his marital status.

"Well, Mama's Missionary Baptist through and through, but Daddy's a little heathenish like me. He used to be religious as anybody, but Sandy's death changed him. He won't talk about religion anymore. I'm sure he still believes. He just won't talk about it."

"Nothing wrong with that," Davis Lee said.

On the ride to her house, she noticed him clasping and unclasping his hands, being fidgety. He furiously chewed his Dentyne gum.

"Don't be nervous," she said and reached to touch his hands.

"I got something to tell you," he said.

"All right," she said and put her hand back on the steering wheel. His tone scared her.

"Could you pull over for a minute?"

She slowed and pulled into a grocery store parking lot. Her heartbeat had accelerated and her hand trembled as she turned off the ignition switch. How tenuous her security was these days.

"Last night after you dropped me off, Brenda come to the trailer," he said and looked at her. He might as well have said, *I found out I'm dying*, for his grave manner and the way her heart sunk.

"Oh," she said.

"Brenda had Jim out in her car, but he didn't come in. She said she'd thought about the divorce—you know I told you I'd made it plain to her I wanted one—"

"Yes," she said and waited.

"—and I was glad to hear she'd thought about it, and I told her so. Maybe we could get this business settled, once and for all, and get on with our lives. I told her not to worry about the money, I'd take care of that part of it, someway—"

I'd help, Esther thought.

"—but then she said things was a little more complicated

than that and she was figuring on keeping Jim with her all the time, seeing I'd been spending my time with a woman—"

"Meaning me?" Esther asked. How did she know?

"—and things could get nasty, though she didn't want it that way."

"But you haven't lived together for some time."

"Two years."

"Then what does it matter if you see somebody? Does she expect you to be faithful to her after two years? That's not logical."

"Brenda don't think logical. She ain't growed up in her mind enough to think logical."

"So she's threatening to sue you for complete custody of Jim?"

"I reckon," he said.

Lord, Esther thought. What a mess.

"How do you feel about that, Davis Lee?" she asked, though she knew the answer.

"He's my son, Esther. He's the reason I married Brenda in the first place. I agree with Brenda that Jim should live with her most of the time. She can do more for him, I know. But if she was to keep him away from me, sooner or later he'd forget me."

"I don't know that he would forget you, Davis Lee," she said.

"Well, I know what it's like to lose a daddy and not have one to turn to when you need him."

Esther couldn't imagine not having her daddy. Though something in him had died twenty years ago along with Sandy, and she and he hadn't communicated much in recent years, she still took great comfort in his presence. She knew if she really needed his guidance, he would offer it without hesitation, and nothing could replace that.

"I don't know what to tell you, Davis Lee," she said. "Maybe you need to talk to a lawyer."

"I reckon," he said, though she knew she might as well have suggested he fly to Los Angeles. He looked completely bewildered.

Neither of them spoke for a while.

"What do you plan to do, Davis Lee?" she said.

"Brenda told me she'd forget about taking Jim if I'd call off the divorce. I told her I wasn't planning on calling off nothing."

"I'm glad you made that clear," she said.

"But that ain't all of it," he said. "When she come in, Jeff asked her where Jim was, and she said he was out in the car, but not to bother him. Well, this didn't set right with Jeff. You know how attached he is to Jim. Jeff's a friend to everybody and don't understand why somebody wouldn't be on his side. I think Brenda still ain't forgive Jeff for piercing Jim's ear, though she ain't stopped Jim from keeping the hole in it. She's raised hell with *me* over it, though," he said and rubbed his hand over his brow. This was the first time Esther had heard Davis Lee use profanity.

"Did Jeff not go out there?"

"Naw, he didn't go, but he stood at the front door and looked out at Jim the whole time Brenda was in the house. I reckon he was thinking Jim would wonder why he didn't come out to the car to see him and that broke his heart. After Brenda left, he asked me what I figured on doing—he heard all her fussing—and he said she needn't think she could keep *him* away from Jim. He said he'd pick up Jim and take him with him to New Orleans and nobody'd ever see them again. He's declaring he's going to New Orleans on that motorcycle—"

"I know," Esther said. "But he can't take Jim. That would be kidnapping."

"I know it," Davis Lee said, agitated. "I told him not to worry. We wouldn't lose Jim, neither of us."

She thought for a minute and said, "Do you think your wife would really try to take Jim away from you?"

"I wouldn't put nothing past her. If she couldn't get me back, she'd do anything to hurt all of us. She knows I love you. I reckon Jeff's let that slip. And I didn't deny a thing to her."

His words stunned her, the roundabout way he said he loved her. *I love you, too, Davis Lee*, she thought, despite the tangled mess his life seemed to be.

"I wanted to tell you this," he said, "because I may have trouble with her. She's got it in her head that I've knowed you all along, since before we separated, or at least she's pretending to think that."

"Jeff could help you straighten that out, couldn't he?" she asked.

"Jeff's too upset to do anything to help. He's saving his money like crazy, what little he has to spare and the extra he makes on his wood work. I don't see how he's saved as much as he has, but he says he's had some things up his sleeve that I don't even know about. You never know with Jeff."

"Maybe he's entering motorcycle races," she said, trying to help.

"I don't know," Davis Lee said. "I didn't sleep last night. Too much has happened."

"And now you're going to meet my parents," she said. "Maybe we should call this off if you have too much on your mind."

"Naw," he said and looked at her. "This is the only thing I have to look forward to. I might make a fool of myself, but I'll take that chance."

"It'll work out, all of it," she said and pressed his arm.

He looked at her hand and touched it with his fingers. Leaning over to her, he kissed her lightly on the lips.

"I want to believe you," he said. "I want your mama and daddy to like me. I don't want you to worry about nothing."

"Well, let's work on impressing my parents first," she said and started the car.

Davis Lee stayed two steps behind her from the time they left her car in the driveway till they came onto the front porch and entered the house.

When they came into the front room, her daddy looked up momentarily and she said, "Daddy, this is my friend Davis Lee I've invited for dinner."

He stood and shook Davis Lee's hand. "'llo," her daddy said, his voice low and formal.

"Good to meet you, Mr. Robertson," Davis Lee said, stiffly. She could tell he was nervous.

Her daddy sat and resumed his T.V. viewing of a political panel. When they sat on the loveseat across from her daddy, Davis Lee looked at her and clasped his hands together. He cracked his knuckles and turned his eyes to the T.V. screen. He stared blankly and she felt his tension.

"Let's go see Mother's garden," she said and stood. He stood up and followed her into the kitchen and out the back door. Her mother stood at the edge of her garden, at the compost pile, tapping unused dough and flour from a mixing bowl. A mist of flour caught the breeze and settled around her shoulders.

"That your mama?" he asked and she said, "Let's go see her."

She worried about introducing him to her mother. Her daddy's lack of response wasn't rudeness. He simply was more interested in the debate on T.V. She didn't know what to expect of her mother, though. She knew Lyla was still smarting over the time she had spent away from home lately.

When they joined Lyla at the garden, Esther said to her, "Mother, this is my friend Davis Lee I told you about."

"Hello, Miz Robertson," he said and held his hand out, almost seeming to offer a handshake, but then as quickly dropped it.

"I won't get flour on you," Lyla said, holding the flour bowl against her like a shield. "Been feeding my compost pile."

"You got some fine vegetables there," he said and surveyed the rows of cornstalks and green bean vines strung from post to post.

"This morning I pulled some corn and dug potatoes for dinner," she said. "But my corn ain't much this year. I had to replant twice, and the ears that did make is scrawny. Not like the sweet corn my mama raised. Her corn was always full and tender."

"It looks good to me," he said. He glanced at the leaning sunflowers that bordered one side. "Pretty sunflowers," he said and pointed to them.

"Let's go to the front yard and see my dahlia bed," Lyla said and handed Esther the bowl.

"Esther was telling us about your dahlias yesterday," he said, seeming to relax.

"You and your mama?" she said.

"Yes, ma'am," he said and followed her around the house.

"'s that in Spruce Pine?" Lyla asked and he nodded *yes*.

"I reckon it's cooler over there," Lyla said and showed him her different flower beds: dahlia, zinnia, petunia.

"Your mama raise flowers?" Lyla asked, kneeling to pluck a blade of grass from her petunia bed. She could spot a weed a mile away, Esther thought. She'd even seen Lyla picking weeds on the Parkway. "Mother, you're not supposed to destroy anything on the Parkway, not even a snake," Esther had told her, but her warning hadn't fazed Lyla.

"Cora's got some giant marigolds," Esther said. Lyla shot her a glance when she spoke the woman's name.

"*Marigolds*," Lyla repeated as if the word were foreign.

"Yellow and orange ones," Davis Lee said. "She likes to sit a vase of them on her eating table."

"Mama used to do that," Lyla said. "Mama didn't have no

vases, though. She used Mason jars."

Esther and Davis Lee looked at each other and smiled.

"That's what Mama does, too," he said.

"Flowers do brighten a table," Lyla said. "D'you see these touch-me-nots I got mixed in with my petunias?" she asked.

He knelt to examine a cluster of pastel flowers. He reached and stroked a petunia's purple petals. "It feels like velvet," he said and leaned to put his nose in the flower's bell. "I never knowed petunias had such a strong, sweet smell."

"They're easy to grow," she said, standing and dusting off her apron. "You can end up with more vine than flower, though. That's one thing I don't like about petunias. I always favored dahlias."

Davis Lee stood, too, and the three of them looked at her flowers until Lyla said the oven was preheated; she'd better get in the house and put her biscuits in. She took the flour bowl from Esther and headed around the house. Davis Lee and Esther followed her.

When they reached the back yard, Davis Lee looked up in the sky, deep blue and cloudless. "You got a good view of the sky from back here," he said. "No streetlights to interfere." Lyla didn't answer, though he seemed to be talking to her. Esther knew he was thinking about star gazing.

"My daddy and I used to come back here at night and look at the stars," Esther said. "He said when he was little, you could see the Milky Way a lot clearer than you can now."

"I don't doubt it," Davis Lee said.

"My mama used to plant by the signs," Lyla said. "Everybody back then did. Mama planted her corn and beans and potatoes in the dark of the moon. And she wouldn't dream of planting a thing on Rotten Saturday."

"What's Rotten Saturday?" Esther asked.

"I heard my granddaddy talk about that," Davis Lee said.

"Rotten Saturday's the Saturday after Good Friday," Lyla

said. "You don't plant nothing on Rotten Saturday."

Lyla shook her head, her expression as stern as a preacher's.

"Did you know if you'd gone out about five o'clock this morning, you could've seen the planet Mars, bigger than any star?" Davis Lee said.

"No," Lyla said. "I was up, but I didn't think to come outside and look at the sky."

"It was there," he said, "plain as could be." With a quick glance to make sure Lyla wasn't watching, he reached and took Esther's hand. He leaned close and in a voice too low for Lyla to hear, he said, "I thought about you when I saw it. I wished we'd been at the cabin and seen it together."

She squeezed his hand and nodded, looking her mother's way. She released his hand.

"I didn't have my telescope, though," he said to Lyla. "I couldn't make out its color, just a flicker of red now and then, but you could tell it was Mars."

Inside the house, Lyla said, "You're the caretaker at Oak Grove Cemetery, ain't you?"

"Well, I don't know if that's my proper title," he said and Esther directed him to sit with her at the kitchen table. "I been there since March. I cut grass mostly, but since I live next door, I keep a eye on the graves and flowers, too."

"Ain't that dreary work?" Lyla asked, stooping to set the pan of biscuits on the oven rack. She would let the bottom of the biscuits brown first and then move the pan to the upper rack and reset the oven to broil to let the biscuits' tops brown.

"Naw, ma'am, I don't look at it that way," he said. "I feel like I'm helping people."

"That's part-time work, I reckon," Lyla said. "I heard most cemetery workers are hired part-time and don't have a job after mowing season."

Esther looked at her mother. "Where'd you hear that, Mother?" she asked, and Lyla said her preacher had worked at a cemetery before he got his calling, and he knew all about it.

"He said they wasn't any future in it. It was good summer work, he said, but it wasn't stable work."

"That's right, ma'am," he said, "about some cemeteries. But I'm looking to get a job at a private cemetery in Spruce Pine. There I'd have more responsibility. I'd cut grass, but I'd work with burials, too, opening and closing graves and so on."

"Would that be full-time work?" Lyla asked.

"Mother, I don't know if that's our business," Esther said, though she wondered why Davis Lee hadn't mentioned the job change to her.

"I asked about that," he said to Lyla, intent on satisfying her, "and at Memorial Gardens I could make between $250. and $300. a week year round, and the work ain't too demanding, depending on the number of burials."

"And that's in Spruce Pine?" Lyla asked. "You planning to move to Spruce Pine?"

"I got a place there," he said, glancing at Esther. "I'm aiming to fix it up."

"Esther's a college teacher here in Milton," Lyla said. "She'd got her master's degree. Did she tell you that?"

"I know she's a teacher," he said. "That's something to be proud of."

"Her daddy and me have always been proud of her and wanted the best for her."

"He knows that, Mother," Esther said, a cold feeling in her stomach.

"Yes, ma'am, I can understand that," he said, looking at his knees. "I got a boy myself, so I know how that is."

"Esther ha'n't started her family yet. We're still hoping she'll meet a man who can take proper care of her. She needs younguns of her own."

Esther looked at her mother, who'd turned her attention back to her biscuits. Since when was she so interested in grandchildren? Back when Esther and Richard had tried to conceive and failed, Lyla didn't seem disappointed. And during the same time, Esther's Asheville gynecologist had given her a clean bill of health—*Just keep trying,* he'd advised—but Lyla didn't encourage her. She'd summed it all up: "Well, it ain't meant to be."

After the separation, Esther was frankly relieved she and Richard hadn't conceived. If a child had come into the picture, would that have made them happier? Maybe Richard. But it wouldn't have changed the fact that he and she didn't feel enough affection—no, enough *sympathy*—for each other to sustain a marriage. His parents considered her inferior. And she had the suspicion that in time—and it might not have taken that long—they would convince Richard and the child also to think she was inferior.

Might she herself still want a child? The notion hadn't occurred to her in so many years that she'd become accustomed to the inevitability of childlessness. And yet, there was still time, wasn't there?

She looked at Davis Lee, his lowered head, and felt sorry for his discomfort at her mother's questions. He was trying so hard to please Lyla, to impress her, and he was failing. She reached and touched his dark head, stroked the soft hair, and he looked at her.

"It's all right," she said and smiled at him.

"Davis Lee and I are going to get Daddy," she said when her mother opened the oven door to move the pan of biscuits. She motioned for Davis Lee to follow her.

In the darkened hallway, she took his arm and pressed her face into his shoulder.

"Maybe this was a mistake," she said, thinking it so strange for him to be standing with her in this hallway where at three she'd ridden her tricycle on the hardwood floor. A few years later she and Sandy played basketball here, throwing a rolled-up sock into a half-gallon milk carton whose top had been cut off and the box attached to a door frame. Had Richard ever lingered here with her? She doubted it. The few times he visited her parents before they married, he always seemed anxious to leave. Rarely, though, did they head together to his parents' colonial-style home in town, *his* house, a home mythic in Milton. Before his family moved there, an elderly lawyer had owned the house and one night had put a pistol to his head as he stood in front of the fireplace. The suicide was part of Milton's history, and when Lyla first asked Esther where Richard lived, she answered, "In Lawyer Porter's house." She thought her mother might be repulsed. Instead Lyla said, "They must be big shots, then," and was pleased. Indeed, they *were* big shots. It seemed only appropriate that old Lawyer Porter's son, who continued his father's law firm, represented Richard in their divorce.

Martin had certainly stood here with her on many nights. He would tease her by pulling the light string of the hallway's bare overhead light bulb to put them in darkness, except for the scant light of the T.V. in the front room that filtered in. At night, her daddy always watched the T.V. in a dark room, no lamp ever turned on. She and Martin could hear her daddy's snoring and knew they were in no danger of being discovered by him. Her mother was in the kitchen reading her Bible at the table, so she too was not a threat.

Martin kissed her in the dark hallway until she heard her mother push her chair back from the table. At this sound, Esther would pull the light string, the sudden, harsh light making them both blink and laugh.

Now as she stood holding Davis Lee's arm, she leaned into him and looked up at his face. He looked troubled, but she couldn't tell if her mother had insulted him. His spicy cologne filled her senses and reminded her of long ago Sunday mornings when her daddy dressed for church.

"They don't want to give you up to me," he said, "and I don't blame them. You deserve better."

"I want *you*," she said and put both arms around him. When he pulled her against him, she closed her eyes and savored his warmth. She kissed his neck and reached to caress his cheek. She didn't care if her mother and daddy discovered them. Nothing mattered but feeling his body, hearing his heartbeat that quickened with her own, letting him cover her mouth with his.

They kissed in the hallway. She felt she knew him now, and in this place so familiar to her, she desired him. She could easily lead him to her bedroom, ask him to lie with her there, and not feel ashamed.

"Davis Lee," she said as he held her after they kissed, "You know I love you, don't you?"

"I was hoping so," he said.

While they stood holding each other, neither offering to let go, her mother yelled from the kitchen, "Esther, did you call Arthur?" and she pulled away from Davis Lee, the smell of his cologne lingering on her skin.

During dinner, the four of them sat chewing quietly, her daddy and Davis Lee leaning over their plates. Her mother had pleased her by frying a skillet of cubed steak, simmered in milk gravy, to go with the pinto beans, stewed potatoes, and boiled corn. Though Esther knew country style steak was her daddy's favorite dish, she suspected Lyla prepared this today in honor of their guest. After their main course, Esther brought her banana pudding from the buffet and placed it on the table. Her mother set out the dessert bowls.

"Go ahead and get some, Davis Lee," Esther said, sitting beside him again, and he filled his bowl with the pudding.

"Would you like a cup of coffee with your banana puddin', Davis Lee?" Lyla asked. "Ice tea don't go with puddin'," she added. "Arthur's having a cup."

Esther was surprised to hear her mother call him by name,

so politely.

"Yes, ma'am," he answered, "I believe I would." Her daddy glanced at Davis Lee when he said *ma'am* and then spooned out some pudding into his own bowl. Davis Lee waited for her daddy to start eating his pudding before he put a spoonful in his mouth. Esther watched him to see his response. "That's as tasty a banana puddin' as I've ever ate, Esther," he said. "You're a good cook like your mama."

"Thank you, Davis Lee," she said, wishing Lyla had heard the compliment, but she had gone to the kitchen to get the coffee pot.

"Daddy," Esther said, noticing his interest in Davis Lee's remarks, "you ought to see Davis Lee's Grafonola."

"Grafonola?" her daddy said and turned his gray-green eyes on her. Had she noticed before how clouded his eyes had become? She would need to take him soon to the optometrist to get his eyes checked for cataracts.

"Yeah, Daddy, across the mountain he has stacks of records like yours. You ought to see them."

"I should've brought some to show you," Davis Lee said and looked at her.

"Maybe next time you can," she said to him, reaching under the table to squeeze his hand.

"Or you could go with me and Esther to see the cabin and we'll look at them there."

"Is that the place you was talking about fixing up?" Lyla said, coming into the room.

"It's the sweetest little place, Mother," Esther said. "Prettiest linoleum rug, like you don't see anymore, and patchwork quilt that Davis Lee's grandmama made—"

Lyla looked at her. It didn't occur to her that the mention of the quilt would arouse such immediate suspicion. Her mother's mind was clicking today—quilt equals bed.

"The house belonged to Davis Lee's grandparents when

they first married. You'd love it."

Lyla seemed to ignore this last observation. She poured coffee into their cups. "My mama always had a hard life," she said, setting the coffee pot on a trivet beside the pudding. After she sat down, she dusted off her apron and said, "Mama never did get what she deserved."

"Who does?" her daddy said and they all looked at him.

"Hard work deserves more than a hard life is what I'm saying," Lyla said.

"Grandmama was happy, though," Esther said. "Or by what I can remember, she seemed to enjoy her garden and her chickens."

"What record labels have you got?" her daddy said to Davis Lee, ignoring her and her mother.

"Oh, I couldn't say for sure, Mr. Robertson," Davis Lee said. "Seems like they's a few Victors and Columbias."

"I saw Vocalion, I remember that, Daddy," Esther said.

"I bet you've got some Okehs," her daddy said, suddenly animated. "They were popular around here. I used to have Roy Acuff on Okeh label, but that's been years ago."

"I hope I didn't break those," Esther said, and Davis Lee smiled.

"I had a few Bluebirds," her daddy added, not hearing her, "'Bring Back My Wandering Boy' by the Blue Sky Boys. I don't know what records I have anymore," he said. "Where'd you put them, Lyla?"

"They're upstairs, Daddy," Esther answered.

"I know I had Cameos, too."

"Davis Lee had some Cameos," Esther said. "They were fox trots. We listened to them."

"In his cabin?" Lyla asked.

"What was the record you used to play over and over when I was little?" Esther said and her daddy looked at her. "You know *when shadows fall* or something like that; it was a sad song." He studied for a minute and said, "Oh, you must mean 'When Day Is Done.'" He nodded, and in a deep voice she'd nearly forgotten, he sang the first words of the song that expressed how at the day's end a loved one is most remembered.

"That's it, Daddy! I love that song."

"That was Al Jolson. But it was a 45 rpm Decca. Not a 78."

"That's right, Daddy, because you'd play it on that old Silvertone cabinet hi-fi we had in the front room. I sat on your lap and you sang it to me."

How could she have forgotten until now how well he sang? At church she'd been proud of his deep baritone voice, as he sang the male echo parts in "Are You Washed in the Blood?"

Until today, how long had it been since he'd sung?

"Where is this cabin?" Lyla asked, still looking at Davis Lee.

Davis Lee had been watching and listening to the conversation between her daddy and her and seemed surprised by her mother's question.

"It's near my mama's house," he said.

"In Spruce Pine?" she asked.

"Yes, ma'am. Where Mama's lived for the past twenty years. That's where all her people come from."

"Twenty years?" Lyla asked. "So she ain't lived there all her life?"

"Naw, ma'am," he said. "Her and Daddy and me lived here in Milton till I was fifteen, then Mama and me moved to Spruce Pine."

"Oh," Lyla said.

"You might've knowed my mama," he added.

"What's her name?" Lyla said.

"Cora Johnson," he said.

"Cora Johnson," Lyla repeated and Esther's daddy said, "Johnson," and Davis Lee looked at him.

"And your family lived in Milton twenty years ago?" Lyla said and looked at her husband.

"Yes, ma'am," he said. After a minute he said, "Mr. Robertson, I think my mama might know you, but I ain't sure."

"Wouldn't that be a coincidence?" Esther said. "Of course, this is a small town. We might even be related."

"I thought your family come from Spruce Pine," Lyla said.

"My mama's people, but not Daddy's."

No one said much else. Dinner over, she left her daddy and Davis Lee watching T.V. in the front room and went back to the kitchen where her mother had started washing dishes.

"Let me help you, Mother, so we can get them done. I thought we all might take a ride on the Parkway. It's such a pretty day out."

"I don't think Arthur would care about it," Lyla said. "He don't seem to feel too good."

"He seemed the happiest today I've seen him in a long time, Mother. Did you hear him singing at the table?" Esther said. "I'd forgot what a beautiful voice he has."

Lyla didn't answer.

"You remember that Al Jolson record he used to play, don't you? Is it still around here somewhere?"

"Esther," Lyla said, "that man ain't got a thing in the world to offer you."

"Mother," she said, surprised this would come up so soon, "don't talk so loud, he might hear you."

"He's good looking. That's turned your head. But that ain't enough."

"No, he's more than that," Esther said. Yet how could she explain what she saw in Davis Lee? He read poetry. He appreciated classical music. He looked at the stars and dreamed. When he was a child, he helped his mother. After his daddy was gone, he helped raise a brother and now he helped care for a brother and a son. When he held her, he gave her a sense of peace she'd never known. He made her feel desired and beautiful. In a way, he'd become *her* caretaker and she guessed she'd become his.

"Well, right now you might think he's more than that, but you'll learn different soon enough. A man his age that don't have a car to drive and has to ask a woman to haul him around is nothing to brag about. I'd be ashamed if I was you."

"If you were me?" she asked.

"And a wife to boot," Lyla said. "You'll live to regret him."

"I wish you wouldn't say that," Esther said, shaken by her mother's words. So much of what Lyla said was true, yet she wanted to believe in Davis Lee.

"You know I'm right," Lyla said.

"I don't know, Mother," she said.

"There's so much you don't understand," Lyla said. "We're just trying to protect you."

"I love him, Mother."

Lyla didn't answer.

"Esther, we didn't raise you—take you to church and Vacation Bible School and P.T.A. meetings and school plays through the years and then help put you through college so you could have a career—to turn around and throw you away to the garbage. You'll understand when you have a child of your own—"

"What makes you think I'll ever have a child? I couldn't do it before, why should I be able to pull it off now?"

"You might have been better off staying with Richard."

"Mother! I can't believe you said that. You never liked Richard. You know we didn't love each other."

"People adjust," Lyla said. "Love ain't everything in a marriage. People work together to make a home. That's called security."

"Davis Lee makes me feel secure."

"I can't see how."

"Daddy seemed to like him. You have to admit Daddy

seemed happy today. He and Davis Lee could be a comfort to each other. Davis Lee lost his daddy when he was young. And Daddy lost his son."

"Your brother wasn't lost," Lyla said. "He was stole from us."

While she drove Davis Lee home, she waited for him to say something about the meeting with her parents, but he'd offered no reaction.

"I think Daddy liked you," she said. "You could tell he was interested in your old records. It's like he came out of a dream," she said. "Did you hear him singing?"

"He's a fine singer," Davis Lee said. "That must be a pretty song you and him was talking about."

"Did he say anything to you after dinner?" she asked. "While you were in the front room together?"

"Naw, not a word. He just watched T.V."

"Well, Daddy's not a talker. Especially when the T.V.'s on. But I think he liked you."

"Esther, I wish we could go someplace where nobody cared about us one way or the other. Where I didn't feel guilty to spend time with you or feel like I did you harm by my company. Nobody seems to want us together."

"People just care about us, I guess," she said. "That makes them get in the way."

"I reckon," he said and touched her knee and looked at her. "But I love you."

She laid her hand on his. So now he had said it directly.

"I wish I'd seen Mars with you this morning," she said. "I was awake at that time and thinking about you. I wish we'd been at the cabin."

"I feel like I'm your husband there," he said.

She thought about this. "Yes," she said. "I feel like your wife there, too."

The rest of the drive he leaned his head against the passenger window, his eyes turned up toward the sky as if he searched for some answer there. But the sky was empty, clear and blue.

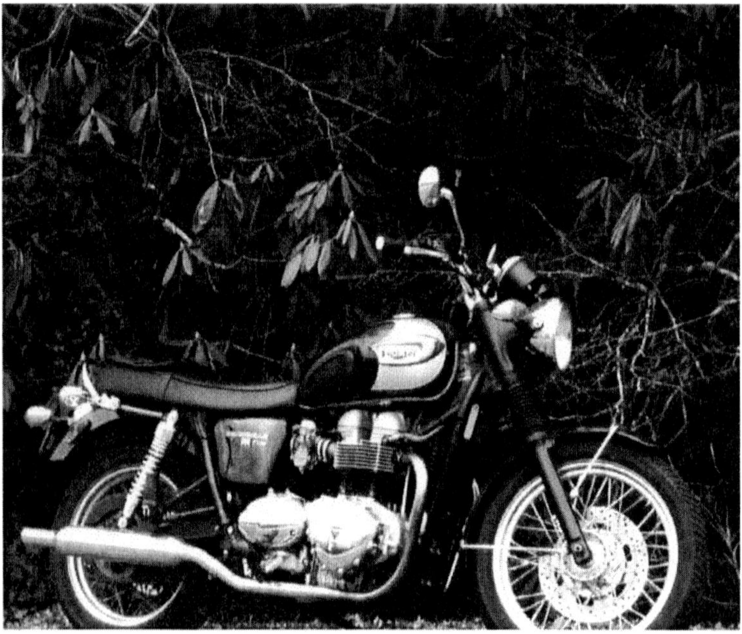

They would see each other the next weekend, they decided as they sat on the front porch of the trailer. But before she left, he asked if she wanted to go for a walk.

"Can we walk through the cemetery?" she asked, preferring the solitude of the graves to the sidewalk next to the highway. She wanted to be alone with him, away from the stares of passing drivers.

"That's what I meant," he said and took her hand.

In the garden cemetery, they walked up shady hills by family plots, some stones so old the engravings had worn away. She stooped at a child's headstone.

"I think she died in the 1800's, but I'm not sure," she said, tracing the indentions with her finger.

"They's some old ones here," he said and took her hand again. His hand was warm and strong and when she squeezed it, he squeezed too, an unspoken message sent to each other.

At the crest of a hill they stood hidden from the highway by a line of tall mimosas. He turned to her and took her face between his hands.

He pressed his lips to her forehead. She took his hand and led him to a wide oak tree close by and leaned back against it. She put her arms around his waist and pulled him closer. He kissed her mouth in a long, moist kiss and moved his lips to her ear and to her throat. She nuzzled her face against his, savoring the heat and fragrance of his skin, the slight scratchiness of his lip and chin. And as he kissed her mouth again, pressing his body closer still, she felt his arousal and shared it.

After the kiss she looked at him. His eyes were dark, the pupils dilated with desire, and his expression tender. She reached to lift back a strand of his hair that had fallen down on his eyebrow, and she caressed his face, warm and flushed. She touched the dimple in his chin and raised up to kiss it.

"I love this feature," she said and touched his chin again. "It's so sensual."

He didn't answer, but closed his eyes as she touched his face.

"Such lovely eyelashes," she said and drew his face down to kiss his closed eyelids, the long, dark lashes. He really was beautiful, she thought.

"Esther," he said and took her hand and pressed his mouth to it. "I wanted to stand up here with you, like this, the first time I saw you driving by. Do you believe me?"

"Yes," she said. "I think I probably wanted that, too," she said and laughed. "I wanted to know you," she said. "I thought about you all the time."

"I wish I'd knowed that," he said. "I watched for you everyday. Some days I wouldn't see you and you don't know how that dragged me down. It made me scared I'd never see you again. I only dreamed in time we'd be here on this hill like this, holding each other. But I knew I didn't deserve you. I might be dreaming now."

"You're not dreaming, Davis Lee," she said. "Unless I'm dreaming, too."

They stood and held each other, quiet for a while, savoring their time alone together. Then they continued walking along the winding road, passing through shade and sunlight.

"You want to go by Sandy's grave?" she said and they headed toward the railroad tracks.

At his grave she looked around the stone, surveyed the area nearby.

"Davis Lee," she said and looked at him. "His flowers are gone."

"I swear," he said. "I've looked after his grave, his especially," he said and swore under his breath. He peered across the surrounding graves. "His ain't the only one bothered."

She looked and noticed that many of the flower

arrangements in the newer section were missing.

"It probably happened when you were gone," she said.

"Maybe yesterday evening," he said, "while we was at the cabin. More likely last night after dark, for the thief not to get caught."

"Can't you report this to the Public Works Director? That's what I'd do," she said. "This isn't right for people's flowers to be stolen. It's robbing from the dead."

"I can't understand it," he said. "Who would steal grave flowers? Unless somebody's turning around and reselling them. That's a pretty sorry way of making money. But people will do anything."

"I guess so," she said. "But it's not right."

"Naw, it ain't."

She looked at Sandy's bare grave and noticed a woman standing at a grave nearby and realized she was the same well-dressed woman who'd been there before. Today she wore no hat, her white head uncovered.

"I wonder if her flowers were stolen?" Esther said and Davis Lee looked at the woman.

"She looks like somebody that could stir up trouble if she wanted to," he said. "She must keep her church clothes on all day."

"She probably dresses up like that all the time," Esther said. "We talked here one Saturday, and she said she knew my daddy. Mother didn't seem to like that idea when I told her."

"I reckon she didn't," he said, scanning the cemetery.

The woman caught Esther's glance and started toward them.

"Haven't I talked to you before?" the woman said when she reached them. "Oh, yes, you're the girl I saw on T.V. I'm glad you took my advice and didn't come here alone. My son's standing over there, see him?" She pointed in his direction.

Esther and Davis Lee looked and saw the woman's son who

had parked on the edge of the road and leaned against his station wagon.

"We're just taking a walk," Esther told the woman and Davis Lee stood silent beside her. He unwrapped a piece of Dentyne gum and offered her one. When she took it she said, "I bet you need a cigarette." He nodded, putting the gum in his mouth.

"You notice the vandals have hit again? Stole a $40.00 chrysanthemum spray from my husband's vase. I just bought it last week, and now it's gone. There're thieves hiding behind every lamp post in Milton. That's why my son and I live in the country."

"We decided somebody probably steals the flowers to make money," Esther said.

"Idn't that terrible? The law needs to get involved," the woman said. "I called them, but I wonder if they've even looked into it."

"Somebody needs to be called," Esther said. "At least the Public Works Director."

"I'm going to go tell my son now," the woman said. "Maybe he can do something."

They watched the woman head toward her son's car.

"Let's go," Esther told Davis Lee. "If we don't leave, she'll be back here talking for an hour."

So they, too, started down the hill.

Later as they stood at her car, Davis Lee said he'd ask Jeff if he'd noticed anybody suspicious hanging around the cemetery last evening.

"If anybody'd know, he would," he said.

"Well, let's not let this worry us too much," she said. "People can't get by with crime for long. Sooner or later, the thief'll get caught."

Before she pulled out of his driveway, he leaned and kissed her through the open window. How natural their kisses had become, she thought. His touch and taste were so familiar and dear now, as if she'd always known him.

At least they'd had a few minutes alone in the cemetery, she thought, before the world, as usual, intruded.

She didn't mention to her mother about going to Sandy's grave, especially about going there with Davis Lee. In fact, she scarcely talked to her mother that evening. But she wanted to talk to her daddy about him, to affirm that he did like Davis Lee. It would mean so much to her to get her daddy's approval. His opinion had always been important to her. It had propelled her through college, seeing him pleased by her high grades and the scholarships she'd won. It was he who had opened her a bank account at the age of eight, so she could begin her college savings, and had emphasized to her for years how important a college education was. He had arranged to have an *Encyclopaedia Britannica* representative visit and had bought her a set of encyclopedias for her college dorm room. Those books now rested in a book case in the front room. Through the years she'd earned money from both her parents by working around the house: mowing grass, washing the car, dusting and vacuuming. And then in the summer before college and during semester breaks, she'd worked at a local shoe store to add to her college fund. In her graduate school years, she drove to Milton two evenings a week to work part-time at the technical college where she worked full-time now. But her bank account never seemed enough to cover tuition, room and board, books, gas, clothes. How many times had her mother bought her a coat or a pair of boots for the cold Boone winters? And how many dollars had her daddy placed in her hand over a span of six years when she drove the fifty miles home to visit?

She knew college was a luxury most people in the working class, like her family or Davis Lee's, couldn't easily afford. Of course, the technical college had helped improve this situation in Milton. Even the poorest people now could have some hope of a higher education. This is what she loved most about her job. But when she graduated from high school in 1974, most of the kids who went on to the colleges or universities were, like Richard's family, more affluent than her family. In that day, it wasn't assumed that every smart or talented child would attend college. And those, like her, who managed to get through college, did so only because of their families' work in the mills or factories and scholarships hard won and the little money their own jobs and lifelong savings would provide. And along with this was some good luck too. Her brother Sandy, of course, didn't have that luck.

She had felt luckiest when she saw her daddy's delight in her successes. At the two ceremonies during which she received her degrees—B.A. and M.A.—her daddy wore his best suit and shook every professor's hand with a vigor that scared a couple of them. But even they recognized a father's pride in that handgrip.

Now she wanted his approval again. Deep inside she felt that if her relationship with Davis Lee had her daddy's blessing, all other obstacles could be overcome.

She caught him after *60 Minutes* as he sat in the rocking chair on the front porch. The air was cool there, and she sat in the swing across the porch from him. Lyla was in the house, rolling her hair.

"It's nice out here this evening," she said. "That breeze makes it seem like fall."

"They dragged in another trailer down the street today," he said. "Sunday didn't stop them."

"Some trailers can be fixed up nice," she said. "Underpinned and front porches added. Maybe they won't all look run down."

"That takes work," he said.

She wondered if he could know Davis Lee lived in a trailer.

"Did you enjoy dinner today?" she asked and wished her

voice hadn't sounded so high-pitched and pleading. She seemed to already be apologizing.

"Lyla tells me he's married," he said. "He has a boy."

"He's getting a divorce, Daddy," she said and felt she'd already lost the battle.

"You're too old for me to tell you what to do, Esther, but I don't want to see you hurt."

"I won't get hurt, Daddy."

"Just be careful, honey," he said, in the lilting tone he'd used with her when she was a child.

"He's a good man, Daddy," she said. "He's poor, but that doesn't matter to me."

"I don't want you to high-hat anybody, Esther," he said. "But I don't want anybody pulling anything over on you."

She didn't ask him outright if he liked Davis Lee. For him to say *no* would hurt too much. Instead she let the subject go for the moment and just sat quietly with her daddy on the porch.

She looked over at him, dressed in his shirt-sleeves, work pants, and work shoes—his standard uniform as long as she could remember—and watched him staring into the darkening sky.

"It was good hearing you sing today, Daddy," she said.

He didn't answer. The only sound that came from his end of the porch was the steady *creak* of his rocking chair.

The following Tuesday morning she had a message in her faculty mail slot from Brenda Johnson. Esther looked at the name *Johnson*—the name Davis Lee had given his wife—and she felt a pang of jealousy and hurt. The note scared her a little, too, though it wasn't completely unexpected.

The phone number the woman had left was for a rural section of the county. After her literature class, Esther went to her office and dialed the number, her fingers trembling. A child's voice answered.

"Jim?" she said.

"What?" he asked, his surprise evident in his voice's high pitch.

"May I speak to your mama?" she asked.

She heard the phone receiver drop and Jim yell, "Mama, it's some woman. I don't know—"

Esther heard the woman's voice in the background saying, "I bet it's her." And then "Jim, you go on outside for a while." The woman and her son's private conversation embarrassed her. She'd been privy to such dialogues when she returned calls to students: a mother or husband grumbling in the background, "I don't know who it is!," these words spoken as if the caller couldn't hear.

The voice that had spoken before and now said "Hello?" was slow and heavily accented, enough to let her know the woman was backwoods.

"Yes, this is Esther Robertson at Milton Technical College returning your call." This response seemed the safe way to approach the woman. Nothing personal, strictly business.

She waited, her heart tapping.

This wasn't the first time she'd been confronted by a rival. On the Saturday morning of her fifteenth birthday, a woman called to say she had spent the past weekend in Gatlinburg, Tennessee, with Martin Faulkner and, as a matter of fact, had spent many nights with Martin for the past year.

How could that be? she thought. Martin was sick last weekend. He had called her on Thursday evening to tell her he had strep throat and couldn't come over the next evening; he called her again on Saturday to say he was still sick. Surely that second call couldn't have come from Tennessee. Then when he finally came to see her on Sunday evening, nothing seemed different. In fact, when she first opened the front screen door to greet him, he kissed her, though her daddy sat a few feet away watching T.V. How could he have spent the past two days and nights with a woman in Tennessee and yet seem the same with *her* afterwards? When they stepped out onto the front porch that Sunday evening, he took her in his arms. *I missed you, Babe,* he said.

I'm glad you're feeling better, she said and stroked the back of his head, his hair silky and smelling of Prell shampoo. She herself recalled too well the fever of strep throat, the needle-pricking sensations in the tonsils, the nausea and diarrhea. How many times had her daddy and mother taken her to Dr. Benedict's office, where she lay on the vinyl sofa in the waiting room, too sick to sit up, dreading the inevitable penicillin shot in the hip.

I feel better now, Babe, he said and kissed her deeply.

It had all seemed so normal. Yet less than a week later the woman would call to say, *I thought you ought to know about me and Martin.*

How could this be? Martin had told her he was a virgin, just as she was. The first time that he made love, he said, would be to her on their wedding night. It was his vow.

You're lying, she told the stranger on the phone, whose voice sounded raspy and mature, someone too old for Martin, who was now twenty-one.

I know all about you, the woman said. *At the store we told Martin he was robbin' the cradle. He told me you wouldn't let him touch you.* The woman laughed at this. *Well, let me tell you, he touches me. He builds up steam at your house and comes to mine afterwards. You're crazy if you think he's saving himself for you. You ain't nothin' but a baby. You don't know a damn thing about men.* Then the woman hung up.

That same evening Martin came to see her. When she opened the screen door, he held out a small, red foil-wrapped box tied with a shiny red ribbon—a gift that seemed more suitable for Valentine's Day than for her birthday. She didn't take the gift, but asked him to come sit with her in the front porch swing, she needed to talk to him. Her voice was steady; she was determined to remain calm and had rehearsed this talk in her mind all day.

They sat together and he placed the birthday gift beside him in the swing.

Her composure left her as soon as she began to repeat the woman's words. Martin listened as she cried and asked him *Why, Martin? I thought you loved me.* He leaned forward, putting his head in his hands, his elbows on his knees, his fingers in his dark hair. He shook his head and began to cry.

I do love you, Esther! he said. *I wanted to tell you. I wanted to tell you from the first.*

Who is she? Esther said, looking at him through her tears, though he kept his head down. *How could you talk to her about me?*

She's nobody, Esther, he said. *She's just a woman I work with. Her husband left her, and she needed somebody to talk to. I never said anything bad about you, Esther.* He looked at her now, his eyes red, his eyelashes wet with tears. *How could you think that? I won't see her again,* he said, *I swear to God. I'll get another job. She's nothing to me, Esther. I want to marry you, Esther.* He tried to take her hand, his hand trembling, but she pulled her hand away.

Suddenly despite her own sadness, she became calm, almost detached.

I can't marry you, now, she said. *You've spoiled everything.*

He didn't answer this, but made a pained sound, his mouth pulled downward, almost like a pouting child.

You need to go now, Martin, she said.

That evening she cried so hard she was ill in the bathroom. Her daddy knocked on the bathroom door to see what was wrong. "Leave me alone!" she growled at him, words that would haunt her always.

But later that same night she sat on the front porch with her daddy and told him how Martin had hurt her.

"I won't let him come back here," her daddy said.

That night she also confided to her mother what Martin had done.

"He's a whoremonger," Lyla said. "I could see this coming. You're better off to know now before he took advantage of you and ruined your reputation."

Why couldn't she herself see it coming? The drive-in restroom graffiti had warned her. Still, she had believed in Martin.

Martin left behind the red birthday package on the porch swing. When he was gone, she opened it to find a gold box. Inside this box was a glass cylinder of *Joy* perfume. She unscrewed the bottle and touched her nose to the tiny hole, closing her eyes. The gold liquid's floral fragrance filled her senses. She screwed the cap back on and replaced the bottle in its little casket. She hid it upstairs in a cedar chest, where it remained to this day. Only years later would she appreciate how expensive this gift must have been and guessed it was Martin's guilt that caused him to be so extravagant. Or perhaps he had really loved her.

In any case, despite Martin's phone calls after that, begging her to let him come back, and despite her temptation to let him come to soothe her loneliness, she told him *You can't come anymore*.

In time he stopped calling.

But he'd left an emptiness in her, a cavern that would remain cold and vast until Richard grinned at her on Main Street.

Now nineteen years later, the same sick feeling she'd felt on her fifteenth birthday overcame her as she waited to hear what Davis Lee's wife would say to her.

Maybe because of her nervousness she couldn't make out the first words the woman spoke. When her brain and body calmed enough to allow her to hear, she heard, "He didn't mention divorce till nine days ago, and don't that tell you something?—"

"—This divorce business will blow over," the woman continued. "Davis Lee and me've been married for thirteen years and knowed each other long before that, and that counts for a lot in my book. We ain't educated like you and we got a youngun between us. Me and Davis Lee's alike and we belong together. If you make Davis Lee push this divorce idea, I'll take Jim. I'll see that happens," she said.

"This is between you and Davis Lee," Esther said, hoping the college switchboard receptionist wasn't listening in.

"Naw, you're part of it now," the woman said.

"I don't know what you want me to say," Esther said and a silence lapsed. For a minute she thought the woman might have hung up.

"You don't have to say nothin'. You just think about what I said to you," the woman added.

What right did this woman, a stranger, have to give Esther an order? Rarely, *rarely* did any student, regardless of how upset or indignant over a grade or a criticism, ever take this tone with her. Her first instinct was simply to hang up the phone. Or to tell the woman to watch her tongue. This was her office, after all, hard earned, and she demanded respect here. But she neither hung up the phone nor reprimanded the woman. She just listened.

"Well, I thought you ort to know where I stand," the woman said and then a click and then silence.

Esther put the receiver down and stared at the phone. So this was Brenda.

She sat numb for a few minutes and then gathered her books and papers in her bookbag and went to her car.

On the drive home when she passed by Davis Lee's trailer, she saw no indication of anyone there, though a few clothes were strung on the porch clothesline. This was a good sign, since Brenda usually took their clothes to the Laundromat on Monday. Could this mean she came by here yesterday and was told to leave? Maybe that's what prompted her phone call this morning.

Davis Lee really needed a washing machine and dryer, Esther thought. Or at least a way to get to a Laundromat—not the one Brenda went to, though. She could drive him there herself.

She wondered if Brenda could cause Davis Lee the problems she threatened. In her own divorce no custody issues were involved, since no children were involved, at least not directly. Their infertility was a cause of the divorce, of course, so in that sense unconceived children, like little phantoms, hovered around the case. But the divorce was simple, uncontested by her, and settled like clockwork a year following their separation. They hadn't acquired anything during their two-year cohabitation: no property or home or savings accounts. So there were no assets to be divided. Richard paid all the legal fees—he insisted, probably to ensure there were no hitches—and so she left the marriage unscathed financially. She suspected his parents handed him the money, eager for him to get on with his life.

Talking to Davis Lee's wife made her think again, as she'd so often thought before, that it was a blessing that no child had been conceived in her and Richard's paltry two years of sexual intimacy. She doubted a child would have made them feel closer to each other. In fact, she often suspected it would have caused a power struggle between her and Richard and his parents—one against three. It certainly would have made the inevitable divorce more complicated. *Things work out for a reason*, her mother had said through the years when Esther brought up the subject of her divorce.

It occurred to her now that maybe the reason for her divorce from Richard was because she would someday meet Davis Lee and want to be with him. If she'd still been married to Richard, would that have happened? When Esther was a teenager, her mother declared that the reason Martin's running around came to light was to free her for Richard. *Now ain't you glad that woman called you?* Lyla asked. *She did you a favor.* At the time, relieved and flattered by Richard's attentions, Esther had said, *Yes, I'm glad*, though the raspy woman's phone call twisted her inside every time she thought about it. Thankfully, she thought about it less and less.

But today, Brenda's words brought back that same sick feeling. Still, she refused to accept that this turn of events was for a reason. She couldn't imagine her life now without Davis Lee. Being with him again, touching him, was what she had to look forward to.

When she approached home, she saw a motorcycle parked in the street in front of the house. She stopped, amazed to see it there. Why would a motorcycle be here? She knew only one motorcyclist.

She parked in the driveway and went to the motorcycle to check the raised inscription on the gas tank. *Triumph.* Yes, it was Jeff's. His black helmet rested on the seat. She didn't realize Jeff knew where she lived.

Her mother met her on the front porch and said, "That Johnson man's here, Esther. He come a few minutes ago."

"Jeff Johnson?" she asked.

"No," Lyla said, impatient, "the one you brought here yesterday. He's been here thirty minutes. He's sitting in there in the front room with Arthur."

"What did he say?" Esther asked. She didn't even imagine it was Davis Lee who'd ridden that motorcycle here. What could he be saying to her daddy?

"He said he needed to see you. Your daddy let him in; I was in the kitchen. I didn't even know anybody'd knocked on the door. Did you tell him to come here this evening?"

"No, Mother," she said. "I didn't have any idea he was coming." She handed Lyla her bookbag and opened the screen door. When her eyes adjusted to the darker light inside the house, she saw Davis Lee sitting on the loveseat. When he saw her, he stood.

"Esther," he said, shamefaced.

"Davis Lee," she said and went to him. As she passed between her daddy and the T.V., she glanced at him and said, "Hey, Daddy." He lifted his finger and nodded, hardly noticing her intrusion. She went to the loveseat.

"I'm sorry I've come here without being invited," he said in a low voice. "But I needed to talk to you." He looked at her grimly, grinding his chewing gum between his teeth.

"It's all right, Davis Lee," she said and touched his hand. He grasped her hand. "Let's go outside," she said, glancing at her daddy.

"Daddy, we're going out on the porch," she said and her daddy nodded, his attention on his talk show. Davis Lee let go of her hand and followed her outside.

She looked for her mother when they stepped out on the porch, but Lyla wasn't on the porch or in the front yard. She must have gone to the back door, Esther thought, to avoid passing by Davis Lee in the front room.

"Let's sit over here," she said and they sat in the swing.

"I saw the motorcycle," she said, "but I didn't dream it was you."

"I ain't been on a motorcycle in years," he said. "I like to wrecked it coming here."

"What's wrong, Davis Lee?" she asked.

"I know Brenda called you this morning," he said. "She called me a while ago and told me she'd talked to you at the college."

"She called you?" Esther asked. She would have thought Brenda would keep their conversation private, since it had been akin to an obscene phone call.

"Just before I come here," he said. "I got here as soon as I could, hoping to talk to you about it. I was afraid you'd be mad."

"At you?" she asked. Even if she'd been tempted to be irritated at him, seeing him here, his face troubled, would have melted that urge.

"I never wanted you to get tangled up in this. If I'd've thought she'd bother you, I swear I'd torn out her telephone. She ain't got any business calling you."

This anger was a side of Davis Lee she hadn't seen before. Or maybe it was fear she saw in his wide eyes and heard in his wavering voice.

"It's okay, Davis Lee," she said, taking his hand, wanting to calm him. "We didn't talk long. She didn't say much. I don't think she'll call me again."

"You don't know Brenda," he said. "She don't think before she speaks or for that matter before she does something. She's always been like that—blunt as a hammer."

"She said you'd known each other a long time."

"I can't deny that," he said. "We went to school together in Spruce Pine."

"High school sweethearts?" In saying this, her voice wavered a little too. She couldn't deny a pang of jealousy when she thought of Davis Lee having a wife or even a girlfriend; having a life—long before she'd come into it.

"You know what I told you about me and Brenda," he said. "We just come together, and that's about the sum of it."

"You must have loved her at some time, Davis Lee," she said. "She said you two were alike," Esther said.

"Well, that last part may be true," he said. He propped his elbow on the swing arm and cupped his head in his hand, as if he had a headache. "But I ain't proud of it."

He didn't speak for a minute and she wondered if she'd offended him.

"I told you when I met you, everything changed for me," he said. "What I might've been before don't seem right now. I settled for things I can't settle for now. Can you understand that?"

"I think so, Davis Lee," she said and held to his hand, though he seemed to be leaning away from her.

"I always felt like life had passed me by," he said. "It seemed like one day just led into the next and it all would lead to what I keep cleared every day."

"The grave?" she asked.

"Seemed like it," he said. "I never had what you'd call a romance or felt the things poets talk about. I thought such feelings must happen for some people, but not for me. My mama and daddy never had it."

"No," she said, realizing she could confess the same about her parents.

"But I believe my granddaddy and grandmama must have had something like that, at least in the beginning, with the way he built the cabin for her—"

"And the quilt she made," Esther added.

"—That's what I mean," he said. "But I never felt that way for Brenda, and I don't reckon she ever felt it for me. I ain't proud that I didn't make her happy either." He stopped here for a minute, composing himself. "But the worse thing is Jim's tangled up in the middle of it."

"Brenda seems to still want you, Davis Lee," Esther said, forgetting her own feelings for a moment. "Why else would she want to hold onto you?"

"I think she wants what she knows she can't have," he said. "I think that's what makes people steal. It ain't because they really need something, it's just the idea that it belongs to somebody else."

"Do you belong to me, Davis Lee?" she asked and he turned to face her.

"I do, Esther," he said. "As much as I could belong to anybody. You made me see that when you come along. I'd never even thought about wanting to belong to somebody till I first saw you."

"On T.V.?" she asked, smiling a little.

"Well, I reckon it was somewhere about that time," he said.

She reached and kissed his cheek. Then she lifted his hand to her face, turned his palm up, and pressed her lips to it.

As she held his palm to her lips, he watched her.

"Nobody ever did that before," he said.

"You have beautiful hands," she said and turned his hand over and traced the length of his fingers. "Like a pianist's." She thought about the plaster cast of Chopin's hand she'd seen in photographs.

"I never played the piano. For a while, Mama kept one and played it, but she had to sell it when she moved us to Spruce Pine."

"My grandmother had one, too," Esther said. "It was an old Remington player piano, but the player mechanism didn't work anymore. I used to sit and pick out *Away in a Manger*—simple melodies like that. I mostly banged. I couldn't read music," she said. She'd always regretted not studying piano and learning to read music, as much as she loved classical music now.

"I always played the fiddle by ear, too. Granddaddy'd play a tune and I'd pick it up."

"That's a gift, to be able to hear something and then play it."

He laughed lightly. "Well, I don't know if you'd call my playing a gift," he said. "But I been working on it."

"Can I hear you play sometime?" she asked.

"I aim for you to," he said and she realized they'd forgotten for a while why he'd come here today in the first place. It seemed nothing could keep them down once they were together.

But she had to talk to him about the situation with Brenda.

"Davis Lee, Brenda said some things to me about keeping Jim away from you. Maybe you should see a lawyer about this."

"I don't like lawyers," he said. "Or the law for that matter. But if it'll clear the way for you and me, I'll do what I have to.

When I left Brenda two years ago, me and her decided Jim should live with her and I'd keep him whatever weekends we agreed on. Of course, I was happy to keep him more than that, but it seemed to me a boy that age needed his mama more. Neither of us seen the need to get a lawyer involved. I don't reckon either of us figured on marrying again."

"What if the lawyer advises you not to see me for a while, I mean till this custody problem is settled?" The thought pained her.

He looked at her as if she'd slapped him.

"I won't stop seeing you," he said. "Nothing Brenda can do will make me stay away from you. If Jim has to live with Brenda from now on then that's how it'll be."

"Don't say that, Davis Lee," she said. "I think you'd regret that."

"It's how I feel, Esther," he said. A slight edge of resentment seeped from those words. She looked at him, his face shadowed in the waning light.

"I just don't want you to be hurt, Davis Lee," she said.

"There's only one thing that can hurt me," he said and stared at her. He gripped her hand tighter. "And I ain't going to let that happen."

"Let's try not to worry," she said and leaned back in the swing, the air cooling her face, feverish from their conversation. "Whatever happens is meant to be."

"I believe that too, Esther," he said and relaxed beside her, as if he had settled in for a while. He held her hand in both his now, their hands resting on his thigh. It felt natural to her, touching his leg like this.

She knew her mother had spied on them from behind the front screen door and peered at them through the front window blinds. But it didn't matter. Her feelings for Davis Lee and their moments of touch couldn't be hidden any longer.

"I've thought about it, especially the last couple of days," he said, looking to the sky and distant mountain ranges. "Maybe all this *is* meant to be. Last night, I walked up into the cemetery and looked at the stars. It's the most peaceful place at night, Esther, not too much traffic on the street down below, so no sounds but wind in the oaks or night birds calling, and up on the top of the hill, near where the woods join the cemetery, I stood and looked at the stars and thought about you. I thought about us walking together there Sunday evening. How we saw each other less than two months ago and was strangers, but wanted to know each other. Now we're together. I'm closer to you than I've ever been to anybody, Esther. Do you believe that?"

She nodded *yes*.

"Well, I am. When Brenda called me and said she and me had to get back together, all I wanted to do was die. But then I thought about you and wanted to come here. All of a sudden, I was afraid I'd dreamed about us and it wasn't real. So much of my life's seemed like sleepwalking anyway."

"For me too," she said.

"I had to come here and make sure it wasn't a dream and you still wanted to be with me."

"It's not a dream, Davis Lee," she said. "And I do want to be with you. More than you can imagine."

"Do you think we could sit out here for a little while longer?" he said. "Then I'll go."

She leaned her head against his shoulder and they sat, enjoying the breeze that carried a hint of fall.

"I wish I'd knowed you twenty years ago," he said.

"When I was fourteen," she said.

"I'd have loved you then," he said. "I bet somebody sat in this swing with you then. That person you still think about."

"That's a long time ago, Davis Lee," she said. "He was just a young boy, but he really hurt me."

"And you're still hurting over it, ain't you?" he said and looked at her.

"Well, no," she said.

"But you ain't forgot him either," he said, his voice intimate.

"No," she admitted. "But I don't think about him so much anymore." Especially since I met you, she thought.

"I'm sorry he hurt you."

"Hurt's part of life, Davis Lee. We can't get around it."

"That's a fact," he said.

"He just made me scared to trust anybody, that's all. You know, to trust my feelings with somebody."

"You can trust me."

"I hope so, Davis Lee," she said and nuzzled closer to him, pressing her lips to his shoulder, so lightly he might not have noticed. At this moment, she would have trusted him with her life.

"What happened to that boy?" Davis Lee asked.

"I don't know," she said. "He's still around here, I guess. Back then, I learned something about him and I made him go away. I haven't talked to him in nineteen years."

"You've counted the years," he said.

"I guess I have," she said.

"Did you still love him even though you made him go away?"

"That's not important now, Davis Lee," she said.

"But the past comes back sometimes, don't it?"

"Yes," she said, thinking of how easily a song could take you back.

"I wish I'd knowed you then," he said again.

He stayed a while longer, until the clouds in the evening sky had a rosy hue, and then she walked with him to the end of the sidewalk where his motorcycle was parked. He pulled her close to him and kissed her. As before, she felt his arousal and her own body pushed a little closer to his in answer.

"I wish I didn't have to leave you," he said, his face close to hers, his breath warm and sweet. His eyes searched hers.

"I know," she said and held to him. "If you need to call me here *anytime*, I'll give you my home phone number. You won't find it in the phone book."

"I know," he said and smiled. "I looked."

When she told him the number, he said, "I'll remember it."

She released him, and he strapped on the helmet and mounted the motorcycle. Before he turned the ignition key, he leaned and kissed her again.

"Don't get chilled on the ride home," she said and rubbed his bare arm, her fingers moving up inside his tee shirt sleeve. The flesh of his bare shoulder was warm and soft, and his arm tensed at her touch. She squeezed his shoulder and pulled her hand away.

"Bye, darlin'," he said and then cranked the motor. He roared away, and she stood and watched him for a minute before going into the house.

In the kitchen, Lyla asked her what he'd wanted.

"Just to talk," she said. "He has some problems."

"And he means to make them yours," Lyla said.

"He needed somebody to talk to," she said, wishing she could tell her mother more.

That night, she lay in bed and thought about the warmth and softness of his bare flesh. Beneath the bed sheet, she reached and slipped down the satin strap of her nightgown and caressed her own shoulder, pretending it was his hand touching her.

14

That night she dreamed about Martin. In the dream they were parked at the drive-in theater, and she was so sleepy she rested her head against his shoulder. He'd brought a blanket to cover them. She was aware that no one had come to see the movie except them, and fog had settled in the surrounding spaces. The movie screen loomed out of the fog.

She told Martin she couldn't stay awake and was afraid they'd both fall asleep and stay there all night. Maybe they'd better go home now, she said. He put his arm around her and said he would take care of her, not to worry. He wanted to spend this night with her. *Tomorrow, we'll be apart again. I've not seen you in nineteen years*, he said. Then she realized they were in the present.

She looked at him.

You've hardly changed at all, she said. *Your hair's still dark*, and she saw he was still handsome and young looking.

I've waited for you, Babe, he said.

I can't believe we're together, she said and nestled into his chest. She fell asleep and when she awoke, she realized he was driving them through the cotton mill village.

Isn't this your street? she said when they came to a steep street, this section seeming even poorer than the others, the front porches cluttered by discarded couches and oil heaters. The yards were covered in a fine mist and dawn had begun to break. The mill clock shone in the distance and read six-fifteen.

I'll take you home now, he said. *This life's not for you.*

He drove her to her parents' house and parked in the driveway.

Before he left her, he said, *Nothing changes.*

She was sad to leave him, knowing she might not see him again.

I've missed you, Martin, she said and then he was gone.

When she awoke from this dream, just after dawn, she lay

and thought about him. How strange to dream about him so vividly. It wasn't the first time, of course, but never had the dream left her feeling as if she'd actually been with him. His scent, laced with *British Sterling* cologne, was distinct. His voice, the mild Southern accent, rang true. How real was the comfort she felt as she rested her head against his shoulder. Just as it had been so long ago.

She felt intensely alone now, but gratified too. The dream seemed like a gift to her.

Had Martin been thinking about her to make her dream about him? She pondered this possibility.

Martin, she said and then remembered Davis Lee sitting beside her in the porch swing last evening and their conversation about the past.

Maybe she did think about Martin more often than she'd led Davis Lee to believe. And maybe the hurt *was* still there from all those years ago.

The dream stayed with her, all that day and into the evening, carrying her through her classes and lurking behind conversations she held with others. In the library, the administrator who'd formerly asked her out approached her as she stood at the front desk.

"I heard you're seeing somebody," he said. "That surprises me, Esther," he added, a note of irony in his voice.

"Why does that surprise you?" she asked, fitting a library book into her bookbag, hoping the librarian who stood nearby was not listening to them. Who could have said something about her and Davis Lee?

"I thought you'd taken a vow of celibacy," he said. "Now I'm personally offended." He knitted his brows, giving her a mock frown, and then grinned, the skin at the corners of his eyes crinkling. His eyes were paler than she'd remembered, almost silver-blue against his tanned skin. He must have spent many summer days on the golf course.

"You're silly," she said, smiling despite herself. She could not imagine taking this man seriously. "You don't seem too offended to me."

"Well, life does go on," he said. She assumed this meant he'd met someone else. Probably a divorcee at his country club.

"Yes, it does," she said and they went their separate ways.

But her heart held a secret. Nineteen years hadn't changed what she had felt for Martin nor what he felt for her, if she could trust her dream.

The next morning the dream remained with her. And when she got home from work later that day, she looked to see that her mother was outside in her garden, gathering tomatoes, and her daddy was safe at the T.V. She wouldn't be disturbed.

She went upstairs to a corner in Sandy's bedroom, where a tall powder blue crib held a stack of blankets. Her mother hadn't removed the basketball team posters from the walls, though the edges had yellowed and curled. A Duke University pennant was tacked over Sandy's desk, which stood bare. His bed with its wagon wheel headboard and blue and white bedspread sat aloof beneath a window.

She went to the crib. Underneath it sat a box marked *Arthur's Records*—her daddy's collection of 78's that Lyla had stored here.

But what she'd come to this room to find was inside the crib.

She folded back the blankets until she found the cedar chest of mementos she'd hidden years ago.

Opening the chest, she discovered what she'd come for: the gold perfume box. She opened it and removed the ridged glass cylinder of *Joy* perfume. She tried to unscrew the cap, but it wouldn't budge. After some effort, the cap began to turn, and she lifted it off and held the tip of the bottle to her nose. How keen and fragrant was the smell, like a rose garden in full bloom.

At the time when Martin gave it to her, she opened it once and then put it away. Only later, after Richard had come and gone, had she taken the bottle out of its box again and removed the cap a second time to breathe the perfume's fragrance. Though at that moment in her maturity she appreciated the gift's worth, she still refused to forgive the one who'd offered it to her. Again, she hid it alongside her other souvenirs of Martin.

Now she screwed the cap back on and put the perfume bottle in her skirt pocket. She sorted through the chest: an initial ring—its *M* in elegant script—he'd given her to wear on a chain around her neck that showed they were going steady; a Valentine's card in which he'd written *Forever*; a four-leaf clover he'd found for her on a summer picnic to Chimney Rock Park; a bracelet of colored love beads he had strung for her. No photographs were in the box; oddly, he'd never given her one of himself, though she'd presented him with several of her. *Why didn't he return your pictures?* her mother had asked after she and Martin broke up. *They was studio portraits.* This was true; her mother had taken her to a Milton photographer's studio on Main Street and had portraits made of her when she turned fourteen. *You won't ever be prettier than you are now*, Lyla had said at the time. Esther had wondered what Martin had done with those photographs of her. Did he, too, have a memento chest stashed away somewhere?

As she placed the cedar chest back under the blankets, she felt something else hidden there. Pulling it out, she saw it was her mother's old scrapbook. For years Lyla had taped photos and newspaper clippings onto its black pages. Why was it here? Esther wondered. Since Sandy's death, the scrapbook had always been stored in Sandy's desk drawer.

Opening the album's satin-covered front piece, she saw the family pictures she'd almost forgotten, among them a portrait of her daddy in his white Navy uniform; an informal shot of her mother sitting in the porch swing with baby Sandy on her lap; and a group shot of the four of them in their church clothes. According to the note at the bottom, this family picture was taken Easter Sunday, 1957. Sandy wore a white sailor suit and saddle oxfords, his face thrown back with a broad grin. He would have been four years old then, she figured. Her mother, in a two-piece rose-colored suit and matching hat, stood behind Sandy with her hands on his shoulders. Beside Lyla stood her daddy, in a gray suit, holding her, a year-old baby, in his arms. He looked down at her, rather than at the photographer. Esther studied the picture to see where they were standing. She noticed tulips in the background, so maybe it was her grandmama's yard.

She leafed through the album until she came to the newspaper clippings. The yellowed obituary notice of her maternal grandmama and that of her paternal uncle Dave were taped next to each other. She turned the page to find a memorial section devoted to Sandy. Here were his obituary, sealed in plastic; the *Milton News* article that reported the accident—*the Ford Mustang flipped three times*—probably read a hundred times by her mother; a letter to the newspaper editor, written by their own Baptist preacher, denouncing the evils of alcohol.

Stuck in the back of the album was a Milton Funeral Home register, *Cherished Memories*, in which people who'd come to view Sandy had signed their names. She noted that Uncle Dave's signature was first on the list of names. Inside the register, she also found the funeral program that explained where and when the service was held, listed the surviving family, told the place of burial, and featured a poem:

God doth not promise
A sky always fair...

Stored here in the register, too, were cards taken from flower arrangements that had been sent to the "Robertson Service." She sorted through these cards and noted the names of the senders, some of whom she could only vaguely place from past church years or from the neighborhood, many now dead.

One card stopped her.

The card, stamped by Milton Florist, noted the sender's name *Mrs. Carter Johnson.* She stared at the name. That was Davis Lee's mama! So his mama did indeed know her family. She'd even sent flowers. It stood to reason, then, that Esther's parents knew Cora Johnson too. Why hadn't they just told her this? She stuck the card in her pocket beside the perfume bottle.

She placed the flower cards and funeral program back inside the register, put the register back into the scrapbook, and closed the scrapbook. She laid it in the crib, alongside her cedar chest, and covered it with blankets, as her mother had done, though she couldn't imagine why or when. She wondered if her mother had sometime discovered her memento chest.

With this on her mind, she sat on Sandy's bed and looked around the room. The room hadn't changed much through the years. It still looked like a high school boy's room, with the basketball team posters and Duke pennant, but it was neater than it should be. No inside-out basketball socks lay dangling over the bed's footboard; no high top sneakers turned on their sides on the floor; no *Sports Illustrated* magazines scattered on the desk. This was a ghost's room, rarely entered by the living. She doubted her daddy had been up here over a couple of times in twenty years. It was getting harder for him to climb stairs anyway. She'd noticed the last time he climbed up their front porch steps, he stopped midway and leaned with his hand on his thigh to catch his breath.

She went to the small closet, opened its blue curtains, and looked at the shelves. Here rested a basketball that Sandy's remaining team members had signed and presented to Lyla at the funeral; a stack of Beach Boy albums she'd heard playing a hundred times from behind Sandy's closed bedroom door; a box of his beloved baseball cards that he'd collected for years—Mickey Mantle, Roger Maris, Sandy Koufax, Don Drysdale. No clothes hung on the metal rod; no shoes sat on the floor. They had been boxed and donated to the Christian

Clothes Center years ago.

She went back to his bed and sat. *Sandy,* she thought, *so much has happened since you sat here and spread out your baseball cards. You wouldn't know our street anymore. Most of the old people have died, and our friends have grown up and moved away. Remember the pasture down the street where Mother and I picked blackberries? It's been cleared for a trailer park. I went to college to be a teacher, Sandy, and I got married, but not to Martin. Do you remember Martin? We had just started dating when.... I'm divorced and living back home now. I try to help Mother, Sandy, but she wants to do it herself. You know how she is. Daddy's lonesome without you, Sandy.*

She felt forlorn, not so much because she missed him, but because at this moment she could hardly remember him at all. She tried to see his face, hear his voice, but her mind had gone numb.

Across the stair landing from Sandy's room was a second room. Once a bare, unfinished room with exposed rafters and a clothesline strung from one side to the other, this second room was now a den. Lyla's lifelong dream was to have such a room, so after Esther moved back home, she hired workers to hang sheetrock and install a ceiling, sand and finish the floorboards, and wire the room for outlets, a power switch, and an overhead light fixture. She and Lyla painted the walls an antique white and then went to a local furniture store and picked out a braided rug, couch, easy chair, and floor lamp. Later Lyla added a telephone table, an extension phone, and a cabinet radio. Esther's daddy trudged up the staircase once to see the completed, furnished room, and for a couple of years Lyla regularly visited the room to sit in the easy chair and listen to the radio or read her Bible. It was her little refuge.

But in time, this den, like Sandy's bedroom, had become unoccupied and silent.

Now, as Esther came here to use the phone, she noticed a thin layer of dust on the table scarf, on the phone's receiver, and on the radio. She would have to come back later and tidy up, she decided, and turn on the window fan to air out the room that was stuffy and hot. But for the moment that would have to wait.

She picked up the telephone directory—an outdated 1985 edition—and opened it.

Until her dream night before last, she'd forgotten Martin's voice, but the dream brought it back. Something she'd wanted to do for years she would do now. God help her, it might be a mistake, but she'd do it anyway.

She turned to the yellow pages and looked under the heading *Furniture* and searched until she found a small ad:

RESTORATION SHOPPE
 Furniture Stripping and Refinishing
 Repairing/Ornamental Work/Reupholstery
 Martin Faulkner, Owner

A business address and phone number were also listed. The address was in the southern end of the county, an area she never had cause to enter. But he was still in Milton, she thought, probably had been throughout the years.

She presumed the business was located at his home, maybe in an adjoining workshop, and she wondered what kind of house he lived in and with whom.

Let's say she took a chair to be repaired. Would he know her if she hadn't called in advance to tell him she was coming? Would he answer the door? Or would she have to speak to a wife or one of his children?

Then again maybe he, too, was childless.

She took a deep breath and dialed the number, her fingers trembling. I'll hang up on the fifth ring, she told herself, but before she had the chance, a voice answered.

"Restoration Shoppe," the man said, and the voice was low-pitched and deeply accented. Martin's voice was neither. Maybe this was an assistant.

"Yes," she said. "Is this Martin Faulkner?" Could he hear the tremor in her voice?

"Yes, ma'am, it is," he said. "What can I do for you?" His voice sounded impersonal, impatient. Had she interrupted his work?

"I have a chair," she lied, "a recliner that has a broken spring. Could you fix it?"

"I'd have to take a look, ma'am," he said. "You got a way to get it here? A pickup truck?"

"Well, no," she said, feeling trapped.

"Well, I reckon I might could get my boy to come by and get it. How far away you live?"

His *boy*. So he'd had a son sometime along the way, one now old enough to drive and help out his father in the business.

"I might have to wait a while," she said, trying to untangle herself.

"Well, just let us know," he said.

She didn't speak for a minute. If she told him who she was, would he want to talk to her for a while? Would he want to see her?

Before she could answer, she heard the click.

And she felt she'd lost him forever.

Her dream was a hoax. This man she'd spoken to on the phone wasn't the Martin she remembered; the young Martin in her dream didn't exist now. And she wasn't the fifteen-year-old Esther who had told him he had to go away, that he couldn't come anymore.

She stood and reached into her skirt pocket to feel the perfume bottle.

We lost our chance then, Martin, she thought to herself. We both threw it away.

"Everything changes, Martin," she said aloud.

When she went down the stairs, she held to the stair rail with her left hand, but her right hand grasped the glass cylinder in her pocket.

Her mother had come into the kitchen and was washing tomatoes.

"Where've you been?" Lyla asked. "I wanted you to help me pick these tomatoes. I need to get 'em canned tonight."

"I was upstairs," she said, "using the phone. I couldn't hear for the T.V., so I used the phone up there."

"I don't see how Arthur stands that television so loud," Lyla said. "His hearing ain't good, though he wouldn't admit it. It's all the machines he worked around that's ruined his hearing."

"I didn't mind going upstairs," she said. "I need to go back up there, though, and do some dusting."

"Who'd you call?" Lyla asked, sweeping her hair back with her wet wrist.

Esther could tell by her mother's tone that she thought Esther had called Davis Lee. From the time Esther was a teenager, Lyla had warned her against calling boys.

"Let the boy do the calling," she'd said. "He won't respect a girl who has to call him."

She'd obeyed her mother all those years ago and had never called Martin. How funny, she thought, that now, nineteen years later, she called him for the first time.

"It was business," she said.

"Oh," Lyla said, unconvinced. "I heard something on the radio this morning about the cemetery," she continued.

"What?" Esther asked.

"It was vandalized, they said. Did you hear anything at school about it?"

"No," Esther said. "Do you mean Oak Grove Cemetery?"

"They said a woman reported her husband's grave had been bothered, flowers took, and the Police Department was investigating it. I thought we might ought to go out there this evening and check on Sandy's grave. I wouldn't mention it to Arthur, though. No need in upsetting him. If he asks where we're going, tell him we need to run to the Winn-Dixie."

"I passed by the cemetery a while ago, and I didn't see anything." Of course, she already knew about Sandy's missing flowers and the woman's missing chrysanthemum spray. But on her drive home, she'd been so preoccupied with her dream about Martin that she hadn't even looked toward the cemetery when she passed by. "I don't see any need in going," she said.

"If you won't take me, I'll get Arthur to."

"No," she said, knowing her daddy hadn't started his car in months. "I'll take you."

After supper they drove to the cemetery and stopped near Sandy's grave. A light rain had begun to fall, so she told her mother they'd have to hurry.

"I brought my rain kerchief," Lyla said and wrapped a plastic bonnet around her head. Esther wore her blue hat.

"They're gone," Lyla said, when she saw Sandy's bare grave. "Somebody has stole from my dead son. They ought to be shot for doing that."

"They'll get caught, Mother," she said. "Don't worry."

"The caretaker around here ain't good for much," Lyla said, as cruelly as she could. "He ought to be reported too."

"I don't think he's necessarily the caretaker," Esther said. "He just took on the responsibility of watching over things because he lives next door. He can't see everything that goes on. Thieves could come in the night."

"Why you defending him?" Lyla said.

"He does the best he can," Esther said. "He's not a policeman."

"He sat at my kitchen table and told me he kept a eye on the flowers. He told me that. You heard him tell me that."

"He does the best he can."

"It ain't good enough," Lyla said and turned. She started walking toward the car.

"You want to go?" Esther asked, glancing around to see if

Davis Lee were nearby. She needed to see him now.

Lyla didn't answer but got into the car and sat there, staring straight ahead. The rain had started falling harder, so Esther headed to the car, too.

When they pulled out of the cemetery, Esther looked toward Davis Lee's trailer and saw a Milton Police car parked in the driveway. A uniformed officer was getting out of the car. When he turned and looked their way, she realized he was her former student who lived in the trailer park on their street. He recognized her, too, and nodded and grinned. In his official uniform he looked more dignified, a little intimidating.

She hoped her mother hadn't noticed the police car or the officer, but when they drove through town Lyla said, "Well, I saw the law out there. Was that that man's trailer?"

"You mean Davis Lee?"

"That Johnson."

"Yes," she said hesitantly. "They're probably asking Davis Lee about the flowers, since he works at the cemetery."

But she wondered why they would specifically be talking to Davis Lee. He wasn't the only maintenance worker, after all. There was Jeff, of course, though they wouldn't be talking to him since his motorcycle wasn't parked there this evening. And other men worked in the cemetery; she'd seen them buzzing around on their riding lawn mowers. They might know something.

"Don't tell Arthur about this," Lyla said.

"I didn't plan to."

Esther's mind was busy, but she tried to stay focused on the road. She would call Davis Lee tonight. She needed to hear his voice, to tell him she had let go of the past.

15

When she called, Jeff answered.

"Jeff," she said, "I need to speak to Davis Lee. Could you get him for me?"

A silence lapsed and she thought Jeff had put down the receiver to go get Davis Lee, but then he said, "Can't you see we got trouble as it is?"

She waited for an explanation. When none was offered, she said, "Can I speak to Davis Lee, Jeff?"

"You ever caught a lightnin' bug in a jar, Esther?" he asked. "Watch him sit there in the bottom of the jar, shinin' his light like a Christmas bulb, then remember you forgot to punch holes in the lid to give him air? Then you notice his light's gone out forever. You ever caught a lightnin' bug like that, Esther?"

"I guess so," she said.

"That's the way you kill something, Esther," he said. "Catch it, take it from its family, make it yours."

"Is Davis Lee there?" she asked, tired of his nonsense. She didn't know how to handle Jeff when he acted this way.

"Why'd you ever have to come here, Esther?" he asked. "You've th'own everything off."

And he hung up.

Well, she thought, he's mad at me.

She started to dial the number again, but decided maybe she should just drive back out there and talk to both of them. She set the receiver back on the hook, and when she stood to leave the room, the phone rang. She grabbed the receiver.

"Esther?" he said before she could say *Hello*.

"Davis Lee?" she said.

"I saw Jeff talking on the phone and heard him call your name, but before I could get there, he hung up."

"I called to talk to you, Davis Lee," she said. "I'm glad you called me back. I think I upset Jeff."

"No you didn't, Esther. We've had a commotion here this evening. A law man's been here talking to Jeff. He ain't been gone long."

"So it was Jeff the officer came to see?"

"What?" he said.

"I had to take my mother to the cemetery, and I saw the police car."

"Yeah, it's been a mess here. The man talked to me, said people'd complained about missing flowers, and Jeff come in about that time, soaking wet from the rain and mad as a hornet, and the law man took him aside. I didn't hear what they said, but Jeff's been nervous as a cat since then. What did he say to you?"

"Oh, he didn't say much, Davis Lee," she said, not wanting to stir up bad feelings between Davis Lee and his brother. "I could just tell he was upset."

"It's no wonder," Davis Lee said. "Jeff don't like nobody challenging him, including the law. He's always been that way. When Mama took him in, he'd been too hard for his own folks to handle and they'd put him in a children's home. I reckon Mama thought we could do him some good—Mama's always been good-hearted that way. By the time Mama adopted him, he'd settled down right much. But he's flared up from time to time. I hope he didn't say nothing to hurt your feelings. I wouldn't stand for that."

"No, he didn't hurt my feelings, Davis Lee. He just thinks I'm causing your family some problems. He's probably right about that."

"You ain't causing nobody nothing but good, Esther. Jeff's worried about not getting to see Jim. I know that's it. He's always looked forward to Jim's weekends with us."

"I know he has," she said.

"I'll talk to him when he gets back, Esther," Davis Lee said. "He spun off on that motorcycle a minute ago, but he'll be back. When he gets bothered about something, he rides. Why, back in the past I've seen him take off without a helmet and ride out into the night without his headlight on. I told him time and again the law was going to get him if the undertaker didn't first. And by golly, he just about ended up six feet deep. But when Jeff gets in these moods, you can't talk to him. Mama stopped trying a long time ago, but she still worries, and so do I. He may be thirty, but he's still my little brother."

"I worry, too," Esther said.

"Well, that's sweet of you, Esther, but you needn't trouble with it."

She heard the stairs creaking and looked through the doorway to see her mother standing on the landing. She wore her housecoat and her hair was rolled.

Esther put her hand over the receiver's mouthpiece and said, "I'll be off the phone in a minute, Mother," but Lyla didn't budge.

She spoke more quietly into the receiver. "I'll come by the cemetery on my way to work in the morning," she said. "I have something to tell you."

"I'll look for you," he said. "But I wish I was with you now. I want to hold you."

"I know," she said.

"Well, goodnight, then, darlin'."

"Goodnight, Davis Lee," she said and hung up.

She found her mother still waiting on the landing.

"What is it, Mother?" she asked. "Why don't you go on to bed?"

"I hope you told him your brother's geraniums was stole."

"He knows."

"The radio said this wasn't the first time Oak Grove's been vandalized. I think they need a better caretaker, if you ask me, and I'm liable to call and tell 'em that."

"It'll be taken care of, Mother. Go to bed and don't worry."

"I can't sleep. What's the point in going to bed?"

"Then watch T.V. with Daddy," she said. "He'd like the company. I'm going on downstairs."

She started down the stairs, and Lyla followed her. At the foot of the stairs, Lyla said, "Why was you talking to him for so long? You been upstairs a hour."

Esther laughed. "It's not been that long, Mother."

"What could you have to say to him so long? And why did you go upstairs to talk to him?"

"It's just quieter, Mother. And private."

"People sneak when they've got something to hide."

"Well, that may be true," she said. "But you shouldn't worry about it."

Lyla stood and looked at her, and Esther couldn't help feeling sorry for her in her tattered terry housecoat. When had her mother grown so small? The housecoat suddenly seemed two sizes too big for her.

"You worry too much," Esther said and patted her mother's shoulder.

"Somebody has to," Lyla said and Esther left her to go to her bedroom.

Later in bed, she thought about Davis Lee's words, *I wish I was with you now.* She touched the empty place beside her.

"I wish you were here too, Davis Lee."

The next morning, she pulled into the cemetery drive and saw him at the crest of a hill, his weedeater leaned against an obelisk. As she drove toward him, he looked, shading his eyes in the sunlight, and motioned for her to come. She stopped beside him and he came to her window. When he leaned down to speak to her, she noticed how haggard his face looked.

"Esther, I need to show you something," he said. "Let's ride on up near the railroad tracks."

"All right," she said, surprised they couldn't just walk. He opened the passenger door and slid into the seat. She looked at his red tee shirt, a hole in its sleeve and patches of sweat on its front. She reached to pick a blade of grass from his hair. "Davis Lee, I'm so glad to see you," she said. "I missed you."

"I missed you, too," he said, though he didn't sound convincing. His face was intent as if he were in a hurry.

"Have you been working hard?" she asked and started driving. "You look worn out."

"Esther," he said, "we got problems."

When they pulled up alongside Sandy's grave, she saw what he meant.

A chunk of the stone's curved marble top lay on the ground beside the grave. The name had been disfigured too.

"Oh, Davis Lee," she said and hurriedly parked the car. She went to the stone and knelt in front of it. She traced his name, the word *Robertson* almost indistinguishable.

"The Police Chief said somebody must've took a sledge hammer to it," Davis Lee said, his voice barely audible. "Then he took the broken piece and chipped the name off."

"Davis Lee, when did this happen?"

"I found it this morning," he said, standing beside her, his hand on the jagged edge of the grave stone. "I hated like everything to have you see this." He moved his hand to her shoulder and gripped it.

She frowned and then blinked back tears. "How could anybody be so mean?"

"That's what I been wondering," he said.

"This will kill Mother," she said.

"Your daddy won't like it either," he said.

"Oh, I forgot about having to tell Daddy," she said. "How am I ever going to tell them?"

"I'll go with you," he said.

"Oh, I don't know," she said, knowing Davis Lee's presence would be a disaster, especially with her mother.

"Esther," he said and knelt beside her. "I'm pretty certain it was Jeff that did this."

"Jeff?" she said and looked at him.

"There's a lot I don't know, but Jeff come home last night around eleven-thirty—three sheets to the wind and he ain't never been one to drink—and I heard him bumping around in his bedroom, like he was hitting or kicking the wall, and when I opened his door and asked him what was wrong, he told me not to bother him, nobody better bother him. At first I thought he'd been crying, his voice sounded all shaky. His hair was wild, like he'd been riding without his helmet, and his face was blood red. His eyes was watery and wide open. I wondered if he might've got poisoned by liquor; I've seen my daddy drunk and raving like that, like somebody having a fit. But Jeff ain't never spoke a hard word to me, Esther, in all our years together. But last night I thought he might kill me. I left him alone, you can bet on that."

"Davis Lee," she said and looked at him. "What made him act that way?"

"It must've been the law that scared him, and you know he'd been upset about Brenda's threats to keep Jim away from us." Davis Lee touched the broken stone and stood, looking down the slope toward the railroad tracks. "He didn't stay around long, though. He went out the door and I didn't offer to follow him. Then Brenda called me after midnight to say he'd been over there and she'd called the Sheriff's Department because Jeff had threatened to take Jim. She said she wouldn't let Jeff in, and he stood in her yard yelling Jim's name. She said Jim woke up and wanted to go with Jeff, and she had to hold him back. You know how much that boy looks up to Jeff."

"Did the sheriff go to her house?"

"Naw, not right then. Brenda said the dispatcher stayed on the line till Jeff left—he didn't stay long—and she told the dispatcher she'd use her pistol if he come back. Jeff had give her that revolver himself. He always said he was worried about her and Jim being so far out in the country by themselves. I told her to call the Sheriff's Office right back and ask them to come patrol the area. After that, she called me and said a deputy had come by and would be patrolling. That's when I reckon the law started looking for Jeff."

"So you don't know where Jeff is now?" she asked, standing. She rubbed her hands together to brush off the marble dust.

Davis Lee still looked toward the railroad tracks. He shook his head. "I don't know," he said.

"Did Jeff steal the flowers here at Oak Grove?"

"When I talked to the Police Chief this morning, he said they'd suspected Jeff all along of stealing from the cemetery. Some third shift mill worker had spotted him hanging around the graves in the night and called the law. And when I called Brenda this morning to make sure everything was still all right, she mentioned Jeff had give her flowers a lot of times and had been borrowing her car for something. We reckoned he was hauling flowers to a buyer."

"And nobody has any idea where he is now?" she asked again. She recalled his weird talk about the lightning bug and his hanging up on her.

"The police found his motorcycle about a mile up the road, near the railroad tracks, the key still in the ignition, so he must've took off on foot or jumped a train. I can't believe he'd leave that Triumph behind as much as he thinks of it. One way or another, he won't get far. Now that he's tried to run off with Jim and messed up your brother's stone, he's in more trouble than he knows. I'm going to have to call Mama back. I talked to her this morning to see if he was there, and now she's worried to death."

"Where would he go?"

"He might be headed to New Orleans, for all I know. I wouldn't put it past him."

"That's a long way," she said.

"Distance don't mean nothing to him," Davis Lee said and looked at her, his eyes strained in the sunlight. "He's like a boy;

he wants something, he thinks he ought to have it. Same with New Orleans. He's had it in his head for a long time that he needs to go to New Orleans because of that movie *Easy Rider*. He ain't thinking clear."

"Well, when he gets there, it won't be Mardi gras," she said, more to herself.

"He won't get there," Davis Lee said. "Like I told the Police Chief: in the past, I didn't hold Jeff responsible for everything he did—I didn't think he knowed any better—but this time he went too far. I've always took care of my brother and defended him, but I can't abide him causing my son or you and your family any harm. Nothing this bad's ever happened before."

"I'm going to have to go back home and talk to my parents," she said. "I need to call the college and tell the Dean I can't come in today. My mind's too muddled now to teach anyway."

"I'll go with you," he said.

"No," she said. "That wouldn't be a good idea."

"I reckon this means we won't be seeing each other tomorrow. I guess everything's changed now."

"I don't know, Davis Lee," she said. "I don't know what's going to happen."

Before she left she said, "I wonder if insurance will cover this."

He didn't answer, but looked again toward the railroad tracks as she pulled away.

What have I got myself into? she asked herself as she drove home. He's everything I could want, but everything that means trouble for me.

No one in her life had ever been on the wrong side of the law until now.

But it wasn't Davis Lee. It wasn't *him*. She had to remind herself of this over and over until she pulled in her driveway.

She found no one in the house, and after she called the college, she went to her room to change clothes. There on her bed she found the *Milton News*. On the front page the headline read *Oak Grove Cemetery Vandalized*. Mother knows, she thought. She's left this for me.

She sat on the bed and read: *Jefferson Dale Johnson, 30, a maintenance worker at Oak Grove Cemetery, is being sought for the recent theft of grave flowers and the vandalism of tombstones at Oak Grove.* Thus far her family's name wasn't mentioned, nor Sandy's stone specified. She scanned the article, continued on page two. She turned the page and read that the suspect had also voiced threats to leave the county with a minor relative.

Davis Lee Johnson, brother of the suspect and maintenance worker at Oak Grove Cemetery, noted his brother's recent restlessness but expressed surprise at his brother's actions.

The article's next paragraph stopped her, though. She read it twice and realized that her mother had left the newspaper on her bed for these words:

The suspect was adopted by the widow of a man murdered in Milton in 1970 after an incident concerning the sell of illegal whiskey to minors. Carter Johnson was murdered by the father of a teen who purchased the illegal whiskey and subsequently died in an automobile accident that also took the lives of three other Milton High School students.

Yes, and my brother Sandy was one of those other students, Esther thought.

Mrs. Carter Johnson was not available this morning for comment.

The article described Jeff's physical appearance—blond hair, brown eyes, medium height and build—and concluded that the suspect was thought to have fled by foot on the railroad tracks near the cemetery. It said that anyone having any information on the case should contact the Milton Police Department immediately.

She folded the paper.

It was your daddy's sorry profession that killed my brother, Davis Lee, she thought. And your mama knew it all along.

And her own mother and daddy must have suspected it, too.

Now Davis Lee's brother had killed Sandy again, in a sense, ruining his tombstone and smashing the name as if it meant nothing. He did that to get back at her; it was *her* name too, that he was trying to destroy. And obviously, he didn't have any scruples about hurting his own family, too.

Have you known more about the past than you've admitted, Davis Lee? she wondered. It just didn't seem possible. He seemed to be the most sincere person she'd ever met.

Johnson, she thought and now understood why the name was a curse to her mother. Suddenly it seemed there was so much she understood. And yet she needed more than ever to talk to Davis Lee to ease her mind.

She went to her vanity and opened the drawer. Inside she found the florist card she'd discovered last night in her mother's scrapbook and had sneaked downstairs. *Mrs. Carter Johnson* the signature read. You sent flowers for my brother, Esther thought. You may have come to the funeral. You were trying to make amends. But now your son has desecrated my brother's grave. What a horrible thing for someone to do to the dead.

While she sat there, she heard someone in the hall.

"Mother?" she asked and the door opened. "I didn't know what Davis Lee's daddy did," she said and then, "Do you know about Sandy's stone?"

"The Chief of Police called," Lyla said. "He said it was tragic that these things happen. Then that boy that lives in the trailer down the street come and talked to Arthur."

"The one who works for the Police Department?"

Lyla nodded.

"What did Daddy say?"

"You know Arthur," Lyla said. "He won't let his feelings out. Even when Dave died, as close as they were, he just complained that his head hurt. It all stayed cooped up inside."

"Does he want to go see the tombstone?"

"He won't go there," Lyla said and picked up the newspaper.

"Your caretaker played a trick on you, Esther."

"Davis Lee didn't know his brother would do something like this. He was as hurt as anybody about this."

Lyla didn't answer. Esther knew her defending Davis Lee would antagonize her mother, but she couldn't help it.

"I'll put up a new stone," Esther said.

"I wish we could move your brother out of that cemetery."

"I'll put up a new stone and it'll be all right. They'll catch Jeff Johnson and that'll be the end of it."

"There ain't no end of it," Lyla said, "so long as you keep us tangled up with that family. I'd hoped to never have any dealings with them again. But here you go and bring them back into our life. And I know you good enough to see you intend to throw everything away for this man." Lyla stopped here and tightened her lips. "If you don't care about your own reputation, you ought to at least care about your daddy."

"I don't mean to hurt Daddy," she said. "And this isn't about Davis Lee. I wish you'd see that. He's done nothing to hurt anybody."

Lyla stared at her.

"Where is Daddy?"

"He's out at the garden looking at the sunflowers."

"Looking at the sunflowers? Why's he doing that?" Her daddy should be watching his morning game shows.

"Maybe it helps him forget," Lyla said and turned to leave.

Outside, Esther saw her daddy at the garden.

"Why're you not at work?" he said when he saw her. In the sunlight, his silver hair looked thinner than she'd realized and his complexion was ashen. During her girlhood, her daddy's skin would turn a rich reddish brown by summer's end, and he would go shirtless while he did yard work. She remembered how stout and strong he looked then and realized how proud he must have been of his physique.

"I'm not going in today," she said. "I thought maybe you'd want to go out to the cemetery and see the stone."

"You and Lyla can go," he said and turned back to the flowers. His hands were stuck in his back pockets, and he looked up toward the sky as if he were a farmer checking the weather.

"I'm sorry this happened, Daddy," she said. "I guess Mother showed you the newspaper."

She waited for him to say something, to ask what she knew or condemn her for being a part of it, for didn't they consider her a conspirator with the Johnsons? But he said nothing.

"Daddy," she said and stooped to touch a purple morning glory that grew wild by the garden, "do you blame me for falling in love with him?"

"I don't blame you," he said. "I just don't want to see you hurt."

"I don't plan to get hurt, Daddy, but I can't guarantee it won't happen."

"No," he said. "You can't always see it coming. We all have to take our chances, I guess."

"That's right, Daddy," she said. She hesitated. "But I wanted to tell you that I didn't know about his daddy's connection with Sandy."

"Maybe he didn't know everything about his daddy either."

"That's what I believe, Daddy," she said, so relieved in this hint of confidence in Davis Lee that she could have hugged her daddy. "That's why I can't hold it against him."

"But you both know the truth now."

"I still love him, Daddy," she said. "I can't help it. I don't know what else to say."

"You'll do what's right," he said, looking at her with cloudy eyes.

"Do you think so, Daddy?" She felt her tears welling. Suddenly she felt like a little girl being consoled after a fall.

But he didn't seem to hear her last words. He'd turned again to the sunflowers that leaned their heads toward him, as if they shared in his grief.

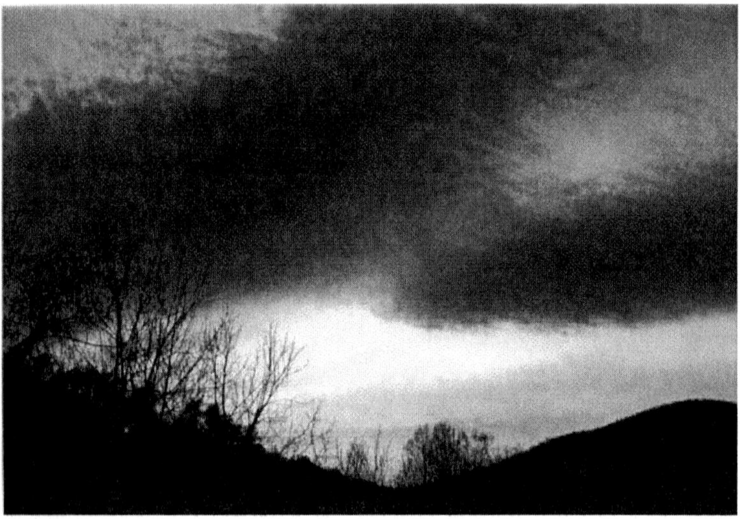

16

That same Friday evening she waited for Davis Lee to call her, but he didn't. And when she drove through the cemetery the next day and again the next, he wasn't there. She dialed his phone number, but no one answered.

It was a long, sad weekend.

Her colleagues at the college heard about the incident with Sandy's tombstone, and on Monday evening some asked her what had happened, though she suspected they knew the details. Earlier that day the *Milton News* had published a follow-up article on cemetery vandalism and included a photograph of Sandy's broken stone. Suddenly Milton's citizens were reminded of a forgotten automobile accident, the bootlegger who sold liquor to cause it, and an adopted son who years later would allegedly desecrate the grave of one of the victims. The scandal was revived with a vengeance.

At home, during the following days, she and her parents didn't talk about the vandalism. Her mother, she knew, had clipped the recent newspaper articles and stored them upstairs. She also knew her mother watched her when she went upstairs to dial Davis Lee's number and listened at the foot of the stairs to hear her hang up when he didn't answer. She could imagine her mother's sigh of relief.

Another Saturday morning came, but she still hadn't heard from him. Panic swept over her as the minutes of the day passed. She had no one to turn to. She fretted over Davis Lee's recent conversations with Brenda. Surely now they would stay in close touch, for Jim's protection if for no other reason. That was understandable, but it didn't make it any easier to bear. What was to say this crisis wouldn't make them emotionally close in a way they'd never been? Concern for their son might melt any past differences. Perhaps he would even ask her and Jim to come home again.

Where had he gone? She called the Public Works Director, but there was no answer there.

She tried to call Cora, but every time she dialed, a busy signal stopped her. Esther imagined the woman might have taken her phone off the hook to avoid prank calls, or calls from indignant preachers, or calls from the law to say Jeff had been found dead.

She even considered calling Brenda. But what if Davis Lee answered? She couldn't endure that possibility.

She drove to the cemetery again. She found no sign of life at the trailer; no motorcycle parked in the driveway, of course. Maybe the police had seized it for evidence. She left, more frustrated than ever.

When she pulled into her driveway, she saw her mother standing behind the screen door. As she stepped onto the front porch, Lyla met her and handed her a post card.

"This come for you in the mail," Lyla said.

She looked at the front of the post card and saw an illustration of a World War I soldier and a woman, his wife maybe, whose hand rested on his shoulder. The printed message underneath read *Don't Worry About Me*.

She turned the card to find a hand printed message:
I'm at the cabin if you want to come.
Davis Lee

"I guess you read it," she said to her mother.

"A post card's not hard to read. How did I know who it was for till I read it?"

Odd that Davis Lee would send a post card that anyone might read. Maybe it was all out in the open now anyway. People would think what they wanted to.

"Well, I'm going to see him."

"Even with what he did to your brother?"

"It wasn't Davis Lee," she said.

"I mean what his family did."

"I need to see him. Can't you understand that? I need to talk to him."

"You can talk to us, Esther. We're your family. They're not stealing *you* from us, too."

"Nobody's stealing me," she said. "I'm going because I want to. Daddy understands."

Lyla stared at her.

"I talked to him, Mother. He trusts my judgment. Don't make me feel like I'm betraying my family."

"You'll do what you want to, regardless of what I say," Lyla said. "But mark my word, you're asking for trouble."

"All right, then, I'm asking for trouble," she said.

She went inside, bathed, and then went to her bedroom where she sat at the vanity. She pulled open the drawer and removed the bottle of *Joy* perfume.

She moistened her fingertip with the gold liquid and touched her throat and stroked the skin between her breasts. After she dressed, she slipped the purse-sized bottle into her jeans pocket.

She brushed her hair, gold highlights gleaming in the lamplight. She noticed how much longer her hair had grown this summer, her bangs now parting and joining the rest of her hair that hung below her shoulders.

Massaging moisturizer into her face and dabbing gloss to her lips, she took a final glance in the mirror, as if to reassure her she was ready for this, and left the room.

Her mother and daddy both sat on the couch in the front room—odd to see them sitting together—and she stopped there to tell them she was going.

"I'll see you later," she said.

"Be careful going across that mountain," her daddy said. "And drive slow coming back down."

"I will, Daddy," she said.

"Bye, Mother," she said. Lyla kept her eyes on the T.V.

When she stood on the front porch, getting ready to go

down the steps, she heard the screen door smack and looked to see her mother standing there.

"Mother, don't worry about me."

"That's what that post card said," Lyla said.

"It'll be all right," she said and reached to squeeze her mother's arm. "You know I have to do this."

"Watch out for other drivers," Lyla said. "They'll be drunks on the highway tonight."

"If I'm driving tonight," she said.

"Well," Lyla said and turned to go back in.

"Mother, keep him company," she said. "You know you could be a comfort to each other."

Lyla didn't answer. She had already gone inside and shut the front door behind her.

Before Esther backed out of the driveway, she sat in the car and looked at the house. For the first time, she noticed that the chicken wind chimes she'd bought on the Parkway had been taken down.

On the drive to Spruce Pine, she listened to Chopin ballades to calm her mind and wondered what she would say to Davis Lee. Surely he'd seen the newspaper articles about Sandy's accident and his daddy's murder. She imagined this publicity is what drove him from Milton. Or maybe he wanted to support his mama. Whatever the reason for his leaving, she was relieved he still wanted to see her.

A light rain had begun to fall and when she approached the farmhouse, she saw Jeff's motorcycle in the dirt driveway. Davis Lee stood on the front porch.

When she opened the car door, he came to her side. He spread his denim jacket over her shoulders.

"Let's go to the cabin," he said and wrapped his arm around her.

"I'm glad to see you," she said and leaned against him as he guided her.

The path to the cabin was wider, undergrowth slashed away and pine limbs trimmed to let them through.

"I done some clearing out," he said. "I been working on the cabin too."

He held the cabin door open for her and she went over the threshold.

Inside, the first thing she noticed was a black potbellied woodstove that stood on a mat in front of a wall. "Look at that little stove," she said. "Daddy said there used to be one like that at the Company Store when he was a boy."

"It's a old one," Davis Lee said. "It'd been stored in the tool shed long as I can remember. It took some cleaning and some flue work and a new stove pipe, but it burns good."

"Did the delivery man help you move it?" she asked.

"The delivery man from the food market, you mean?"

"The one who helped you bring the Grafonola out here."

"Yeah. But lately I'm thinking he's more than just a delivery man to mama. Don't tell her I said that, though."

"I won't," she said and smiled. She could imagine a man wanting to court his mama, as attractive as she still was. It must be a comfort to Davis Lee, she thought, for someone to come by and help his mama pass the time.

"I bet the stove's cozy," she said.

"I've started us a little fire," he said, "in case it gets chilly."

"It looks so homey in here," she said, noticing the white scarf on the Grafonola's lid and the linen cloth on the table. She walked over to the telescope, its shiny white tube pointing toward the window.

"You've cleaned your telescope," she said. "Have you been looking at the stars?"

"I been meaning to," he said. "Some say the stars can give you answers."

"Maybe we can both take a look then," she said and smiled,

feeling lighter.

"Can we sit at the table?" he said and pulled out a straight chair for her.

When she sat, he removed the kerosene lamp's clear globe, no longer smoky as before, and lit the wick. He put the globe back on and adjusted the flame.

"I was afraid you wouldn't come," he said and sat across from her, the lamplight casting a glow on his dark eyes.

"But you were waiting for me, weren't you?"

"I was hoping," he said. "But I smoked a pack of Mama's Winstons today while I waited. I told you I quit smoking cigarettes, but I couldn't help it. But I'll give them up again now." At the moment he was chewing gum.

"I wanted to come," she said. If only he knew how much she'd feared he didn't want to see her again; how long her nights had been.

"I ain't sure you ought to have come," he said. "But I need to talk to you."

"I wanted to talk to you too, Davis Lee," she said. "I wonder what your mama thinks about me coming here; she's bound to see my car."

"She knows I wrote to you. She found the post card for me in Grandmama's trunk."

"I was glad to get it."

"Mama said that card belonged to Grandmama's brother who was in the First World War. I reckon he never got around to sending it."

"I hope he didn't get killed in the war."

"Naw. Injured but not killed."

"I always thought if Sandy had lived he might have gone to Vietnam," she said.

"Esther," Davis Lee said, "I know your brother's on your mind a lot now, especially with what's happened at the cemetery. And with all the past stirred up again, Mama thinks you won't be able to forget what my daddy did to your brother."

"I've just learned about your daddy, Davis Lee," she said. "I've not even had time to digest it all."

"Esther, I just learned about your brother's part—."

"I know that, Davis Lee," she said. "If you'd known before, you would have talked to me about it."

"Like I told you, I was fifteen when Daddy got killed. It happened out in the yard, but I heard the shots. Then the law come to the house, looking around, asking questions, driving Mama crazy. After that trouble, when her head cleared enough to think, she moved us here to the mountains. She tried to protect me from people's talk, but I still knew that my daddy was shot over the whiskey he sold. It was all over the newspapers, even one in Charlotte. But I didn't know the connection with your brother till now. Mama's spent the past twenty years trying to live all that down, but now it's come up again with Jeff."

"I need to tell you that our life wasn't nice back then, Esther. Before Daddy got killed, he had Mama working for him, carrying bags of beer or whiskey to the cars when men would stop in front of the house and toot their horns. Then when the men started making vulgar remarks to her, thinking maybe she could be bought for a few dollars too, he put me to working instead of her. Mama hated that, but she didn't stand up to him."

"Was she afraid of him?"

"Nobody challenged Daddy. He never lifted a hand to me, but I've seen Mama cower around him when he took his drunk fits, and she told me to stay out of his way. First person I thought of when Jeff was raving the other night was Daddy. After Daddy died, Mama forbid alcohol in our house, like she was trying to make up for all the past sins we'd committed. But the reputation sticks."

"Reputation," Esther said. "That's all I've heard all my life."

"Respectable people think that way, Esther. That's why I wanted to talk to you. I know the kind of remarks you'll be hearing about my family and about me. My daddy was a bootlegger, and his son ain't much better. The first girl I went out with I got in trouble. I tried to make it right by marrying her, but that marriage was a lie. I've tried to help take care of Jim with the income I've earned and be a daddy to him the best I knowed how, but it ain't been enough. Jeff could talk to him and get him to laugh and make him feel important in a way I never did."

"But you're his daddy," Esther said. "Jim knows that."

"Esther, I want to work out this problem with Brenda to make her see I can be with Jim without being with *her*—I ain't going to give you up to please her, Esther—but I don't know what's going to happen."

"I'll help you make her see," Esther said, not sure how she would live up to this promise.

"But it's other things too. My jobs ain't been nothing to brag about, though they've been respectable enough. Before I started at Oak Grove, I worked in mills and sold scrubbery and did some carpentry jobs, and my brother Jeff was right there beside me. But seemed like something always happened to mess things up for us. Up till now, Oak Grove's worked out good, though I wanted a better situation—more responsibility and better pay, thinking I might have more to offer you and Jim, so I looked into a cemetery here in Spruce Pine. But likely they'll not hire me now with all this scandal about my brother and my family's past. Why would a cemetery hire somebody whose brother had just vandalized and stole from another cemetery? Now that the law's got Jeff, there's no telling what he'll admit he's done."

"They found him?"

"He didn't jump a train; he just walked till he took up with a family along the tracks. You know how friendly he is. One evening at the supper table he told them what he'd done and where he was heading, and they turned him in. I guess it never occurred to him they would do that."

"So he's in jail?"

"I reckon so. He called Mama a couple of days ago and told her the law had him. I don't know how long they'll keep him or what's going to happen, but I'll know soon enough. Mama's wanting to go see him, so I'm going to pick up my car first thing Monday morning. Likely I'll have to appear in court to testify. That's the thing, Esther. I know my name will be in the paper again and it won't bring either me or Jim or you any honor. I don't blame your family for worrying about your reputation."

"This is not about you, Davis Lee," she said and reached to take his hand across the table. The evening's shadows were falling and the air within the cabin had grown cooler, despite the woodstove's heat.

He took her hand.

"But everybody'll think it is," he said. "And if enough people think it, it might as well be so."

"I won't think it," she said.

"Maybe not, but in time you might."

"I'll take that chance," she said.

"Well, then—" he said and leaned across the table and she met him half way and they kissed. After the kiss, when his face nuzzled hers and he sighed in her ear, she realized why she had panicked to think they wouldn't be this close again. She was not complete without him.

He stood and led her to the bed and asked her to sit. He reached in his shirt pocket and handed her a cassette tape. She saw that it was the Tartini violin concerto she'd let him borrow.

"You didn't have to give it back."

"I'm finished with it," he said.

He squatted by the bed and reached underneath it. He gently brought out something wrapped in cloth. When he stood and uncovered it, she smiled.

"Your fiddle," she said and reached to trace its rich, straight grain.

"I wanted to surprise you," he said. "I don't usually keep it under the bed."

"You're going to play for me?" she asked.

"I told you I aimed to," he said and stood in front of her. He plucked the four strings with his forefinger to listen to the pitch, and when he adjusted the tuning pegs and seemed satisfied, he lifted the fiddle with his left hand and positioned his chin on the chin rest, tilting his head to brace it, and raised the bow with his right hand. He looked at her and then closed his eyes and began to play.

It took a minute for her to recognize the melody, but then it occurred to her that Davis Lee was playing "When Day Is Done," the song her daddy had sung to her years ago when she sat on his lap and that he had sung briefly at the dinner table when Davis Lee came to eat with them.

While Davis Lee played the melody, his left fingers pressing the strings on the fingerboard, his right hand gracefully sliding the bow across the strings, he kept his eyelids down and let his body move with the music. The melancholy tones and the beauty of his face in the lamplight, his eyelashes dark and long, made her blink back tears. Yet despite the music's sad, wistful lyrics that she could hear in her mind, the song uplifted her. She was here, yes, but she was also somewhere long ago, in a happy time, before loss and sadness had come into her family.

When Davis Lee finished playing, he opened his eyes and held the fiddle down at his side. He bowed.

"My granddaddy taught me to bow after I played. He said 'Be a gentleman in everything you do.' I reckon he hoped I'd be at the Grand Ole Opry someday, bowing on the Ryman Auditorium stage."

Esther lifted her hands as if to applaud, but instead pressed them together like a child in prayer. "Davis Lee," she said and went to him, "thank you." She grasped his arms and reached up to kiss his cheek. "So beautiful."

He laid his fiddle on the table and they sat together on the bed.

"How did you learn 'When Day Is Done'?"

"I told Mama about you liking that song, and she said she thought Grandmama had a recording of it. I told her I didn't think it was in the Grafonola, and she said it was probably upstairs with the rest of Grandmama's records. Mama said Grandmama had told her about sitting at the radio at night and listening to orchestra music. She was a country woman, but she loved beautiful music, and Granddaddy bought records for her when he could find them. Mama and me went upstairs in the house and sure enough in a stack of records there was the song you liked—it wasn't the Al Jolson Decca record your daddy had; this one was Paul Whiteman's Orchestra on a 78 Victor. I brought it out here and played it on the Grafonola until I had it set in my mind. I'd intended to learn the violin piece that's your favorite, and I'm still working on it, but it ain't ready yet."

"Oh, you couldn't have played anything I would have loved more," she said and reached to touch his cheek. "Do you know how special you are, Davis Lee? I don't think you do. I thought you had the hands of a pianist, but you're not Chopin, you're Paginini."

"I don't know who that is," he said, "but I take it as a compliment."

"Your granddaddy would be proud of you, Davis Lee," she said. "You're a gentleman in everything you do. Nobody ever gave me a gift like you did tonight."

"I hoped it would please you," he said and touched her face, his eyes studying her. "You have such beautiful hair," he said and took some long strands in his fingers. "It looks like spun gold in the lamplight."

He took her face in his hands. As they looked at each other in the dim, flickering light, she noticed the shadows that had settled in the hollows beneath his cheekbones and under his eyes and saw fine lines along his mouth and on his forehead that she hadn't noticed before. He was not a young man. Soon grey would mix with his dark sideburns and the black hair that fell onto his collar. For the first time, she saw him truly for what he was: a weary soul, chased by time and trying like herself to grasp something that had escaped him.

And she found only beauty in this man. She wanted to drink in his beauty, make it part of herself, for truly she knew she had found love.

"Esther," he said as if he had understood her thoughts. He didn't speak anything else, but seemed to struggle with his thoughts. His eyes were sad, troubled.

The rain fell harder outside and pecked like hail on the tin roof. She looked toward the window.

"The fog'll set in early tonight," he said. "It'll be a hard drive down the mountain."

"Let's not think about that now," she said and reached to embrace him. He took her in his arms. She shuddered, suddenly chilled or nervous.

"Are you cold, darlin'?" he asked and held her closer. He pressed his lips to the top of her head. "I'll put more wood on the fire."

He stood and went to the stove, squatting to open its iron door and put in another stick from the pile on the floor.

"Davis Lee," she said and he turned his head to look at her. "Would you mind keeping your back turned for a minute?" He started to speak, but stopped himself. He looked again to the stove, his back to her.

She stood and turned down the wedding quilt, the soft flannel blanket beneath it, and the white sheet.

Keeping her eyes on Davis Lee, who remained quiet at the stove, his head angled as if he waited for her to speak, she undressed. While she removed her shoes and socks, her jeans and blouse, and then her underclothes, she felt strangely calm, as if she were in a dream.

When she slipped into the bed, the boxsprings jingled and the feather mattresses sank and then rose around her. She felt like she had entered a pool of cool softness. The fragrance of her perfume and the scent of woodsmoke and kerosene mingled to make a lovely incense.

She pulled the covers to her shoulders.

"You can come now," she said.

He stood and when he turned to face her, his mouth opened slightly, but he didn't speak. He moved across the room slowly and sat on the edge of the bed, his back to her again. She reached and touched his shoulder, the thin cloth of his checked shirt, tracing the contour of his shoulder blade. He looked around at her for a moment and began to unbutton his shirt and removed it. She touched his warm back and fingered the dark freckles that she'd never seen before. There was so much to discover.

"Do you want me to put out the light?" he said.

"No, Davis Lee," she said. "I want to see you."

She heard the boots strike the floor, *thump, thump*, and then heard him unzip his pants and slip them off. He pulled back the covers and then slid in beside her. She felt his movement as he reached and pulled off his underpants and dropped them on the floor beside him. She realized then that he, too, had been modest and didn't want her to see him naked.

At first he didn't touch her, but lay quietly beside her, as if he were holding his breath. She could hear his heart beating.

She sat up and let the covers slip from her. She closed her eyes as she felt his fingers touch her throat and find her breast.

"Esther," he said, almost whispering, "I've never seen anyone so beautiful."

She lay back while his hands explored her body and kindled her desire, and she heard his *ah* as she stroked his belly and the soft hair beneath it and caressed his dearest, most secret parts. As they touched, he kissed her, allowing her to savor the sweet, hot moisture of his mouth. And when he came into her, the bed like an ocean billowing around them, they were two drowning souls clinging to each other, pressing deeper and deeper, until they rose above the waves and found their joy.

At that instant she knew that something in the most hidden and sacred part of herself had been found by this man; she had found it with him.

They lay quiet afterwards, their bodies moist with the strain and triumph of their union, and she rested her head on his arm. He stroked her forehead with his fingers.

"Esther," he said, his voice tired, "if ever I said anything that was true in my life, what I say now is true: I love you and I'll love you forever."

"I know that, Davis Lee," she said and nuzzled closer to him. "I love you, too, and nothing will ever change that."

"I've never been happy until now," he said. "Ain't that a strange thing?"

"No," she said. "It's not strange. I feel that way too."

Before the fire went out and she would have to rise to leave him, they made love again. This time their touch and movements were quiet, sweet, familiar, as if they had been lovers always.

"I don't want you to go," he said as she stood by the bed and dressed. He sat on the edge of the bed and slowly pulled on his clothes. When she had dressed, she sat beside him and helped him button his shirt. Then she leaned her head on his shoulder and he kissed her temple. "Is this a dream?" he asked.

"It might be," she said. "But I think it's more real than anything that's ever happened to me."

"Yeah," he said and nodded. "But I'm afraid. It seems like when we get away from here, everything and everybody tries to pull us away from each other. I wish we could stay here."

"You know I have to go tonight," she said. "My parents are

probably watching for my headlights. I wouldn't have them worry all night."

"Naw. I wouldn't want that either."

She took his face in her hands and looked into his eyes. "But you know I belong to you now, don't you, Davis Lee? You know that happened here tonight."

"I'm going to do better for you, Esther," he said. "I'll get things straightened out so I can be your husband."

"You are my husband," she said. "Whatever *husband* really means, you're that to me."

Something she had forgotten she felt in her pants pocket. She reached and pulled it out.

"I want to give you something, Davis Lee," she said and put the perfume bottle in his hand.

He held it up and looked at the gold liquid in the scant light. Then he looked at her as if he didn't understand.

"It's to let you know I've given up the past," she said.

"Does it have something to do with that boy you never forgot?"

"Oh, more than that," she said. "It's to remind you of tonight, too."

He unscrewed the cap and held the bottle to his nose.

"It smells like you," he said. "Like a wild rose."

"We'll call it a remembrancer," she said. "Like the song you gave me tonight."

The rain had let up outside and he led her through the woods to her car. Without his arm, she would have been lost in the pitch blackness.

Before he opened the car door for her, he took her in his arms and clung to her.

"This ain't the end of anything, is it?" he said, his voice sounding frightened in the dark. His mama's house was surrounded by fog and the cabin was hidden from sight.

"No," she said. "I promise, Davis Lee."

"We'll be together again like tonight?" he said.

"Nothing can stop that," she said, sensing a trickle of moisture seeping into her underpants, a precious nectar that she would hold inside her as long as she could.

"Well, I'll let you go, then," he said and released her. "But I want you to be careful, darlin'."

When she reached to press his hand to reassure him, she felt his fingers clasped around the perfume bottle.

She drove away from him and looked in her rearview mirror though she couldn't see him in the darkness behind her. But she knew he stood there to see her away.

Lord, watch over him, she prayed.

On the drive home, fog rose like ghosts in front of her headlights, and she passed through it. She knew with God's help, she would safely reach the foot of the mountain.

Tonight she would talk to her parents and make them understand.

Tomorrow she would call Davis Lee and they would find a way.

In the meantime, she took comfort in the memory of his music and in the image of him holding the fiddle to his chin, his eyes closed while he played.